MW00713506

Pent Up Passion

Unleash The Dangers Of Romance

By Hope C. Clarke
Author of Shadow Lover

This book is a work of fiction. Names, characters, places and incidents are products of the author's imagination or are used fictitiously. Any resemblance to actual events or locales or persons, living or dead, is entirely coincidental.

Published by:

A New Hope Publishing
Brooklyn, New York

Hope Clarke@aol.com

Copyright © 2001 by Hope C. Clarke

All rights are reserved, including the right to reproduce this book or portions thereof in any form whatsoever. For information, address A New Hope Publishing

Library of Congress Control Number: 2001090335

ISBN: 1-929279-01-9

Cover Design: Raymond Taylor-Green
Printing provided by: www.BooksJustBooks.com

Dedication

This book is dedicated to my dear friends, Keesha Nance, Desiree James, and Dorothea Williamson. Thanks for being my motivation and inspiration. Friends like you are hard to find but easy to keep.

Acknowledgments

I give special thanks to Gloria Mallette, author of Shades of Jade, for both her friendship and mentor-ship.

Gloria thank you so much for all your help, and guidance. I look forward to a long and lasting friendship in the years to come.

I also give thanks to Berneal Sutherland for her help in getting this project on the way. All of your time and efforts are greatly appreciated and will never be forgotten.

About the author

Hope C. Clarke is a publisher and author of fiction horror of the new Millennium. She unsparingly carries her readers through the bowels of their twisted fantasies and quenches their thirst for the eroticism of sex, and romance in modern language. She takes her readers' greatest fears and amplifies them.

Shadow Lover was the first of her novels to hit the market, and she now unleashes the dangers of passion with her second novel, *Pent Up Passion*. See a preview of her next book, *Missing Births,* at the end of *Pent Up Passion*.

Hope C. Clarke intends to bring to the public a new breed of character and a new taste of fear.

CHAPTER
1

"Hey, Brownie," Keesha Smalls called, observing the dark, sweet, chocolate bunny nearing her. Each time she saw him, it was like seeing him for the first time. Her pupils took in the smoothness of Chris's skin, which reminded her of silk. He was tall with broad shoulders and a narrow waist. She imagined muscles rippling across his chest. A slender man with bulges in all the right places.

Looking in her direction, with his sexy, deep voice, he called out his greeting to her. His Barry White voice vibrated in her ear. She could see his pearly white teeth and those eyes, like Hawaiian sand. She continued watching him, yearning for him in the secret world of her mind. He was far too young for her, and his mother, her friend, would surely not approve.

Keesha was in love. At thirty-five, she found herself swooning over her neighbor's twenty-one year-old son. Yes, Chris' mother, Christine, had raised him correctly. Indeed he was the apple of her eye. Chris was one to be proud of, an achiever. Finishing high school two years before his scheduled time and completing his second year of college at an Ivy League school was another mark of achievement. Majoring in accounting was only a mere stone in the foundation of his life. His excellence had landed him a position at one of the largest and most prestigious accounting firms in New York, Goldman, Thurman & Sacs. His skills made a great deal of money for the firm and for that, he was rewarded with a home on the company's elegant property. Keesha had never had the pleasure of seeing it for herself, but people said it was beyond elaborate.

Keesha recognized their age difference, but he appealed to her sexually. Although she knew Christine would not approve, especially since she was over-protective of her son, she anticipated being ravished by him. Seeing him daily only heightened her desire for him.

Chris, too, had feelings for Keesha. He wanted more than sexual gratification from her. He admired her beauty, intelligence and success. She had a remarkably unmarred almond complexion. It was as though none of life's iniquities had befallen her. This assumption was far from the truth. Keesha sheltered her fear of falling in love again after finding her once beloved in their bed together. She vowed that day to never love another. Keesha's dancer's shape only heightened his attraction to her. Chris imagined her breasts would fit perfectly in his cupped hands, and he loved her petite waist and complementary rear. God it's round.

With all of Christine's boasting of Chris' achievements, and Keesha' continuous nods of approval still didn't warrant Chris approaching Keesha. He did notice a special wink and pout of Keesha's lips, emulated a kiss, but he couldn't be certain enough to act on it.

"Chris, this is Keesha," Christine said with pride, introducing her prized son to her new neighbor. Although they were still new to the neighborhood, Keesha and Christine's friendship just clicked. There was something to be said about this chemistry since Christine was reserved with her acquaintances. Within a two year period, Keesha became like a daughter to Christine, and a wife to Chris though she didn't know it.

Keesha was blind to Chris' physical changes at least he thought she didn't notice. His fear of approaching her caused the past two years to be fruitless. Chris was still a child in Keesha's eyes, her best friend's young son. Why didn't she notice him? he wondered. She wasn't seeing anyone; it was as if she avoided relationships. For the two years Chris had known her, not once, had he witnessed a man in her company. Who wouldn't want her?

During the time Keesha had known Chris, his body developed into a mature sculpture of perfection. Women yearned for him, lusted at his very being, craved for just a mere touch of his flesh. Girls his age, just were not mature enough for him. They had no ambition and no desire to reach the heights Chris was destined to reach. Chris had a handful of women but Keesha was the one he wanted most. Chris realized he was still smiling and waving at her. Keesha indicated her fatigue by holding her wrist while waving at him. Feeling silly, he joined her on her porch.

"How are you? Since I was passing by . . ."

"No explanation is necessary, Chris. You're always welcome. What's up?" She realized that his mother lived just a few houses away.

"Not much. What are you working on?"

"Just some figures for a client."

"Need any help?"

"Nah. I've got it under control. Besides, I'm almost finished, anyway. But thanks for the offer."

"Any time."

This year, March brought pleasant weather, the usual lingering winter breeze was capitulated by the warmth of spring air. Even the flowers began their bloom early, and Chris believed the weather created the perfect setting for him to test the waters with Keesha. "What are your plans for this evening? He asked."

"I'm just going inside to relax. Would you like to come in? I don't think you've ever been inside my home."

"You know, you're right? Why is that?"

"I don't know. Why don't you come in now?" Keesha stood and opened the door.

Chris followed her in. "Wow, it's beautiful."

"What's that, Chris?"

He wanted to say her butt, but indicated the layout of her home instead.

"So, have you set your eyes on anyone yet?" Keesha asked.

Taken aback . . . "No, I'm still waiting for the right girl to come along to match your beauty!"

His retort surprised her. "You'd better stop talking like that! I might just take you up on that offer one of these days!" She watched him as he smiled slyly.

"That's what I'm betting on," he uttered under his breath, not wanting to move too fast. Her words gave him a new sense of encouragement. He sensed their shared attraction, and Keesha had finally admitted it. Keesha began patting her lap, drumming to the silent music. Chris, observing his surroundings, realized that an uncomfortable silence between them. Their inquisitive conversation turned in to silence. "Why don't we pick up this conversation tomorrow, same time?" Chris offered.

"Sounds good to me." She escorted him to the door

"Good night, Keesha."

Returning his salutation, she closed the door behind him. Thinking over their suggestive comments, she asked herself, what am I doing?

This isn't right. A long time had passed since she had been with a man, but Chris wasn't a man. He was just a successful boy who happened to be her neighbor's son. But he was gorgeous and sexy. Damn, I can't do this! Leaning against the bar, she picked up the invitation Christine sent her to a dinner party. I've got to get rid of these feelings before Christine notices it. How can I attend this dinner knowing Chris will be there panting over Christine's son.

Monday evening, about the time Chris usually stopped by, to see his mother, Keesha continued preparing the presentation for her client. This case held great importance because she would gain the respect of her client along with a hefty commission. The doorbell rang. The last thing she needed was an interruption. Hesitating for a moment, hoping the person would go away, the bell rang again before Keesha realized her car was parked right outside. "Just a minute," she called, hurrying to the door wondering who it could be. With all the work she needed to do, she had no time to spend listening to Michelle, the local gossip or to catch up on old news with Christine. Living in a small residential area, with a radius of no more than four blocks each way, there wasn't much room for gossip. Especially since the residents consisted of hardworking, money-hungry go-getters, who often didn't have enough time to say hello in passing. In fact, there were rarely any neighbors to be seen, unless someone's home caught on fire or worse, which was never until she met Michelle. Michelle made it her duty to generate her idea of excitement, which consisted of nonstop gossip although she lived just outside of the community. Usually the neighbors ignored her but at times, Keesha would allow her to come in and chat awhile. Of course, that wasn't often because she picked inopportune moments like this one to visit. Keesha opened the door... Chris!

"I didn't see you on the porch today so I decided to check up on you to see if everything was all right."

"Well, come in," she beckoned him. "Would you like me to take your clothes off, I mean your coat?" Clearing her throat. Chris considered the chances of her making a pass at him and discarded it as a misunderstanding. "Thank you. Yes you may." He was answering both of her questions. Keesha took his coat and hung it in the guest closet. Keesha became moist observing his physical attributes. A yearning, she hadn't felt in a long time, became obvious, giving her a feeling of uneasiness. She had to get rid of him. She had been a friend of his mother

for quite sometime and would never let this kind of thing come between them. Besides, he couldn't really be interested in her anyway.
"Can I offer you something to drink?"
"Yes, thank you."

"Orange, Coke, Ginger Ale, Sunny Delight?"
He smiled. "Coke please." He answered her with a chuckle, recognizing her joking expression when she said Sunny Delight. He observed his surroundings as she escorted him to the kitchen. From the outside, the house seemed modest but the inside was immense. Keesha had class, no doubt. Her home reminded him of someone who was absorbed in work. Purposely avoiding relationships, sterile like.

From the front door into the corridor, the floors were covered with egg-white carpet. The walls were also egg-white with a sculptured ceiling. The detail was lovely. "What's this?" Chris asked acknowledging the first room to his left.

She ushered him into that room, delaying her response.

Her study was admirable. Two walls were covered by cherry-wood bookcases and filled with different kinds of reference books. Another wall was filled with literary material and financial guides. Keesha's desk was situated diagonally at the far right of the room. It, too, was immense and constructed of fine cherry wood. Everything suggested power and greatness. Parquet floors, perfectly polished were partially hidden by a large Oriental rug in front of her desk.

"This is my study," she offered, noticing his amazement. "This is where I see my clients on occasion. Rare though. I prefer to meet at my Madison Avenue office."

Just beyond the study was an empty room, a gallery, Chris presumed. He only saw paintings and sculptures. "You do these yourself?" Her expression encouraged his question.

"Yes. Rarely does anyone come in here. Most of this was done when I was younger."

Chris started toward one of the sculptures.

"No," she called out to him surprising herself as much as him. These are personal to me.

Chris not understanding at first took one last glance at the sculpture and realized that it was a woman grasping a man's leg, crying. The man seemed to be pulling away. "Someone hurt you didn't they?" he questioned her while searching her eyes.

"I wouldn't have brought you through here but I'm having work done through the corridor, and I didn't want you to get paint on your clothes." She offered avoiding his question.

"I didn't smell any paint."

"I know. It's probably dry, I'm just being cautious."

"No need to explain," he offered, feeling embarrassed about his intrusion. Continuing to the living room, Chris was surprised at the furnishings. "Simple."

"Excuse me."

"I'm sorry. I was just noticing that your style changed in here. It's the complete opposite of the other rooms. This one gives me the feeling of tranquility." A bone-colored Italian leather sectional, which had about six parts to it. Looking at the center of the room, he asked "Is that real?"

"Sure is. I had it preserved, petrified and imported from the Caribbean."

"I've never seen anything like it before."

"This plant grows deep in the sea. Of course, the glass was specially made here." Keesha paid special attention to spacing as everything was placed with an obvious purpose in mind. There was a fifty-two-inch color TV made into the wall with a hidden control panel. A bone-colored bar was off to itself on the other side of the living room with four leather stools flanking its mirrored front. The floors were carpeted with a rose-colored floki. The living room was lighted by two rose sculptures with softly lit balls on the end. Chris could see the dining room in the adjoining room from where he stood. There was a large cherry-wood case displaying fine China, crystal goblets and wine flutes. In the center of the diningroom was a large well-polished-cherry-wood dining table. To the left of that room was the kitchen with an island in its center. A four-person table was positioned in front of the window. Finally, just outside the kitchen was a wide stairway, which formed an arc that led to the bedrooms, he guessed.

"You have a very beautiful home, Keesha." He offered after his observance. "I love it! I'm rather impressed!"

"Your mother tells me that your house is even nicer than mine! I would love to see it sometime."

"You can stop by whenever you like. I'll be happy to give you the full tour," Chris said, rocking back and fourth on his heels smiling proudly as he thought of his own accomplishments. While pouring the Coke, Keesha could feel Chris undressing her with his eyes. She experienced an unusual tingling, at the back of her neck. The magnetism that he was giving off was strong. Turning, she said "Ice?"

His lips locked with hers. They were soft yet firm, gentle yet sweet. She knew that she should stop before things got even more out of hand. She tasted his aphrodisiac as he waxed it into her tongue. His tongue traced her neck, lingering for just a moment, causing flutters of emotions to chill her soul.

Fear clouded her mind, as she thought of what his mother might think. After all, she and Christine are friends. How could she betray her this way? Pulling away from Chris, Keesha said, "Chris, this isn't right. We can't do this."

He stepped away from her, still holding her hands, looking into her eyes. "I have waited an eternity to do this. I have been suppressing my love for you for longer than I can handle. Lets not let age come between us." He lowered his lips to meet hers again, caressing her back with his hands. Keesha felt the firmness of his arms tightening around her. Hugging her, Chris declared that he would never let her go. Somehow she knew he meant it. After staring down into her eyes, he picked up the glass of Coke, then took a seat in the living room. Stunned, she followed him. Their silence was thick enough to cut.

Chris broke the silence reciting his goals and aspirations. "I hope that I will someday become a partner of Goldman, Thurman & Sacs. I'm working my butt off, showing my skills, hoping that the partners will take notice of my talents and realize that I am a valuable asset to the company." Sighing, he gazed at the ceiling remembering the words of his accounting teacher during his sophomore year in high school. "Son, you've got potential, all you've got to do is apply yourself and so for what you want." He enrolled him in the co-op program, allowing him to work every other week. In fact, his accounting teacher had found him the position at the Goldman, Thurman & Sacs investment banking. "Asset Management and Private Client Services is my field. I started off as an analyst, then moved to project leader, and now I'm climbing the ladder to VP or maybe to even make MD." Chris graduated high school at the age of sixteen but that was just the beginning. One incident changed everything for him: After four years with the company, he had developed and maintained high-profile clients and earned $200,000 base with hefty bonuses. His inexperience and limited education allowed him to be more innovative than an entire staff of older, well-seasoned account executives with more designations and initials before and behind their names than he could shake a stick at. One of the company's largest and most prestigious foreign clients had been saved because of his simplistic eye. Now, he alone handled that account by the request of the client.

Chris graduated high school earning $45,000 a year, which was a hefty salary for a sixteen-year-old, but was nothing compared to his current $200,000 base. He believed that with his competency he should make partnership but in the meantime, he would have to settle. Of course, four years with a company did not entitle him to the position nor the property that was given to him as a status perk.

"Stopping by sounds wonderful Chris. I'm sure things will continue in your favor. I'm rooting for you!"

"Right now, the partners seem to be impressed. I have been holding down some important clients for them and so far, things are working out well! Of course, having a black man on the board might cause problems with the other board members!"

"Don't think like that. The bottom line is what they think about your work. Keep that in mind!"

"I know, it's just that when it comes to African Americans, no matter how hard we work or how important we are to them, they fail to give us the recognition we deserve! Of course, they pay me quite well. They don't mind paying the salary, it's the title they hold back on!"

"Keep hope alive, Chris. Keep hope alive!"

He smiled at her as she held her right fist in the air chanting the familiar slogan. She told him about what she did to build her business and how, with hard work, it proved to be lucrative. "Life was not easy for me, Chris. I had to work hard for everything that I have. You keep your head up and continue in the way you're going and no one can stop you, no matter how hard they try."

Chris couldn't believe she was giving him inspiration. Most women wouldn't even think he needed it. This woman really cared for him. Chris could feel nothing less than impressed by her declared success, and her home was proof to those who had any doubt that it could actually be done. Right then, he knew that she was indeed the woman for him.

"It's not often you see businesswomen advance in society as rapidly as you have. I like that in a woman." They talked for another hour. "I should be leaving now. Can I see you again or have I ruined the opportunity with my advancement?"

Keesha gave a smile of dismissal. "Don't worry about it. See you tomorrow."

He had a long day ahead of him tomorrow, not to mention he had to get out of her house before his feelings caused him to become more aggressive than was appropriate. Chris was afraid of tainting this opportunity of winning Keesha's love. He wanted to prove that he could give her all that she wanted, satisfy her sexual desires and take care of her emotional needs. She would never want another after him.

"Good night!"

"Good night." She ushered him to the door. He turned and kissed her on the cheek before making his exit. He decided that he would pay his mother a visit before journeying home. He walked down the block to his mother's house and attempted to compose himself before greeting her. His mother was good at reading him.

"Hi, Mom. How are you today?"

"Just fine, Chris. What brings you to the neighborhood today? You seem exceptionally happy. What's new with you? Let me guess: You met the girl of your dreams, and she's agreed to marry you?" Chris could never keep anything from his mother. If he was in love, his mother knew. She reminded him of the time when he was in junior high school and he had a crush on his teacher. When his mother went to open house, from the moment she walked into the classroom, she knew that the lady waiting to speak with her was the apple of her son's eye.

"How did you guess? Well actually, you're partly right, however, she didn't agree to marry me yet but I'll win her with my charm! Hmm, what's that pleasant aroma?" He was evading any further questioning.

"I made your favorite dish today!"

"Barbecue ribs?"

"Yeah, come in the kitchen, and I'll fix you a plate!" Chris followed her into the kitchen, taking his usual seat.

"Were you expecting company?"

"No. You know how I like to be prepared all the time!" She placed a plate of Barbecued ribs, a baked potato and mixed vegetables in front of him. She cast an endearing glance at her son who had made her proud from the day he was born. "I made sweet potato pudding too."

The food was all too welcoming. Christine was content with her guileless living. All of the other houses in the neighborhood had been remodeled by interior decorators. Their lawns treated by the best local landscapers but Christine didn't. She had even refused Chris' offer to pay to have the work done. She enjoyed the obvious dissimilarity her home displayed.

They talked about her day, and how he should visit with her more often. The usual stuff he heard whenever he visited. "So, tell me about her. Anyone I know?"

Chris didn't respond. This wasn't the right time to reveal his beloved. "I can assure you, you'll approve. She's smart, beautiful, successful and very easy to get along with." Christine considered questioning him further but realized that perhaps she shouldn't press him. "She sounds great. I would love to meet her! I take it that she's not one of those local girls. You know how I feel about them, she said, " frowning at the thought. She knew that Chris was smart and hadn't dated a great deal, thus her concern for her son's choices. "Son, there are a lot of wolves in sheep's clothing!"

"I know that mom. You don't have to worry. This woman is really nice and I know that you'll like her. Trust me."

"So when can I meet her? Not to kick dirt, but remember that girl I told you to leave alone after your father died? Didn't I tell you that she would bring you grief?"

Resenting the memory. There wasn't a day Chris didn't regret meeting Rhonda. She was not the ideal woman for him, and it didn't take him long to realize that. It took Rhonda a while to grasp the fact that things were over between them but she finally did let go. He could still remember his first love. He had never been attracted to younger women.

"Soon, but not yet, Mom. I want to wait until things are official and going the way I hope they will."

"So, you've finally found someone who's mature enough for you?"

Chris avoided the question. "Mom, I've got to be going. I'll stop in later this week. How's that?"

"Okay, son, but I know you're just avoiding the question. We'll talk later. You just be careful." Christine was very perceptive and would continue to question him until he would have no choice but to tell her about Keesha. He leaned forward to kiss her before leaving. Chris took a deep breath recognizing the close call he had just encountered.

The drive home was especially long, but Chris knew that he had to stop in to see his mom at least twice a week. She still had gotten used to the fact that he was a man now and their would be different. He would always be her little Chris.

Chris' mind was occupied by the thought of loving Keesha. His mother always said good things do come to those who wait! And Chris would wait. He wanted Keesha to be the mother of his children. Chris would work hard and take care of her. Taking care of the woman he loved is all he'd ever wanted, and no one or anything would come between them. Chris pulled up to the gate at the Enclave Town Houses where he resided. Charles, the gate attendant, buzzed him in, and he drove up to his designated spot and parked. The residence was quiet and peaceful. Fumbling with his keys, he finally located the ones needed to unlock the door. It was late and he desperately needed sleep to be fresh for the next day's events.

CHAPTER

2

All day at the office, and during appointments Keesha continued to think of Chris. She stared deep into her coffee cup and there she saw his face. Get a grip on yourself, she thought, realizing that she was trying to get something she could never have.

Despite her musings, the day proved to be successful. Her client accepted her proposed business agreement. She explained to them the importance of making such business preparations in the early stages of business. The premiums paid rendered her $300,000 richer. All her hard work and effort had paid off. Well actually, she only spent a total of three hours on it, but what the hell, she thought, I earned it! She danced the tootsie roll in front of her thirty-seventh-floor office window. Feeling proud of her achievement, she stared out at the open sky, no longer caring about the ten years she'd spent alone since her last love. Gerald was a bastard and deserved any afflictions he encountered. He made her life hell with his deceptions and lies. Keesha could still see them lying on her silk sheets cuddled in her bed. The couple never noticed her standing at the door as they made promises to each other to be together forever. Keesha silently left the small apartment without confrontation. There was a time Keesha used to wonder if he had made good on his promises, but after becoming engrossed with work and money, it no longer mattered. Besides, he wasn't good for her anyway.

She would probably have still lived in that constricted, dilapidated apartment today if his betrayal hadn't shown her the light. She had wasted five years of her life with him. She was only twenty then, too young to realize the mistake she was making. Things were hard at first since she had no one to depend on. Both her parents died during a hostile drug war between the local project thugs. Ebony, her best friend, had given her a place to stay and helped her finish college and become the person she was today. The last three years of her life had been wonderful. Business was going well, she built the home she had always dreamed about, and now she had the finances to keep things going the way she wanted.

Keesha couldn't wait to get home and share this information with her new lover. Although she knew that Chris wasn't her lover, she entertained the thought anyway. Look at me calling him my lover. I should be ashamed of myself. I don't know what he is, but one thing's for sure, He's mine for now!

Later that evening she anticipated his arrival. As it got later, she couldn't understand why he had not arrived yet. He always showed up around the same time everyday, and now that she had her heart set on seeing him, he had stood her up. Her mind was going crazy. It was eight o'clock. Certainly he should have been there by now. She waited and waited for him to ring her bell.

Keesha could envision Chris sitting home laughing at how bovine she must be to think that he would have some real interest in her. Keesha imagined him making jokes with his friends, saying how he had an old cow swooning over him. Taking umbrage to his imagined behavior, Keesha couldn't help but welcome despondency. Keesha ate the dinner she prepared and followed it with a hot bath to wash her troubles away. Keesha leaned back in her Jacuzzi enjoying the new power jets she had just had installed. She could smell the peach bubbles cascading in her tub and the warmth from the steam penetrated her tired soul. An hour passed, and she awakened from her relaxed stupor and decided that she'd better make way to her bed. She blotted the water off with her towel then went to her bed. Keesha laid down, staring at the ceiling, wondering why Chris hadn't come by as he'd promised. Just as she was drifting off to sleep, she thought she heard the doorbell ringing. She listened again and decided that she had better go check it out. Keesha rushed downstairs and hurried to the door.

"Who is it?" she questioned, while observing the face peering at her through the peephole. Recognizing the familiar face, she excitedly opened the door. The sight of Chris immediately wiped away the despondency she felt earlier. Her heart quickened as Chris patiently awaited admittance. Finally, realizing that she hadn't invited him in, she quickly stood aside, gesturing him in and apologizing for the delay. "Chris, what a pleasant surprise," she said as he entered.

"I'm sorry about being late. I had to get out some work before I left today and realized that it was getting late. I would have called but I didn't have your number." He followed her into the living room, taking a seat together on the sectional, while discussing their days. Keesha told Chris about her plans for the money. Chris had other things on his mind. Gazing deep into her eyes, he leaned close enough to kiss her, speaking softly with a gentle breath tickling her lips ..."I want to make love to you!"

She wanted him, too, but had not expected him to be so forward. "Tell me you want me."

"Chris," she said shyly, not wanting to play into his ego game. He repeated his request but she wouldn't say what he wanted her to, fighting to avoid eye contact. She couldn't admit her desire for him. His brown eyes had captivated her, and she was lost in the abyss of his pupils.

Chris kissed from her neck down to her breasts. His skilled hands undid her buttons. As he fervently sucked at her tender flesh, his fingers loosened the last of the buttons on her dress. Her dress cascaded off her shoulders and made a pool around her on the chair. His hands shaped her supple flesh as he guided his hungry lips to the chocolate mounds of her breasts. She moaned with pleasure.

His hands glided around her torso, resting on her buttocks as he forced her to recline on the chair. He ripped her bikinis from her waist then fell to his knees indulging in an oral inquisition.

"Say it" he demanded. She couldn't. The words were locked in her throat. He spread her legs apart as far as they would go. Keesha leaned back deeper into the cushions of the chair. His lips were warm and gentle against her flesh. His wet tongue softly tickled her. She took delight in the pleasure he was giving.

"Say it!"he insisted, demonstrating his skill in lovemaking.

Keesha remained closed mouthed as he tasted her more aggressively. The feeling intensified. Keesha couldn't resist conceding to his request much longer. Chris' body hardened at the thought of her wetness. He considered the gratification penetrating her would bring, and the supplicating culmination that would follow.

"Say it!"he ordered. Again she remained stubborn, unwilling to give in to his arrogance. As he mentally observed her changing condition causing his own anticipation to intensify, a fire like he had never known built within. Chris imagined himself entering her until the love flowed from his body, and passionately teasing her into submission.

She ached for him, needing him to take her to the ultimate climax. She knew that she couldn't hold out much longer.

"Say you want me!"

Keesha knew she couldn't and wouldn't.

"Say it,"he demanded in a seductive manner. She was becoming so hot she couldn't stand it.

"Say it."

Keesha ached to feel him thrust into her.

"Say it"he said with more command. The pleasure he was giving her intensified. He could sense her near submission. He could feel the heat building in her.

"Say it!"

Her lips trembled, and she gritted her teeth.

"Say it."

She clawed the chair.

"Say it."

She leaned over and gripped the chair.

"Say it."

Ecstasy nearing.

"Say it!"

Her breath quickened. I won't she thought. It was so close and she could feel herself preparing to explode when he stopped. She was panting like crazy, burning with lasciviousness and ardor. Her body pleaded for him.

He came up, kissed her lips taunting her with the smell of her essence on his lips . . . "Say it, and I'll give you what you want. Just say it." He kissed her neck, shoulder and her back. "I'll wait for you, I know that when I finish with you, you'll say it, you'll scream it, you'll even beg for it. So I'll wait for you."

She could feel the blood pumping fast within her veins, rushing in and out of her heart, sending blood to the pulsating, lusting organ that was overheating and beseeching his affection.

"Okay, you want to play tough." Chris touched her hungry body lightly with his, grinding himself against her. She was pleading for his love. She wanted to feel him inside her but he only teased her. Keesha wanted him and knew that she could not resist his arrogant request

much longer. He would prolong it long enough to render her into submission.

"I want you," she cried.

"Want me to what?" he asked.

"I want you to make love to me."

He knelt down between her legs. "It's not love you want tonight,
baby."

"Then fuck me!" she said.

In an instant he threw her legs over his shoulders and began hammering into her. She screamed with passion, satisfaction and pleasure as
he brought out the passions that had been pent up inside for far too long.
She could feel the orgasm knocking at her door. Keesha experienced
eruption after eruption, as Chris penetrated her, carrying her to new
heights of pleasure.

He pulled her arms around his neck, for her to hold on, then lifted
her from the chair. Gripping her buttocks, he slid her up and down his
shaft. Keesha met his every thrust, admiring his strength and agility.

"I'm cumming," she screamed.

"What's my name?" he said.

"Chris," she yelled.

"Whose pussy is this?"

"Yours," she answered.

Their lust succumbed to exquisite orgasm as the two of them experienced the rapture of climax and concupiscence' wrath. Chris carried
Keesha over to the wall, pressing her against it. He continued grinding
himself against her, giving her all of himself until they ruptured into the
final ecstasy. Then, he kissed her. "Don't ever be afraid to express yourself to me. I love you and know all of your needs and will supply you
with more loving than you could ever stand. Don't let our age difference
get in the way of our happiness." He placed her on the sofa and withdrew himself from her, letting her legs slide down his sides to the floor.

Chris found his way to the bathroom and ran warm water in the
shower. Chris enjoyed the massage the water pressure gave as it knead-
ed into his shoulder blades. Chris smiled to himself, thinking that he
finally would win the heart of the only woman he had ever loved. Yes,
he'd had relationships with other women but; they could never conquer
the desires that were deep in his heart the way Keesha did.

After the shower, he found a bed to rest on. Chris wasn't sure if it was a guest bedroom or Keesha's own sleeping quarters.

Keesha went upstairs when she no longer heard the water running. She waited for Chris to return as long as she could. When she reached the top of the stairs, she looked in the bathroom, but Chris was not there. She then headed to the guests' bedrooms, not finding him in any of them. She found Chris sprawled across her bed. Keesha stood there amazed at his body, as well as the self-control he displayed and his ability to make her do whatever he wanted. Keesha felt as though this was her first time all over again but one thousand times magnified. He was indeed magnificent, and she knew then and there that no other woman would ever have him.

Keesha went into her bathroom, and sat on her bidet relaxing as the water cleansed her body. Then she let the shower rinse away the dew of romance. When she soaped her skin, she could feel the lingering pleasures while enjoying the aroma of the peach soap. The steam burned out the kinks of the day. "Ah, how good it feels to make love to a man again and then enjoy the ending finale of the shower,"she said aloud.

She put on her robe and found Chris was still fast asleep. Shocked, she studied and admired the structure of his body. He was a slender man, built like a Greek god. His arms were thick with chiseled muscles, neck wide like a cobra, his chest and back rippling with brawn. This was not the body of an twenty-one-year-old! . He had a long, thick circumcised penis.

She wanted him again but was too tired. Noticing the clock, she realized the amount of time that had passed. Could we really have gone at it for three hours? No wonder he's tired. Keesha pulled the covers over him calling it a night. Crawling into the bed next to him, Keesha kissed his lips then dozed off to sleep.

The next morning she woke up expecting to find him at her side, but he wasn't there. When could he have left, she wondered.

"Good morning!"Chris called from the kitchen. "I got up early and made breakfast."

"Oh, Chris, you didn't have to do that."

"I know, honey. I just wanted us to start the day with a wholesome breakfast." He smiled at her continuing to prepare their meal. After breakfast he got dressed in the suit he pulled from his car while Keesha slept. Chris then headed off to work. "See you later,"he yelled as he walked out the door.

Keesha locked the door behind him and wondered what had she gotten herself into. She knew that a relationship with Chris couldn't possibly work. How could she face Christine knowing that she had slept with her son? She pondered that for most of the day, wondering what she would say if she were to run into her or if Christine decided to stop by.

Chris and Keesha spent weeks enjoying each other's company, doing new things and exploring possibilities. Keesha could feel that love was drawing them closer together. March was coming to its conclusion and the April showers would either make the relationship fresh and clean or wash it away. Judging the circumstances, Keesha already felt the torrent rains washing Chris away. She needed time, time to get away and think things over rationally.

CHAPTER

3

"What are you doing here?"

"Chris, honey, let's not spit venom at each other. You know how much I love you. I was in the area and realized that we hadn't seen each other in such a long time and decided to stop by!"She was smiling at him with eyes filled with the greatest of joy and happiness. She had missed her Chris, and now after such a long time, would reunite with him.

"I told you that things were over between us. You are making this very difficult for me."

"I know we shared some bad times, honey, but that's all over. Let's just start over anew." Chris' ex-lover was seducing him. He had not seen her since his second semester of college, almost two years ago. He could not understand why a woman would waste her time trying to win the love of someone who despised her. One thing he realized was that she had one thing over him. Chris appreciated her good loving and would always fall for her seduction. She was twenty-three years old and acted like she was fifteen. She had a body to die for and the looks to stop a speeding locomotive.

Since Chris did not yield to her pleading, she did what she knew would win at least his body.

"Don't do this,"he insisted. "I told you it's over between us. I don't want to...

Before he could finish his sentence, her lips met his. Making his best effort to avoid her, he turned his head, to no avail. She ignored his rejection while fumbling with his bulging erection. "Honey, your mouth says no, but your body says yes. Which head is the commanding officer? You're so confused."

He wanted her to leave, but his body ached for the magic he knew she would create. He never could break her spell. In an instant, she had freed his staff, gratifying him orally. Pushing him to the floor, without reluctance, he obeyed the conscience of his penis. She positioned herself atop him while he penetrated her with little resistance. Chris was at home, a place where his coat had hung many times before. The fit was perfect.

Her motions welcomed him home, taking only moments to find an appreciable rhythm. A rush of ecstasy pacified their fervent cries of passions. Chris fought to contain himself but couldn't. Her passion was so sweet, not even the Pope with all his glory could deny her.

"Oh God," he cried out.

Her body pounded harder against his, forcing him to want her. His hands gripped her thighs as he forced himself deeper. "Give it to me," she begged as she welcomed his sweet release. The child she always wanted would be hers at last. The love held within her for him was too precious to let go. Nothing would ever come between them. She could feel herself reaching orgasm. He was about to erupt too.

When it was over, Chris' obvious repulsion led him to his bath. If soap could only remove the filth she had just tainted his new relationship with. Chris hoped that he could cover his mistake and avoid the inevitable ruin his new relationship would suffer.

Finally returning to confront his tormentor... "Don't ever come here again!" The words pierced her like a double-edged sword. She could never have imagined her Chris treating her with such cruelty. It was as if he had spat venom into her face.

"You think you're better than I am because you have all this, but it means nothing when there's no one here to love you!"

Chris bit his tongue, resisting retort. He would let her humiliation and disgrace keep her away from him.

"You'll pay for this Chris!" she spat while storming out of the door, almost twisting her ankle on a pair of heels too high for her.

Chris quickly closed his door, not waiting to see her off the grounds. Infuriated at the events, he called the gate attendant, reprimanding him for letting someone onto the property unannounced. The attendant assured him that he had not authorized any visitors. "She must have been here already. When I came in, I checked the grounds before I relieved the other gate attendant."

Baffled, Chris hung up the telephone. He wondered how she was able to get on the property without anyone noticing her. He picked up the telephone again and told the attendant he wanted his locks changed immediately and the grounds searched diligently afterwards.

"How dare he make love to me and throw me out without even giving me the courtesy of cleaning, like I'm a common whore? I loved him and gave him the best of me. Chris will not get away with treating me this way. She wrestled the tears forcing their way through her ducts. He would not break her. Chris would pay for the anguish he had just caused. Suddenly, she had renewed spirits, realizing her desires had finally been met. She got what she wanted . . . "Chris Warner, you will marry me. I'm carrying your child, and you can't take that away from me and I will let the whole world know it too." Her voice echoed through the desolate property. She would force him to love her. Otherwise, she would ruin him.

By now, tears blinded her as she fought to control herself. She would not exit the property by the front gate but use the entrance she had used when she arrived.

Chris went to his bar grabbing a bottle of his best vodka, desperately needing a drink. As the bitter liquid stung his throat, he realized that there wasn't a drink strong enough to wipe away what had just happened. Defeat left a bad taste in his mouth. Disappointment hung over him like a cloak when he realized that he had allowed his ex-lover to waltz into his life once again. He remembered the night before when he had made love and spent the night with the woman of his dreams. "How could I throw it away so easily? I love Keesha and would never do anything to hurt her. How could I let my ex come between us? I should have known better and guarded myself against this kind of problem. Now I have to worry about whether or not I impregnated her! God, please hear my prayer. Give me one more chance. I promise this will never happen again! If no one else can help me, I know you can! Please God, don't let her carry my child!"

CHAPTER

4

It was April 1, and Keesha decided to spend a few days in California with her friend Ebony Thomas. If anyone could take her mind off things, Ebony could. Ebony was one of Keesha's best friends and whenever Keesha needed counseling, she could rely on her. Ebony and Keesha attended elementary, junior high and high school together. During Keesha's second year at college, she fell for one of the students, Gerald. They decided to get an apartment together. That lasted only two years. Broken to pieces with no place to turn to, she took shelter with her friend Ebony. Ebony held a decent job and was able to manage our tuition. She paid for her own with a student loan and used the money her parents put aside for her to pay for Keesha's education. Ebony being the person she is, refused to let Keesha repay her generosity. She said that friendship was something that couldn't be bought and should be prized no matter what the cost. She would always hold a special place in Keesha's heart.

Considering the forbidden relationship she was currently in, Keesha wished she had allowed Ebony to let Jamal Warner know how she felt about him. She wondered what he was doing with himself after all these years. Fearing rejection, she had Ebony swear secrecy. Jamal was very attractive, and many women were attracted to him. "He wouldn't have been interested anyway,"she murmured. "Oh well, he'll never know just how I felt about him."

Keesha drifted, imagining how wonderful life would have been with him. Chris was the only man she had dealt with since she walked away from a relationship ten years ago. Without realizing it, she wanted to mold Chris into what she believed a man should represent. He would be her perfect sculpture. She purposely avoided calling Gerald's name in her thoughts fearing it opening a wound that has been closed so long. She thought of Chris and half regretted getting involved with him.

"I need time to think,"she told herself. "I shouldn't be doing this. How could I have let things go this far?" As much as Keesha wanted Chris, the fear of hurting Christine overshadowed her feelings for her son. On the other hand, she didn't want to let go either. Chris was right! age really didn't matter. She decided that she would take a little time and confide in her friend Ebony.

She called the airline and reserved a ticket to California for an afternoon flight. The agent told her that the next flight was at 12:05. She looked at her clock and realized that she had enough time to make it for the flight. Keesha gave the clerk her credit-card number and paid for her ticket.

Then she called Ebony at work.

"Taylor Financing."

"Girl, guess what?"

"What?"she said.

"I just reserved a ticket to fly to California!"

"You're kidding, when? Next year? You know how long I've been trying to get to you spend some time with me."

"Today. My plane leaves at 12:05. I'm spending a week with you."

"You're coming today? Gee, that's sudden. What's the occasion?"

"Do I need an occasion to see my best friend?"

"No, you know you're welcome anytime, no reservation needed. Mì casa es sù casa. I'll meet you at the airport."

"Good, I'll see you about three. Talk to you later. I've got to get out of here before I miss my plane." Keesha hurried upstairs to her bedroom, quickly packing her travel bag. She called a taxi explaining her rush to get to the airport. When the taxi arrived, she locked her door and hurried to the end of her driveway with her bag. She jumped into the cab and the driver put her bag into the trunk then sped down the street and onto the highway.

Keesha stared out of the window wondering how Chris would respond to her sudden escapade, feeling deceitful for not calling him at the very least to let him know that she would be away for a few days. Maybe, she thought, this is the best way to handle the situation. If she could convince Chris that she was avoiding him, maybe he'd just leave her alone. The thought made her feel sick since she couldn't bare the thought of Chris being with someone else. He needs to be with someone his own age. What kind of person would I be if I hindered this young fellow when I am so many years his senior⸮ She was punishing herself with guilt and knew that she should not be trying to hold on to her friend's baby.

Perhaps when I get to California, Ebony and I will meet some nice men and I can forget all about Chris!" She contemplated many ways that she might rid her mind of the young man she had fallen in love with. Why does life have to be so hard⸮

After a while, she turned her attention back to her destination and asked the driver to speed it up. His eyes widened as he looked up at her through the rearview mirror. "Lady if I go any faster we'll crash through the divider, go tumbling down over the overpass smackdab onto the pavement underneath us and finally mess up your pretty little face. Now we wouldn't want that to happen, now would we⸮" His mark of sarcasm angered Keesha as he continued to glance at her, smiling all the time. He gave her a wink and added a little gas to the engine.

She made a face at him. "Just speed it up, thank you!"

He chuckled, continuing to make his way through traffic. Thank goodness traffic was light affording them to make good time. The driver helped her with her bags. Keesha, feeling grateful and a little embarrassed about her behavior, reached into her purse and pulled out forty dollars, thanking the driver then gesturing with a wave of her hand to keep the change. He smiled, blew a kiss, then hurried to his cab. Keesha picked up her ticket and the attendant hurried her down the corridor to catch her plane, which was almost ready to leave.

Keesha quickly took her seat, fastening her seatbelt , then looked at her watch noting that it was twelve o'clock. It wasn't long before the flight attendant began giving emergency instructions while the plane slowly began to move toward the runway. Keesha stared out of the window thinking about the chocolate bunny she thoughtlessly left behind. I could have at least called him at the office to let him know,"she thought reprimanding herself.

Keesha remembered the way Chris aggressively made love to her. He was sooooo good. Hmm, I'm going to hate letting him go. He has all the qualities I believe a man should have. He's handsome, charming, sexy, intelligent, ambitious, and is already planning his future. God, I love him!"

She closed her eyes deciding to sleep because she knew Ebony would have a full itinerary planned beginning the moment they left the airport. I can hear her now . . . leave your bag in the trunk girl and let's get this party started right! Keesha smiled at the thought and thanked God that she had a friend like Ebony.

Keesha fell asleep, fantasizing about being married to Chris, him working long shifts, her waiting for him to come home and make passionate love to her. There she was standing on the veranda with her hair blowing in the wind, wearing her long champagne, silk nightgown. Chris would greet her with a gentle kiss on the neck. Then spin her around to face him, placing her atop the railing where he made love to her. Afterward, she would be standing close to him staring at the starry blue sky in search of the Heaven that must have brought them together.

Abruptly her eyes opened, and to her surprise, there was a crowd of passengers standing around her smiling. "What's going on? Is everything all right? What is everybody standing here smiling at?"she asked vehemently.

"Girl, someone must have turned you out, because you were talking and moaning passionately in your sleep. As you can see, your premier was good, and everyone fought to get front-row seats!" The attendant sympathized with her embarrassment and said, "Ma'am, you were talking and moaning in your sleep. The other passengers overheard you so I decided I'd better wake you up before you said something you wouldn't want anyone to know."

"Thanks, at least there's someone with some decency around here!" Her voice had a note of mockery and chastisement. The rest of the flight to California was miserable having everyone giggling and whispering then turning their heads when she looked at them. The men winked or blew kisses at her when they caught her attention. She couldn't wait until the flight was over!

Finally, the plane landed, and she jetted off. Someone yelled to her, "Hope to hear from you soon!" A horde of whistles and claps chided her off the plane. Her eyes roamed and scanned the waiting area searching for her friend. "Don't tell me she's late. Ebony is never late. I don't think she's ever been late for anything." There at the concession stand was Ebony flirting as usual. "Hey, girl,"she yelled. "Here I am." Keesha ran over to greet her best friend. She gave her best friend a big hug, grabbed her hand, and they raced off to get the car. "Oh! What about my bag?"

"Girl, your bag got here a long time ago, I picked it up already!"

"How did you know which was mine?"
"Who else would carry a bright orange blind-me bag but you?"
"All right! So my bag is bright and noticeable."
"Yeah, they probably rushed the plane here to drop it off."
"Would you stop making fun of me and come on?"
They hurried off like two teenaged girls who hadn't seen each other in years. Keesha ran behind her best friend Ebony, admiring the sunny skies surrounding her. They raced out to the parking lot. They jumped into Ebony's jeep and rode off into the California sunshine. "So where do we go first?" Keesha asked.

"I thought we'd start at my place and discuss why you spontaneously decided to make this trip to Cali. Certainly there must have been something on your mind that couldn't be discussed over the telephone, and I want you to spill your guts before you do something you'll regret for the rest of your life!"

They arrived at Ebony's house and pulled onto her stone driveway. Ebony unloaded the bright orange bag, taking it into the house, before it drew the attention of the neighbors. "I'll take my bag to the guest room."

"No you won't, you're going to leave it at the door and accompany me to the sitting room to spill your guts."

"Ebony, do you remember that young boy that I told you would break someone's heart someday? Well, I think I may be falling in love with him!"

"How did that happen? Didn't I tell you that he was too young for you when you first mentioned him? You've got to cut that short, girl! It will never work out! Young men are nothing but heartaches and grief to older women! Don't you know it takes a man seven years to catch up with a woman! Girl, he's got a great deal of growing and maturing to do."

"I know, but he seduced me and now things have gone too far. I thought that after we made love that it would just be a fulfillment of my greatest fantasy, but now we have been spending a great deal of time together, and I don't know how to handle the situation. His mother would kill me if she knew that I was with her son. You know how she worships him. No woman is good enough for him."

"Hey, you're good enough for him, too good if you ask me! But he is too young for you, and you need to leave that snack alone before you get yourself hurt or at the very least a heart full of pain!"

"I can't just drop him!"

"Girl, a woman isn't a woman if she can't change her mind! Remember that. Don't let that kid make you feel guilty. He'll get over it and if not, too bad. This is all about you and what will be in your best interest!"

"Yeah, I should just tell him that the sex was great but I have to leave him now!"

"No, you don't have to say it like that. Just explain to him how you feel."

"That's the problem, I think I'm in love with him, and I'm sure that he can sense it. So how can I explain stealing away and returning? With a `little harp song'? So Dr. Ruth, what do you think, how should I handle it?"

"If you really like him, go for it, and his mother will have to just deal with it. Now if on the other hand, you were just exploring and wanted to remember what it was like being a teenager . . . you will hurt him in the end. Then I'd say let him go now before you ruin that young boy. Keesh, we never talked about Gerald. Does this have anything to do with him?"

"No, why would you bring him up after all these years?"

"I just felt that after you left without calling or confronting him, perhaps there's still a little insecurity festering in you."

"No there isn't! I'm fine. I've been over him since I walked away. Look at me, I have everything."

"Not everything. You're lonely, Keesha, and this young guy isn't the answer."

"Ebony, I thought you were my friend. How can you criticize me like this?"

"I'm not, I'm trying to help you. I know you, Keesh, and this is not what you need, but if this is what you think you want, as I said before, you have my blessing."

"What do you think about young men?"

"I think no one can be more exciting and exploratory than they are . They are the most energetic, strong and sexiest people you will ever meet and no old man can give you the longevity a young man can. Not only that, a young guy will kill himself trying to please you because he feels he has to prove himself and he really gets off on you enjoying what he's giving and finally he really wants to please you. They are the desired forbidden fruit!" Ebony took a deep breath ... "So let's go and have some fun and you'll decide what you want to do about Mr. Romeo after this weekend."

"Did I mention that I didn't call him to let him know that I was leaving?"

"No, you didn't. If you think you're lonely now, wait until you get back, girl. He'll be long gone, yes, he will," Ebony sang the old familiar song by Bobby Womack.

Ebony stood up, dismissing the conversation feeling confident that her friend was not on the verge of mental breakdown. "So you're saying I should call him?"

"No, I'm saying you should consider what you may be doing by not calling him and decide if the repercussions behind not calling are worth the suspense you'll get when you return."

"Maybe after this trip you may find that you want to be with him, and if you're starting off this way, you may lose him! Is that what you want?"

Keesha shrugged and gave it some thought. "You're right. I'll give him a call when we get back!"

"Stalling, huh? Okay, come on."

They went everywhere. Ebony took Keesha sightseeing showing her the monuments and landmarks of California. She showed her the ritzy neighborhoods of the rich and famous. They had lunch at the Pavilion where they were served the best club sandwich in town. Then later in the evening, they ate dinner on the beach blowing kisses at the hunks in trunks, who resembled roasted peanuts.

"Oh, by the way, Keesha, I have a surprise for you!"

"When will I get it?"

"Soon."

"Soon like when?"

"Soon like in soon! No more questions." Ebony laughed knowing Keesha would ponder on her surprise until she got it. Ebony was good for being mischievous. Ebony, sipping a Sex on the Beach, dismissed Keesha's questions about her surprise. Keesha knew that Ebony was up to something but she would never be able to put her finger on it. Ebony was always good at surprises. Suddenly a nicely tanned man walked over to where they were sitting. He was drop-dead gorgeous. Keesha had to lower her shades to get a better look at him. She wanted him. "Now that man I would put all my morals on the side for. I'd take that sexy string he has around his waist off and make passionate love to him."

"I'm sure that he's hoping you feel that way!"

Keesha looked at Ebony in surprise. Usually Ebony wanted all the play herself. It was all about competition to Ebony, and now she was almost throwing the man at her. "What do you mean?"

"Hi, ladies," came a husky voice. "Care if I join you?"

"No, of course not," Ebony answered with that sly provocative grin of hers, realizing that Keesha hadn't remembered him. "This is Keesha."

"Hello, Keesha. Mind if I join you?"

"Please do," she said provocatively. The stranger kissed Keesha's hand and sat between them. Keesha stared at him wondering where they had met. Not wanting to be embarrassed, she decided not to ask Ebony until later. Instead, she observed his manly qualities. His muscles were firm and tight, body crisp and brown like a Park's Hot & Sagey sausage.

Jamal knew Keesha didn't recognize him so he decided to play along and see how long it would take for her to remember. He could almost see her mental wheels turning as she tried to be inconspicuous. "So ladies, where are you currently residing?"

"Well," Ebony started, knowing he was just making it more difficult for Keesha , "I live here in California and Keesha lives in New York."

"That's great! I've always wanted to go to New York. Maybe now I'll have a reason," he said with this boyish grin.

Ebony excused herself and said, "Maybe you two want to be alone and catch up on lost time."

"Oh by the way Keesha, surprise!" She walked away and some husky, fine brute snatched her up, and ran off with her. Keesha listened while her friend's giggles faded as they disappeared down the beach. It's just like Ebony to know all the guys, she thought.

"So Keesha, what brings you out here to California?"

"Oh, I just felt like getting away."

"That's nice that you take time to treat yourself. Many women spend a lifetime in one place and never get to see the world and don't even think about it. Their main concern is how much money and jewelry they can con a man out of!"

Keesha wondered whether she should be insulted, or appreciate him noticing her class. Of course, she didn't need his money, if he had any. She was financially set and really couldn't think of anything that she longed for, other than a good loving man her age to fall in love with.

"So, do you live here?" Keesha asked.

"No, I live in Virginia now."

"What do you do in Virginia?"

"I'm a surgeon, specializing in gynecology and obstetrics."

"That's interesting. Do you like it?"

"Yes, I do. I think God was very artful when he created women. So I wanted to know more about them and how they operate."

"Then I guess being a gynecologist, you should specialize in pleasing a woman," she flirted.

He laughed. "No, not really but I'm sure that I can please you!"

"Oh, you can?"

"That is if you want me to of course. Most women don't reach an orgasm because they don't want to. They fill themselves with so much anxiety that they don't allow the man to please them. Unfortunately, the man is blamed all the time. But when I make love to a woman, she will give me all of her attention because I demand it with passion!"

Is he serious? This is either a mark of arrogance or bull shit beach talk. Either way, he's good-looking and I think I will take him up on his offer. Her mind was going overtime. Suddenly she came to her senses realizing her outward lust!

"Ice cream?" he offered. "You look a little hot!" His statement struck her funny, and he joined her in laughter. She really did feel a little hot for him.

Jamal wanted her so desperately but the timing wasn't right. He wondered how she would feel about him if he continued his advances. Trying to divert his attention from her appetizingly desirable body…"So, pretty lady, tell me about yourself. What do you do for a living?"

"I am a financial planner for large business owners. I mainly handle funding business agreements, pension plans, establishing liquidity for buyouts during the premature death of business owners or retirement of disabled partners."

He had heard enough, with his mind going overtime, he had to take his chances. "Liquidity, I like that word. Are you liquid, Keesha?"he asked, hoping not to frighten her away.

"Doc, are you being dirty?"

Just, what he needed to hear. She was thinking along the same lines. "Yes, you like it?"he asked with apprehension. Keesha went along with his teasing as she was hoping to relieve herself of the forbidden desires she had developed for Chris . . . "I do!"

"Shall we?"

"We shall!"

"So let's go?"

"Where?"

"To my place!" At first, Keesha felt a sense of guilt. She wondered if maybe she was allowing things to move too fast. Not focusing on morals, she found his offer tempting. Her yearning for him was greater than any known to her. She felt perfectly safe with him and knew he meant her no harm. Today she would have him, and tomorrow...would speak for itself since tomorrow was promised to no one. Disloyalty was something she didn't want to focus on right now. Tomorrow's anxieties would speak for themselves. The entire situation was erotic, something she hadn't felt in a long time. All she knew was that this tall, dark and sexy man, from her past, was driving her to his place, and she wanted to sleep with him.

They pulled up to a beach house, cabin, would be a more suitable description. Jamal got out of the car, making his way to her side, then helped her from the passenger seat. He pulled her face up with his hands pressing his lips against hers in a soft, passionate kiss. "You know, this hot orange bikini is very attractive on you. I spotted you a mile across the beach."

Suddenly, she remembered him, a dark stranger from her past. The guy she wouldn't dare look at twice, fearing rejection. Of course, all the girls wanted him. As quiet as he was, he was the most popular guy in the school. "It's funny how time changes things,"she said, smiling at the thought.

"What do you mean?"

"I used to have a crush on you but I was too shy to tell you."

"I can hardly imagine you being shy toward a man! Certainly not worrying about whether someone would like you. What man wouldn't?" He remembered attending high school in Washington, D.C., sitting behind Keesha in biology. She was bright, beautiful and classy. Keesha never mingled with the guys. Ebony, her best friend was the opposite. Ebony was the only one to know how he felt about Keesha. He wondered how the two of them got along so well. He pleaded with Ebony to hook them up but she always refused.

Many years had passed, and finally Ebony had granted his wish, and all he could think about was making love to Keesha when his focus should be on convincing her to allow him to stay in contact. Jamal considered the situation, reasoning that he had the best of intentions toward her. Keesha would see that over time.

"If I had known you were interested in me then, I would have snatched you up a long time ago. In fact, you'd probably be my wife running along the beach with our children." Keesha was surprised by the statement but something in his eyes showed sincerity, and she believed him.

He lifted her up into his arms and carried her into the wooded area surrounding the cabin. There was a clearing beyond the trees with a picnic table and two benches. He laid her on the table and said, "I like my meat saucy!" as he peeled her bikini down around her ankles then over her feet. He kissed her belly and circled her navel with his tongue. Keesha moaned with pleasure. Jamal gently nibbled at her side and she flinched from the tickling sensation he sent through her waist. Jamal opened her legs far apart and said . . . "I'm going to give you a new meaning to the word pleasure." Jamal gently kissed her belly one last time before disappearing into the woods. Keesha began to worry that he might leave her there. She remained, waiting for his return. After a few moments, he returned with a blindfold, some rope and a few items he bought from the kitchen. He asked if he could have her any way he wanted, and she agreed, as long as she promised not do anything that would humiliate her or cause her pain. Then he explained that he wanted her to use all her senses except her eyes. "I want you to hear, feel and taste my lovin'."

Covering Keesha's eyes, Jamal kissed her nose, cheeks and mouth. She felt him binding her hands and tying them above her head. Then he put a cloth around each of her thighs, separating her legs and securing the cloth to the benches on either side of the table. Jamal told her this would prevent her from premature orgasm.

"A different approach, but I'm for it,"Keesha said. This was exciting for her. Never had she been rendered helpless and appreciated it. She felt something cool and wet around her nipples. "Whip cream, my dear?"he asked while pouring something warm down the middle of her chest, onto her stomach and over her vagina. She smelled the aroma of chocolate. Jamal put his lips to hers and forced her mouth open for a kiss, dropping in a cherry. It was so juicy. Sweet liquid squirted from her mouth. He kissed her again, deeply, and whispered into her ear . . . "Darling, I want you so bad I can almost taste the smell of your skin." He slid his lips down her chin and onto her throat. "Do you like bananas?" Jamal peeled a banana and slid it down her almond-colored belly through the chocolate sauce and down to her vagina. Jamal toyed with her clitoris, sending a sweet sensation up her spine. She moaned from his gentle touch. He brought his lips up to her face and nuzzled her with his cheek until her face turned to the side. Then he whispered into her ear, "I'm so glad you decided to open up and let me in."

He touched the opening of her oyster like organ, using the tip of the banana. "You're so sweet." He came close to her face again, laid the banana across her lips and bit into it. She could feel his lips moving against her own as he chewed the fruit. "You taste so good,"he exclaimed in his deep, seductive voice.

The thought of him sucking her tender flesh caused her yearning to manifest itself into liquid. Jamal knelt to taste her love again, and she pleaded for him to take her.

"Not yet,"he told her. "Enjoy it, love it, feel it . . . it's all for you." He slowly pressed his tongue deep into the crook of her neck, which intensified the feeling and made the sensation penetrate deeper and deeper. It seemed an eternity before he reached the part she wanted him to touch. He sucked at her nipples. She could feel them harden at his kiss.

Suddenly he was gone. She heard him moving around the table. Then he stood over her head placing his erection in her hands. He was humongous. Just the feel of it in her hands intensified her hunger for him. "This is for you,"he whispered, leaning close to her ear. Then he moved in and out of the palms of her hands causing her to masturbate him. He was firm like a frozen sausage with soft hot flesh over it.

Keesha could feel the blood pulsating through the veins coiling on top of his penis. Jamal withdrew himself and returned to sucking the chocolate from her stomach.

He touched her waist with his hands and moved his mouth down to her bushy mound. He then moved farther down to the split, straight down the middle, kissing the outside of her lips, making her beg for him to open it up and do what she knew he would, when he was ready. Jamal parted her center with his fingers, opening it wide while wrestling with the little man in the boat. A yearning like she had never known shot from the top of her head to the balls of her feet. He was the best at this.

Keesha felt an orgasm knocking at the door; beckoning her to it. The feeling was so different from what feeling she was used to, it was a mental culmination. She wanted it, anticipated it.

Keesha knew that any moment Jamal would draw the feeling right out of her. He didn't. Just as she felt the beginning wave, he penetrated her with the head of his penis, stroking her with the tip. "Push it deeper,"she pleaded with him. However, he teased her, making her thighs tremble with desire. Her need for him was great . . . then he withdrew himself.

Jamal caressed her hungry, pulsating organ with his. He spilled his hot liquid onto the mound of her sensitive member then rubbed it in. He rubbed faster and faster, and again she began to tremble. If she couldn't have his staff, she would take his hand. Jamal pressed himself a little deeper stroking her insides. She was filled with his manhood. He continued to move around and around, back and forth, in and out, up and down then round and round. She was aching with lust. He saw her tightening up. Jamal gently caressed her body. "Easy,"he said.

Pressing his hand down on the mound of her vagina, Jamal began to bang a little harder, increasing in speed and intensity. As she ruptured into exquisite ecstasy, Keesha roared like a lion, tearing her hands from their restraints and wrapping her arms around Jamal's neck as he continued to pump faster. Jamal could feel the tightening of her legs as Keesha tried to capture the ecstasy, overwhelmed by the excitement. Jamal continued his pace, hammering and expressing his love and admiration for her. He enjoyed every moment as though it was his first all over again. There was definitely a difference between having sex with someone that you had feelings for versus just relieving yourself. Keesha was good because he wanted her to be. She clawed at his back with her fingers, trying to control him, but Jamal maintained his rhythm. Keesha covered his mouth with hers, fervently sucking his tongue. She couldn't let it go, not wanting to lose control.

She ruptured into a dynamic orgasm, gyrating beneath him. Jamal audibly expressed his pleasure. Squeezing each other, Jamal and Keesha fought to seize what they needed so urgently. Jamal put everything he had into pleasing her. Their culmination was endless. She ruptured, he ruptured, they both ruptured as the fiery liquid poured from her body like lava. Jamal felt his ejaculation about to begin when he pulled away, just in time! He placed his hands between Keesha's legs, catching her flow, rubbing it over his chest and hers.

As her blurred vision slowly focused, Keesha realized that Jamal looked different from before.

"I hope that this was as good for you as it was for me!"Jamal said smiling lovingly at her. "And to think, we allowed so much time to pass, afraid of each other!"

"Jamal, I'm really glad we finally caught up with each other! You were indeed wonderful! I loved it."Keesha said holding him tightly.

"I hope that we will have many opportunities to share like events as well as other things. I'm playing for keeps, Keesha. Are you ready¿ Don't answer that yet. You may say the wrong thing...think about it. and let me know."

They kissed, then he took her to the cabin and they talked about how things used to be and how he always hoped to run into her again.

CHAPTER
5

Chris wanted to settle things between he and his ex-lover for fear that she would try to ruin things between he and Keesha. What would he do if the woman that he always wanted finally came into his life and he lost her because of someone from his past?

He would try to make peace with his ex-lover and help her to understand that he never wanted to hurt her. Things had just turned out that way. He picked up the telephone and dialed her number.

"Hi, I'm not home right now, so at the sound of the tone, please leave your name, and number and I will return your call." When he heard the beep, he left his name and asked her to give him a call.

While Chris was trying to reach her, she was at the doctor's office waiting for the results from the pregnancy test she had taken about two weeks ago. "Ms. Tanner, would you wait for me in Room Three please? I will be there in a moment." She could feel her heart racing. She already knew that she was pregnant. Ms. Tanner had already begun feeling the joys of motherhood, vomiting early in the morning, sometimes during the day, tenderness of the breast. Occasionally, she felt cramping but nothing that she wouldn't bare for her beloved Chris.

She sat and held a conversation with her unborn child. She was feeling better than any other day in her life. She would be Mrs. Chris Walker and they would be a happy family after all. She would after nine months, deliver a beautiful healthy baby that, would become the apple of Chris' eye. Chris always wanted a child, and now he was going to have one.

When the doctor entered the room, he didn't look like he was baring good news. "Ms. Tanner, please try to understand the difficulty in delivering this news. I do recognize your strong desire for this child. The blood test shows that this child is not growing properly." The doctor paused for a moment to catch his breath. We will have to do some extensive studies to find out the cause of your child's irregular growth. The child's growth pattern suggests abnormality or miscarriage."

"What are you saying?"

"I'm saying that I may have to terminate your pregnancy."

"You can't! I won't let you do this to us. I won't let you take Chris' child from me!"

She was screaming at the top of her lungs. The doctor tried to calm her, but she was hysterical. Nurses came rushing into the room to see what was going on. The doctor was standing away from her because he didn't know how far this hysteria would carry her.

"Nurse Green, would you pull Ms. Tanner's file and see if there is anyone to contact in case of an emergency. Right now, she is unable to make an intelligent decision on her own. I was trying to explain to her that their may be complications when she started screaming!"

"Would you like her to be sedated?"

"I can't, if the child is viable then the medication may cause interference in the child's health."

"So how do you want to handle it?"

"Right now, just get me the information I need and tell security to help us control this patient before someone gets hurt."

"Ms. Tanner, I would like to help you and your child but I will need to do some more tests, if you would just cooperate. Please come out of the corner and stop screaming, you're making me nervous!"

"No, you're trying to ruin my life!"

"I'm sorry you got that impression. I was trying to tell you that we need to look at the child's position in the uterus to determine if it's where it should be or even alive. Please, let me help you."

She looked at the doctor for a moment as if to figure out whether he was friend or foe. Her heart raced with fear. The fear that only a mother would have for her unborn child. She would not let anyone or anything interfere with the birth of this child, no matter what the consequence. She replayed the doctor's words over and over in her head and decided that perhaps he was not against her to destroy her chances of being with Chris.

"All right. I'm sorry. I will allow you to do whatever testing you need to do if you promise to keep me informed of what you're doing and why. Now, if somewhere along the line I find out that you are trying to take Chris' child from me, I promise you that I will hunt you down like a dog and kill you in the worse way! Do you understand me?" Her words spat at him like poisonous venom, and she meant every word.

Never in all his years of medical practice had he run into a patient like this one, which made him, determined to help her. All the excitement made him sick and he needed to get out of there for a moment.

"Yes, Ms. Tanner, I do understand and I promise you that I don't even know who Chris is. Okay?"

She slowly stood from her crouched position in the corner and took a seat on the examining table. There was no way that she would let anyone come between she and Chris. She loved Chris and had given her virginity to him. He would love her if it were the last thing he did or else . . .

The doctor left the room and scheduled her for a sonogram. He swallowed a couple of pills to calm his nerves then washed them down with coffee. He needed something to relax him. Never in all his thirty-five years of practice had he witnessed a client carry on like that. Dr. Nabatian started to feel a building ache in his chest. He reached for his buzzer to call the nurse but he couldn't. The pain intensified, and he started to slowly kneel to the floor.

"Dr. Nabatian, are you all right?"Nurse Green called out to the doctor, as she entered the room. The doctor gave no response. "Oh my God,"she said as she rushed out of his office searching for help. She sent Nurse Wright to cardiology. "Tell them I need somebody right now, Dr. Nabatian is ill. He was just taking his heart medicine when he collapsed! Somebody help us. Dr. Nabatian is having a heart attack!"

A fleet of doctors ran to the aid of Dr. Nabatian. When they entered his office, he was lying on the floor with his hands gripping his chest, his eyes stretched as wide as they would go and mouth open as though he wanted to yell. They straightened him out on the floor and checked his vital signs. No pulse was found. "Damnit, get me a crash cart,"one of the doctors screamed. The cardiologist rushed in with the shock equipment and started administering CPR. "Clear,"the doctor yelled as he forced electricity into Dr. Nabatian's chest. His body shot up. Dr. Porter checked his vital signs. Everyone looked at him…"nothing." The doctor swore and shouted "clear"again. Dr. Nabatian's body shot up again. "Increase the power by two increments. This will be the last attempt. He won't be able to stand another treatment. One more shock at this ration, and he'll be brain dead!"

Nurse Green crossed her fingers, and put her trembling hands under her chin and prayed that the doctor would be okay. He was the only one that had given her a recommendation for reevaluation of her wages and appreciated her work. She had been in several departments of the hospital and she didn't like any of them. Just when she wanted to quit and look for another job, she was transferred to obstetrics and gynecology. Dr. Nabatian became like a father figure for her. Now, because of some crazy, whacked out bitch, her boss was losing his life..."hope she loses that bastard," she said to herself.

When the final charge was applied to his chest the doctor put his finger to his throat to check his pulse and found a vague one. "He's going to make it, everybody! Let's get him hooked up!"Dr. Porter felt a great relief. He never thought that he would have to save the life of one of his own colleagues. "What happened here?"Dr. Porter questioned when things were under control.

"Doctor, the patient in Examination Room Three started screaming at him, and I guess when he got into his office and took his medication, it was too late!"

"Is she still there?"

"Yes, she's waiting for him to return. He was going to schedule her to have a sonogram." Nurse Green went back to the examining room and found that Ms. Tanner was gone. "You better run,"the nurse snarled at the vanished woman.

CHAPTER

6

"Maybe we should be getting back now, Ebony's probably worried."

"You're right." Keesha and Jamal showered together then returned to the beach. As they pulled up, Ebony ran to the car and said, "So Jamal, was she as good as you imagined she'd be after waiting all these years?"

He smiled, thanking Ebony for letting him know Keesha would be coming to California.

Keesha was shocked. "So you both plotted this, huh?"

"Yes, but not to hurt you. I just needed to see you. Ebony has been trying to get you to come here for a long time, when you called her and mentioned that you'd be coming, I booked a flight immediately. Yes, this was a setup and I hope you're not insulted."

"Hey, didn't I say if you felt like it? Oh, by the way, surprise again!" Ebony interrupted. Keesha could not help but laugh.

Keesha enjoyed the rest of the evening with Jamal. Ebony spent her day with another friend, giving her two closest friends time alone. She respected the value of privacy and realized that three was definitely a crowd.

The week went by fast. Keesha spent maybe three of the seven days with Jamal and the rest with Ebony. On Keesha's last night, Ebony asked her..."So, what are you going to do about Chris? Jamal likes you and you do find him attractive and sexy, right? So who wins the prize?"

"Ebony, it's not that easy as one wins and the other loses." Keesha hesitated a moment before continuing. "I've been wanting Chris for a long time, and now that I have him I don't know what to do about it. Jamal, on the other hand, just pops up out of the past and romances me with the best lovin' any woman could have wanted. Let's not mention my age. I'm stuck in the middle wondering who to let down."

"Well, I'll tell you one thing,"Ebony said, "Chris is too young for you and will bring you more heartache in the end just because of his age than any man your age however trifling his behavior may be."

Keesha laughed, "You're right. I'll contact Chris when I return, and I'll let him go easy." Ebony hugged Keesha. "Trust me, girl. You're doing the right thing for all the right reasons. I know that this Chris character must be someone very special to have caught your attention. Poor Jamal has been trying to win your heart since high school. The only reason I didn't mention it is that I didn't think you were ready for another relationship since you know who. He was no good for you anyway. Jamal will make you happy. I mean really happy. Keesha, you deserve so much better and I want you to have the best." Ebony began to tease her, "Remember Brian?"

"Oh, you're kicking dirt now. What are you, an archeologist? Digging up old shit. He wasn't that bad. He had money," Keesha defended.

"Okay, I agree that Brian had the finances, but that's only because his family afforded him that. Besides that, he was an asshole then, he's an asshole now, and I've got to tell you something. He isn't doing that well on his own. He has a business that's about to go belly up any day now. When you get to know Jamal, you will thank me a zillion times. Trust me. He's the one for you."

Keesha wanted to resent that statement but realized that Ebony meant no harm. "Ebony, I'm not settling, I love Chris. I am seriously attracted to Jamal, too, just not the same way. I know he's a wonderful man."

Realizing that she was pushing too hard, Ebony changed the subject. She didn't want Keesha dwelling on her decision. "So, tell me about your time with Jamal."

Keesha went on and on about him, what they did, where they went, how he treated her. "He's wonderful, I enjoyed every moment we spent together. I don't think I've had so much fun in years."

"You mean since you hung out with me, right?"

"Yeah, although your parties go just a tad bit over board."

"Nah, it's fine, you're just square." Ebony drew an imaginary square to emphasize her statement. "Girl, you need someone like Jamal. He's lively, rich, passionate, understanding and wants to make you happy."

"Then why hasn't anyone else tied him down?" Keesha asked skeptically.

"Because Jamal wants you. Why else would he drop everything he's doing to fly down just to meet you here? Trust me, girl, you're fortunate. All the ladies want him, all of them! Look at him, he's gorgeous, very well kept. You had better get him while he's available, he'll eventually get tired of waiting on you."

Keesha gave her suggestion some consideration then realized that Ebony was probably right. During the two years they had known each other, not even once did Jamal approach her for a date. He should have let her know that he was attracted to her. She thought back to their evenings together, how exciting and passionate they were and how happy he made had made her. Keesha went to bed thinking that she had finally found a man she could love, and who would make her happy. She had found a solution to her yearning for Chris, a replacement for the forbidden fruit, yet deep inside she felt terrible. Somehow I still have feelings for Chris and want him to be mine, she thought. No young girl would know how to handle a man like Chris!

She knew it was selfishness that was making her think that way, so she closed her eyes and tried not to think about it.

Ebony woke Keesha up early the next morning, and they went to Joe's for breakfast. It was Keesha's last day in California, and Ebony wanted to make the most of it before her best friend left. Ebony made certain to give Jamal a call at his cabin so that he could meet them at Joe's. Ebony knew Jamal would want to see Keesha off as well. The waiter showed them to their table. Both Keesha and Ebony sat and began to talk about their plans for next week. "What time is your flight scheduled to leave?"

"One-fifteen, So don't try to make me late on purpose. I know that trick already!"

"No, of course not, I just wanted to see if we had time to do something before your flight."

"Nope, we have just enough time for breakfast, then we have to get to the airport." Ebony looked up and noticed that Jamal had arrived. He looked excited. Keesha took note of his arrival as well. In a way, Keesha was excited to see him too. Keesha wasn't the only one who was excited about his arrival, because all the women were giving him goo-goo eyes. He leaned forward and gave Keesha a kiss on the lips then kissed Ebony on the cheek.

"Keesha, I haven't been able to get you out of my mind since our first encounter, and now that I have you I don't want to let you go. So with this thought in mind,"he said, removing his hand from his pocket, feeling the last-minute jitters, as he prepared to relinquish his deepest sentiment. "I thought you should have this." Jamal handed her a little red velvet box. Jamal watched her with anticipation as she clasped the box in her hands, fearing what was inside.

Keesha could feel her heart racing with expectation. Could his expression of love be sincere? Knowing deep down how she felt for Chris, Keesha feared what she would say to Jamal. She didn't know how or what she felt at the present moment. She opened the box finding a diamond solitaire surrounded by whispering diamonds and rubies on either side. It was beautiful. The ring was impeccably made, an antique, something she would probably never see again. He was giving her something that meant a great deal to him. Her eyes met his with a million questions across her pupils, pleading for answers. Interrupting their telepathy, the obvious excitement of Ebony jolted them back to reality.

"Let me see!" The sight of it almost caused Ebony to faint. "Jamal that is the most beautiful thing I have ever seen. Is it custom-made?"

"You could say that,"he answered.

"Ebony, it's for the most beautiful woman I have ever seen or known, and I hope that she will say Yes when I ask her to marry me. " He returned his attention to Keesha. "Keesha will you marry me?"The question was synthesized by Ebony's voice as she posed the question along with him. Keesha had two pairs of eyes on her, as Ebony and Jamal waited for an answer. Keesha couldn't find her voice. She sat there frozen staring at the ring. It was indeed exquisitely made, and she knew deep down inside that she didn't deserve the ring or Jamal.

He cupped her face and said, "This is nothing compared to the things I will shower you with. Take it with you to New York and give yourself time to think about it. I know that this is sudden, and you need time to think about it."

She appreciated his kindness and courtesy. "Thank you,"she said to him and kissed his hands.

Jamal fought the fear that he was making a grave mistake in giving her the ring. He just hoped that with time and patience, he would win her. He cursed the butterflies fluttering in his stomach and focused on instinct, which said that Keesha was good for him.

Another woman overhearing his proposal remarked that she would marry him. Jamal turned to the woman and said, "I'd rather wait for the woman I proposed to. But thanks anyway." He sat and joined them for breakfast. His eyes remained locked on Keesha the entire time as though he wanted to etch her face into his memory.

After eating, he asked if they would mind if he followed them to the airport. Keesha said, "No of course not. Please, I'd be delighted." The three of them walked to the car. Ebony suggested that Keesha ride with Jamal since this would be the last time she'd see him for a while and it would give them time to say the things they needed to say before she departed.

Keesha and Jamal waited for Ebony to park her car and he remove Keesha's bags then continued into the airport terminal to have them checked. The silence was so thick you could cut it with a knife. Keesha heard the announcement that her flight was now boarding, so she kissed Jamal one last time and he held on to her for a few seconds more pressing her against his chest. "You feel my heart racing? It's because I'm afraid I won't ever see you again." He watched her eyes hoping to find something that would give him the slightest inclination that she felt the same way. She assured him that he would see her soon. He released her reluctantly, wishing that he could do something that would make her return to Virginia with him. Keesha walked over to Ebony and bid her farewell.

Ebony could see that Jamal was not reassured that he would see Keesha again. "Listen. Jamal, you're always invited to spend time with Keesha in New York. She's just lost for words right now, she would have said it herself but her mind is suck on stupid right now. You'll see." Keesha realizing her negligence, handed Jamal her card with her address and telephone numbers so that if he were ever in New York he could pay her a visit. She kissed him one more time and hurried through the gate to board her plane.

Aboard the plane, all she could think about was hurting Chris or breaking Jamal's heart. Why is this happening to me? Keesha asked while looking up into the heavens. Why is it that just when I think I've found the right person, another comes along? She was tormented with perplexing questions. She closed her eyes and waited for sleep then decided that maybe she'd better stay awake since the last time she went to sleep on a plane, she spilled her guts.

Upon arriving in New York, Keesha hurried to a pay phone and checked her messages. Chris had left so many messages that she ran out of change trying to hear them all. He seemed desperate. How could I have done this to him? Her heart felt heavy, and she could feel a lump building in her chest. He's so young he wouldn't be able to handle this kind of disappointment, she told herself. She went to the baggage area and waited for her luggage. When her bags finally came through, she picked them up, raced through the door and jumped into a taxi. She had no time to spare and needed to get home.

CHAPTER

7

Chris had been trying to reach Keesha for about a week, and he had become concerned. He knew that it was foolish but he couldn't help but think Keesha found out about his old girlfriend or worse, told his mother. He wondered whether Keesha just didn't want to be bothered with him. Whatever the case, he loved her and didn't want to lose her. He would do anything to keep Keesha's love. He decided to visit his mother to see if she had seen Keesha lately. He was surprised Keesha had not called to let him know she had received his gift.

He drove to his mother's house and could see that Keesha's car was still parked in front of her own house. Chris drove down the block, parked in front of his mother's house and rang her doorbell. "Hello, Mom. How have you been?"

"Oh, darling, I'm just fine." Chris knew that his mother was very perceptive and that he couldn't just ask about Keesha without his mother realizing that he still had a crush on her so he questioned her in a roundabout way. He talked about everything else except Keesha. He knew that his mother would mention the people in the neighborhood eventually.

"I guess Keesha must have gone away again, because I haven't seen her lately. You haven't seen her darling have you? I know that you have been stopping by there. Next time you're over there will you please let Keesha know that I said she doesn't have to stop by and see me anymore if she doesn't want to!"

Chris laughed the way he always did when his mother made that kind of remark. What he didn't know was that his mother was aware of him stopping by Keesha's so often. Why hadn't she mentioned it before? Chris became concerned. Christine noticed his fidgeting and knew that he had already gotten the information he wanted and was looking to make his exit. "Mom, I'd better get going and catch up with you later in the week." He stood and leaned down to kiss his mother, who was seated at the kitchen table. "You don't have to get up. I'll let myself out. You get some rest, and I'll talk to you tomorrow."

"Okay, honey, have a safe trip home. Listen, you want me to tell Keesha something for you? She usually isn't away for long. Is she working on your investments strategies?"

"Yeah, something like that,"he said, knowing that he had better leave before she probed for more information.

Chris felt relieved to know that Keesha had just taken a spontaneous vacation and would be back sometime soon. He knew that she would be returning, so he no longer worried about her responding to the gift he had sent.

As Keesha walked through the door, she searched for Chris' number. "Could I be missing him this much?" It had only been seven days since they'd last seen each other. "Why am I so high strung on him?" She began to realize that she really did love Chris.

She was down on her knees looking for his number when the telephone rang. She jumped up and rushed to the telephone hoping that Chris' voice would be on the other end. Her heart raced. She longed to hold him. The only thing she could think about at the moment was hearing his voice. Keesha was in love with Chris, but her new relationship with Jamal was risk-free. Maybe I'll just take things one day at a time until I have time to see which one would be to my advantage.

She took a deep breath and grabbed the receiver but the machine had already picked up. She waited patiently until her message completed. "Hello, Keesha. This is Jamal. I miss you already and hope your flight was all right. Give me a call when you get settled in." She heard a click as he returned the receiver to its cradle.

Keesha decided that she would get some food burning in the kitchen. She was pulling out a pot and some pasta when the doorbell rang. Now who could that be, she wondered. She walked to the door and opened it. It was her friend Michelle.

"Oh, hi Michelle,"Keesha said with disappointment.

"Well hello to you too. I can see you were expecting someone else! So can I come in?"

"Oh, sure. Come on in Michelle." This is what Keesha needed like a hole in the head. Michelle was annoying, nosey and a straight up pain in the ass. No one really liked her. In fact, word was that she was a little on the crazy side since she broke up with her boyfriend. However, Keesha being the kindhearted person she was could never turn a lonely heart away.

"So who were you expecting¿ Word around here is that you're messing with that young thang everyone talks about. He's been spotted ringing your bell for the past week. You know what else¿"

"What Michelle¿"Keesha asked with a voice reeking of monotony and dismay.

"He's even been in here . . . all night! So what's the scoop, is he rocking it or not¿" It was just like Michelle to be uncouth and get excited over someone else's life.

"Michelle, I'm just getting home from a long trip, let me call you later this week or something and chat okay¿" Keesha decided she would rather try to get rid of her unwanted friend before she caused friction between she and Michelle.

"Sure, kick me out when there's gossip this good. Hey, if you don't nab him somebody else will. I say go for it. Hell, I would."

"That's good Michelle. Now please let me get unpacked and settled in."

"Need any help¿"

"No! Thanks anyway." Finally, Michelle got the message and not a minute too soon as Keesha's patience had reached its final drop. Michelle made her way to the door without Keesha escorting her. If that girl ever got a life of her own, it would be a cool day in Hell, Keesha thought to herself and laughed. It wasn't that Keesha disliked Michelle, she just didn't know when to mind her own business. It wouldn't take Michelle ten good minutes to get the word to Chris' mother and that was definitely a no. The longer Keesha could keep Michelle in the dark, the better.

After dinner, Keesha decided that she would go through her mail. She discovered an UPS slip stating that one final attempt would be made before the package would be returned to the sender. Who would be sending me a package anyway¿ I don't recall ordering anything!

Around six o'clock, the doorbell rang again. Keesha rushed to the door hoping it would be Chris. She opened the door. "UPS, ma'am, I have a package for you." Keesha stood there gazing at him for a moment. "Would you sign for this please¿ I've been trying to deliver it a few days now."

"Yes, sure." It was a pretty heavy box so she asked the UPS guy to put it in the living room. She signed for the package and went to see what was inside the box. Keesha studied the box and then decided to just open it. She cut along the taped area and opened the box. There was a large manila envelope inside so she opened it and read the letter.

> Dear Keesha:
>
> I love you very much and hope that you will take my feelings seriously. I understand that this situation is difficult, but we can work it out. Just give it some time. I haven't been able to think about anything except you and making you happy for the rest of our lives! Please give me a call.
>
> Chris

Keesha noticed a telephone number at the bottom of the page. The area code was from out of state. The added P.S. read They say green outlives any other!

What the hell did that mean? She opened the box and found a plant. A beautiful plant full of thick green leaves with red and white details. At the bottom was a label "Rubber Tree." She placed the plant on the living room table, captivated by it. It was truly a beautiful plant. Chris really knew how to make a woman feel special. His mother taught him well or somebody did.

She opened the blinds in each room to let some sunshine in. In the living room she thought she saw prisms on the wall. She walked a little closer and they disappeared. I must be going crazy, she thought. When she turned again and moved out of the sunlight, they reappeared. She couldn't figure out where they were coming from. She went into the living room and looked around. She couldn't understand why the prisms were reflecting off the plant. She took a closer look. There between the leaves of the plant was a diamond ring. "Holy Sweet Jesus!"she cried out. She sat on the sofa and began to cry. She now had two men ready to commit to her, and both men were wonderful.

She held the two rings side by side. They were both beautiful and carefully selected. Chris' ring had a heart-shaped diamond with an army of perfectly sized diamonds stair-casing the center stone. It was impeccably made. The inscription read, Forever My Love. Keesha removed

Jamal's ring from her finger and placed it in her jewelry box then replaced it with Chris' ring.

She realized that she was putting Jamal on hold. Choosing youth over wisdom, learning over experience, love over love. Keesha wasn't sure if Chris could really make her happy but now he was the only one on her mind, and she wanted to give their love a chance. She still had Jamal beckoning her with his caring ways. Somehow, she knew she was making a mistake.

CHAPTER

8

Jamal sat in his office after a long day. He had delivered five babies, a set of identical twin girls and three boys. He loved the sight of a child being born and he thanked God that he had been blessed with the opportunity to deliver such precious creatures. He knew that someday he would be delivering his own.

Keesha stayed on his mind, and he wondered whether she realized how deeply he felt about her. Jamal examined Keesha's card. There had been many in his past but none like Keesha. She was confident in herself, successful and beautiful. Her success meant nothing to him because he could take care of her anyway. He would marry her if he knew that she was dirt poor and living on the street. She deserved the best and that was what he had to offer her the best.

He wondered if there was someone else in her life that might be his competition. He knew that he couldn't allow too much time to pass. Otherwise, he might allow her to walk right into someone else's arms. The thought made him cringe!

Certainly he wasn't being selfish. She was the only woman that he had ever loved, and he waited a long time for her. He would not let anyone come between himself and his destiny. He thought that maybe he should give his mother a call and let her know that he had finally seen Keesha after all these years and that he gave her the ring.

He picked up the telephone and dialed to his parents' house. He waited while the telephone rang. "Hello"

"Hi, Ma. How have you been?"

"I'm fine, Jamal. I'm so happy to hear from you! Your dad was just talking about you."

"Oh yeah, what was he saying?"

"How he hopes you'll will get married and have children before he becomes too old to bounce them on his knees!"

"At least one of them," Jamal's father said as he picked up the telephone in the other room.

"Hey, Pop. What's doing?"

"I'm fairing well my son. I have this beautiful lady at my side who takes good care of me and now that your brothers and sisters are grown and out of here, I have her all to myself!"

"You stop that, honey. Jamal doesn't want to hear about that!"

She blushed from his statement. Jamal's parents still had it after all these years. They raised five children and enjoyed every moment of it. They had been successful in their day and raised their children to be just as successful. Jamal's siblings all had children, and he alone was left to give his contribution to the family.

His parents longed to love his children. He was their favorite child, and never gave them any trouble. Jamal was destined for success, and he superseded all of his siblings as well as his parents. His parents admired his continued humility. He didn't bring every girl he met to his parents' house, and he was very discrete about whom he entertained. They knew that he was trying to find someone that he could love but his heart belonged to only one. Keesha. He loved her from the moment he saw her. After a long wait, he would finally have the opportunity to get to know her all over again and to marry her and raise a family of his own.

Money meant nothing to him if she wasn't part of his life. He envisioned their first child, a daughter. She would have pretty curly hair like him and nice light brown eyes and a cute little point of a nose like Keesha.

"Mom, Dad, I called because I wanted to let you know that I am finally getting the opportunity to get to know Keesha. I was able to express some of the feelings I have held for her for all these years."

"So, how did she respond, honey?"

"I think she likes me too. I don't know to what degree but I have all the time in the world to wait for her. We will eventually get together. I wanted her to take her time thinking about it."

"So in other words, you proposed to her then postponed her answer!"

"Yes, simply speaking, I didn't want to scare her away. I want her to really think about it before she makes a decision like this. Whatever feelings she has for me will have to surface sooner or later. I've got a good feeling about her, and I know that she will realize that we are meant for each other!"

All Jamal's life he had played the conservative role and plotted his next move cautiously but there was something within him that told him that now was the time to make his move. There was no time to map it out. He would play the hand as it was dealt, and he would make the best of each hand.

"You've made a wise decision, son,"his father said. "A young man of your caliber deserves the best and you will get it whether it is Keesha or someone else! One thing, son. I don't think it's healthy for you to put all your eggs in one basket! Give someone else a chance."

"Sorry, Dad, but Keesha is the one for me, and I will have her!"

As Jamal reasoned with his parents, he felt his beeper go off. He looked down at it, and it read 911 CALL THE OFFICE.

"Mom, Dad, I will have to get back to you, my beeper is going off and there seems to be an emergency. I'll talk to you later in the week, okay?"

"Sure, darling,"his mother said.

"Later, son,"his father said. Jamal hung up the telephone and dialed the number on his beeper.

CHAPTER
9

The doorbell rang. Keesha rushed to the door and didn't have time to wipe her eyes. "Chris!" He walked in with apprehension. Chris watched as she too gazed at him in astonishment and anticipation. Neither knew what to say to the other. Chris continued to stare, fighting the impulse to snatch her into his arms. Her response was so important and detrimental to his being. Keesha, not knowing what to do, stepped close enough to him to place a gentle kiss on his lips. Chris remained motionless, wondering if it was a kiss goodbye or an "I'm glad to see you kiss." Keesha, realizing his hesitation, raised on her tiptoes to whisper in his ear an assuring "I love you."

That was all he needed to hear. He wrapped his arms around her and squeezed her as tight as he could. "I thought I lost you!"he said as he found his voice. She took him by the hand and escorted him to the living room. Immediately he noticed that she had received his gift. "So did you like the plant?"

"Yes, I loved it." The sparkle from the ring caught his attention, and he smiled at her. Feelings he never experienced before were swelling in his chest. He got on one knee and said "Keesha, I love you. I promise that if you agree to be my wife, I'll love you forever and take care of you and our children till the end of time." He held her hands in his and searched her eyes for an answer.

She could see that his intentions were good and that there was nothing but earnestness in them. "Chris, I need time to think about this. I do love you and always will but this is a difficult situation for me, and I'm not sure I can handle the pressure that will come in the near future."

"You mean you're worrying about what people think?"he questioned as concern and dread came over him.

"No, it's just that I feel like I've betrayed your mother. How can I face her knowing how this would make her feel? This would only cause hatred and resentment between us!"

"Keesha, she would love the idea of you and me getting together! My mother is very fond of you and she could never resent you. If I love you, what could make her more happy than for the woman I love to love me back?"

"In her eyes I will be robbing the cradle. She would feel that you are too inexperienced for me. You need to ¼"

"Wait, wait, wait. Let me decide what I want for Chris, not my age, not my mother, the nosy neighbors or anyone else. The only person, who can separate us, is you. So if you're turning me down then I'll accept this loss and carry my hurt, but I want you to be sure that this is the choice that you want to make and not fear talking."

Keesha didn't know what to say or to do. She felt a great deal for him, but, her senses were telling her that she should leave him alone. She gave herself a few minutes to weigh her next answer before she spoke. "Let's take it slow? Let the idea grow on me, and when I feel more comfortable about the situation, then perhaps it might work out. Is that acceptable to you?"

He agreed with her, rose from his knees and locked lips with her. The kiss was so sweet and tender. She could feel the desires building inside her. She kissed him more diligently. Keesha asked him to accompany her to the bedroom. He picked her up then carried her upstairs.

Keesha ran her hands down Chris' broad chest then stroked his tight stomach continuing down until she reached the swollen vessel in his pants. She unbuttoned his pants and pulled down his zipper. Upon being opened, it protruded through his boxers. She reached for it and it struck out at her hand. It was sensitive to her every touch.

She pulled his shirt over his head, casting it to the floor. Keesha moved her mouth away from his lips to suck at his broad neck. His breath quickened with every touch. Gently, she kissed his collarbone sending a chill through his stomach. His heart was pounding, and he wanted to take her, show her exactly how she was making him feel. He caressed her back as she straddled him. He pressed the firmness of her buttocks with his hands. She moved down to his chest and encircled his nipple with her tongue. Keesha could feel his staff jumping excitedly, hoping to, at the very least strike some portion of her body. She pushed him down on the sheets and moved her tongue across his belly, over to one side and then to the other. Keesha nibbled at his firm waist teasing him. She knew that kissing him so close to his lower section would cause his lust for her to continue to his pulsating member. Finally, she aggressively took the tip of his manhood into her hungry mouth. He moaned with pleasure as his hands fumbled with her long tangled mane. He massaged her scalp. "Not yet!"she said in a seductive voice. "I'll make it so sweet." She played with his corona with the balls of her fingers and stroked his shaft. His hips began to rotate with her strokes. "You like that baby?" She crooned, gently pushing his sac with her tongue. The intensity was so great, he tried to pull her atop of him to no avail. She was not finished torturing him, making him nebulous and lustful. She bit at his shaft with her lips and felt the blood building in his vessel. He begged for her. He wanted it. "I love it. You love it? She said."

"Yes, I love it, I love you, stop teasing and let me please you!" He said. He knew that she was only paying him back for the sexual torture he put her through the first time they made love. "Keesha, let me take you!"

He fought for control and gained it. Pulling her by her thighs, he forced her to tower over him as she propelled herself on his aching staff. The feeling was more gratifying than they had bargained for. They yelled cries of elation. He hammered himself up into her, and she forced herself against him. Finally, they were consumed by an incandescent rapture. He could tell that Keesha had a little fight left in her so he pushed her onto her stomach and completed his duty from behind.

He wanted her to be his, so he did the only thing he knew that could keep two happy people together. He removed the condom and projected himself into her.

Afterward, he placed the condom into the receptacle next to the bed. They spent the rest of the night holding each other. Not a word was spoken, as the gratification was enough to tell how they felt at that moment. Keesha thought about how wonderful it was to finally find someone who would love her as much she loved him. She went to sleep in the comfort of his arms.

CHAPTER
10

"Ms. Tanner. Hi, I'm Dr. Schwartz, I will be taking over the studies that Dr. Nabatian mentioned to you the last time you were here."

"Why isn't Dr. Nabatian doing the studies himself?" The doctor searched for the right answer to give her without sounding spiteful. Dr. Nabatian was a good friend of his and his knowledge and kindness had helped Dr. Schwartz make it through medical school. Dr. Nabatian was the best in his field, and Dr. Schwartz was fortunate to be chosen as his understudy. All his skills and mastery were owed to Dr. Nabatian. Every time he performed a complex surgical procedure, he could feel Dr. Nabatian at his side, coaching him. Now, he had to help the woman responsible for his predicament.

"Dr. Nabatian suffered a terrible heart attack and is currently unable to work."

"Oh, how awful. He seemed so healthy when last I saw him!" she said with astonishment.

The doctor could feel his anger building as the woman pretended not to know what had happened to his friend. It was her fault, and she didn't even have the courtesy to apologize.

"Ms. Tanner, I have a great deal of patients waiting for me, so needless to say, I don't have time to explain to you the damage caused to our distinguished colleague. I'll give you some time to change into a gown and I will return to perform the sonogram."

Dr. Schwartz left the room and went to his office to compose himself. The sight of that woman filled him with an anger he had never known. Dr. Nabatian was like his father and she was responsible for his condition. Dr. Nabatian would be here if it were not for her foolishness. Dr. Schwartz counted backward from ten then returned to the examining room where Ms. Tanner patiently waited for him. This time, the nurse accompanied him. There was no way she would allow any more of their doctors to be left unattended with that crazy woman.

"Okay, Ms. Tanner," he said in a calm voice, while applying the cold gel to her abdomen. He slid the sonogram device through the gel and looked for the pregnancy that the blood test showed. Nothing could be seen. He added a little more gel and pressed a little deeper. Still, there was nothing to be seen in her uterus. It was now one month into her pregnancy and certainly something should be visible. Especially since the blood test reflected a definite pregnancy. He would have to search with a more precise device to confirm natural abortion. Her body must have rejected the embryo by miscarriage.

The nurse smiled in spite of the woman that lay before her. This would certainly be a just reward to someone who would cause such a catastrophe to someone as undeservingly as Dr. Nabatian.

"Ms. Tanner, I am going to have to do an internal sonogram." Dr. Schwartz picked up a penis-shaped device, covered it with a condom and applied gel to it.

"What are you going to do with that?" she questioned him. "I will need to insert this into your vagina to get a closer look at your uterus."

He inserted the device inside her and sought the growing life inside her. Still, to no avail. Just when he was about to give up the search, he spotted it. "All right, Ms. Tanner, I have found the pregnancy."

"Is everything all right?"

"I'm not sure. The embryo seems to be in a very vulnerable spot. We will need to keep you under close observation. In the meantime, I would like blood studies done to give me a good idea of what condition the child is in, and what are our chances of making this a successful birth."

In his heart, he could care less but the knowledge of medicine and the years of study compelled him to do all he could to make this another successful event. Not to mention, it would make Dr. Nabatian proud of him. Nothing meant more to him than to win the esteem of his superior. With this in mind, he would go out of his way to make sure that things work out for this woman.

Ms. Tanner sat there thinking about the man who fathered her child. She knew that everything would work out, it had to, that was her only hope of winning his heart. She loved Chris, and she would never let anyone come between them.

Then she considered Keesha's relationship with Chris. What does she have that I don't? It can't be the body or the sex. Anyway, I'm carrying his child, and I will have him. So for now, she would allow her to parade around with Chris and pretend to have his heart but his love belonged to her, and there was no way Keesha could take that away. Not to mention that Keesha being the kind of person that she was, would eventually lose interest, especially in him when his mother found out about them.

Her friendship with Mrs. Walker would definitely take precedence over her feelings for Chris. She entertained that thought for a while. Then decided that maybe she should help his mother find out about Chris and Keesha to speed things up a little. Christine would kill over her son. Chris and I are made for each other and no one would come between us.

The nurse watched her as though she could read Ms. Tanner's thoughts and hear the plotting in her head. I hate her, she thought. Frankly, she wished that she would be grief stricken by the death of this child. No one like her deserved to have a child. Besides, any child would be miserable with her. The nurse continued to think about Ms. Tanner while she extracted blood.

She placed the last tube on the needle and the blood filled the tube.

"Okay, Ms. Tanner, you can get dressed now. The results should be back in a week. Make an appointment at the front desk."

Ms. Tanner thanked her and waited for the nurse to leave the room. The doctor stood outside the examining room, complimenting himself for doing the right thing. Feeling good about himself, he greeted his next patient as he entered Room Six.

CHAPTER

11

Keesha and Chris spent the rest of the week shopping and visiting places they would never have thought to go alone, but somehow the company of each other made life worth living to the fullest. I really do love him, Keesha thought. They spent hours dining at the French coffee shop located in Upper Westchester. They went on for hours discussing their feelings.

"Good evening!"Chris greeted her as he walked in from a long day at work. After planting an affectionate kiss on Keesha's cheek, he continued into the kitchen to see what smelled so good. When he opened the lid of the first pot, the aroma caused his stomach to churn with hunger.

Keesha laughed, watching Chris massaging his belly. She tortured him by naming the items on the menu. "Chicken in mushroom sauce, surrounded by yellow and red peppers with broccoli,"Keesha said in a proud, cheerful voice. Her pride in her cooking was obvious from her expression when she talked about it. Chris admired her cooking. In fact, he loved everything about her.

"Umm, sounds delicious. Let's eat."

Chris helped set the table then held the chair for Keesha before being seated himself. He listened to her rambling on and on about her day and what she did before he finally interrupted her. "Keesha, I really do love you, and I am so glad that you are giving me this opportunity to shower you with the best of me." Chris wanted to pour out his innermost feelings to Keesha and show her how sincere he was but he felt that maybe he sounded ambivalent.

"Well, Chris, I find you extremely attractive, ambitious and sexy. There is nothing that I could ever want more than to spend my life with you. I would never do anything to hurt you, and I do want us to be happy but what about your mother? Have you told her about us yet?"

"No. Didn't you tell me to give you time to adjust to the situation? I would have mentioned it to her a long time ago."

"I don't think your mother would be too happy about this!"

"Well, it's something she would just have to get used to. It's my life, and I've chosen to spend it with you if you'll have me. Will you have me?"

"Oh Chris, of course, but how do you think it would make me feel if your mother resents our being together? It's not just a matter of Christine disapproving, but it's also a matter of our friendship. Can you understand that?"

Chris took her hands into his and kissed them, "Yes, sweetheart, I do understand where you're coming from, and whatever you decide, I will respect your feelings! However, I must make one request!"

"What's that, sweetheart?"

"Please don't string me along. I want you to be absolutely sure of what you want whichever way you decide. That way I will always respect you because you have respected me and my feelings."

"Hold that thought, the doorbell is ringing."

Keesha rushed to the door. Now who could that be? She wondered. She opened the door. "Christine, how are you? What a surprise!"

"Girl, why don't you come by to see me anymore? What have you been up to?"

"I was just about to lay down I haven't been feeling well these past few days, and I've been working like a dog."

Christine totally ignored Keesha's hint for her to leave, walked in and found herself a seat in the living room.

"So what's for dinner? Something sure smells good in here."

"Oh, just chicken, something I threw together, you know how I am!" Christine, can I get back with you maybe tomorrow? I'll stop by your house tomorrow evening. Would that be all right? I really hate to dismiss you like this but I'm really feeling sick right about now!"

"Oh, I understand,"Christine exclaimed. Besides I stopped in unexpectedly anyway. Feel better, and I'll see you tomorrow if you're up to it."

Keesha escorted her to the door and hugged her and told her farewell.

"Who is it honey?"Chris shouted from the kitchen. Christine hearing her son's voice spun around in amazement.

"Chris, is that you?" Recognizing his mother's voice, Chris stepped into the foyer to greet her. If ever there was a better time to give her the good news, now was the time. Chris was smiling excitedly not noticing Keesha's uneasiness. Christine, uncertain of the situation began to question them, looking from one to the other. "What's going on here?"

Keesha's mouth became dry and tight. At least a thousand explanations came to mind as she examined possibilities to deceive her friend. "Christine, I can explain," she stammered. "Chris stopped by to visit, and I suggested he stay for dinner."

Christine, known for her perceptibility, made Keesha's task all the more difficult. Expecting the worse, Keesha anticipated Christine's next response. "Girl, I'm not worried about that!" Christine answered with a chuckle. Keesha was relieved to see that Christine wasn't concerned about her son being at her home. "Did my Chris tell you about his engagement? My baby's getting married! I haven't met the girl yet but I raised my son well, and I'm sure that he picked a lovely woman to wed and I would approve of her. He told me that he wasn't sure that she'd marry him. I told him a woman would be crazy to deny him her life." Christine babbled on and on about her excitement in meeting the mystery woman who won her son's hand in marriage.

Keesha interjected, "So, you're not even the slightest worried about who he's marrying?"

"Why, no, it's his life, and my son is very careful and if he says she's successful, beautiful and there's no other for him I know I don't need to worry!"

Christine spoke very well of her son and was confident in his ability to make the right decision. Never did he bring home anyone that she disapproved of, so she had no reason to feel insecure now.

"In fact, my son said he wouldn't settle for anyone else. Could you imagine he said he'd die if she refused him? Between you and me, I know she must be special!" she whispered to Keesha and gave her a nudge with her elbow.

Chris was fully out of the kitchen now and his mother was halfway out of the door.

"Mom, I would like you to meet my wife-to-be!"

"Oh, darling, is she here, too? How could you introduce her to Keesha before you introduce her to me? Keesha, you know Chris always had a crush on you but I told him that you were too mature for him.

Isn't that funny? Kids!"

Keesha could feel herself shrinking faster and faster as they talked around her as though she wasn't there. "Ma, I asked Keesha to marry me! I love her, and I hope that you'll understand that I can't live without her!"

While Chris continued to express his feelings for Keesha, Keesha felt herself shrinking and sinking lower and lower as Christine's eyes flared at her.

"This is a joke, right?" Christine bellowed. "This is all a plot by the two of you to get me all worked up over nothing. You both saw me coming and decided to play a trick on me, right?" Chris could see right away that his mother was not taking the news lightly and was definitely not pleased. Regretting his words, he wondered how to fix it. He could see that Keesha was not comfortable either.

Keesha's mouth now completely dry, and she refused to take part in the confusion. Just then, a ray of light reflected off the engagement ring Chris had given Keesha and Christine caught sight of it. She turned her attention to the ring on Keesha's finger. Christine examined the ring with scrutiny then realized that it was the same ring that her son showed her the other day and this fiasco was not a sick joke.

"Chris, we talked about this," she said in a high tone, almost yelling.

"Mom, please control yourself. It's not as if you didn't know how I felt about Keesha. Now I love her, and you said that you would be behind me no matter whom I chose, so let's not make a mountain out of a molehill! Right now I need your support and your blessing!"

While Chris pleaded for his mother's understanding, Keesha could see the fire flaring in Christine's eyes.

"Keesha, what's going on here? You and I are friends. How could you do this? How long has this fiasco been going on? Tell me, how long have you been stabbing me in the back. I trusted you."

"Christine, I don't know what to say. I didn't plan this, it just happened."

"I asked you a question. How long?"Christine asked, raising her voice just a pitch higher causing a shrieking crackle in her voice. "A little more than a month." Keesha searched her mind for the right words to express to her dear friend. She knew from the start that Chris was forbidden fruit. She should have left him alone. Instead, she allowed a night of romance to build into something greater than any words could describe and now she had to face his mother, her friend and mentor. She loved Chris with everything in her but she could not let this impossible relationship ruin the friendship that she built with Christine. She could see from Christine's response that there was no understanding to be found in her heart and that she could either continue this relationship with Chris or lose a good friend.

Christine attempted to be calm, but the words a little more than a month repeated in her head, tormenting her. "What interest do you have in my son? He's too young for you! What would you do with him other than break his heart and make him useless to anyone else? You've crossed the line, Keesha. You've crossed the line."

Christine felt anger and rage welling inside her along with an urge to kill Keesha. How dare she seduce my son, how dare she, Christine repeated with her eyes sharply focused on Keesha, challenging her.

Keesha stepped back a few paces fearing the blow she felt coming and putting a little distance between them. Chris must have felt the same tension because he stepped between them and put his arm around her.

"Ma, I love Keesha. Please don't make me unhappy. All my life I worked hard to please you. I maintained an A average, attended the best of schools and now I am successful in my job. I was the best son that any mother could ever want, and now I'm asking you to give us your blessing and not take my dreams away."

Chris gave his final plea for Christine's motherly blessings. She turned from Keesha for a moment and looked at her son.

"Chris, I pushed you to work hard so that you wouldn't have to struggle all of your life. I will not benefit from it one way or the other. Sweetheart, trust me on this, I know that you are making a mistake, and right now you're in love with a woman that has experienced many things and is by far, more advanced than you. This is a mistake, and you will get hurt in the end. I'm sure that the sex may be wonderful, something that no young girl could ever give you but has it ever occurred to you that she must have learned that through years of experience?"

"Ma, please stop. This is not about sex. I really love Keesha and have felt this way for a very long time, and we deserve each other. Don't make this difficult for me! His tone became calm and weak. His eyes moistened with tears and his heart became sick. He kissed Keesha's hands and walked over to his mother...

"Mom, listen to me. I love Keesha and I want to marry her. She is special to me and I'm happy with her. If you mess this up for me, I will never forgive you!"

His eyes pleaded with Christine for understanding. She turned from them and walked out the door. Chris exasperated, kissed Keesha on the lips and went outside behind his mother. Keesha felt sick. She stood with her back to the door wondering how she had gotten herself into this mess. Maybe she should just go on with life and leave Chris alone. How could something that feels so right be so wrong? she thought to herself. After a few moments, Chris returned and wrapped his arms around Keesha. She could feel the acid building in her stomach and a foul taste came to her mouth as she searched for words.

"Nothing will come between us,"Chris vowed in a very low voice, imploring her understanding. She watched his eyes and could tell that he had been crying because they were swollen and red. The windows of his heart seemed gloomy and bare. He stood there with his hands hung at his sides wishing that she would say something that would make him feel that all wasn't lost.

"What did your mother say?" Keesha hoped that there was an understanding when Chris attempted to talk with his mother. Keesha knew that he loved his mother more than anything in the world. He would never do anything to hurt her. The question now was how deeply did he feel about her. Keesha knew that without Christine's blessing, what ever decision she made would be wrong.

"I told her that I had to follow my heart and that with or without her approval I will not let you go, and if she came between us I would never forgive her." The sound of those words rung in Chris' mind as he remembered how hard his mother worked to provide him with the funds to reach the financial position in life that he now held. She worked two jobs days, nights and weekends, to make ends do more than meet. He attended the best private schools, got the best grades because she made certain that there was someone to teach him the things that she did not know. Of course, she didn't finish school because she had him, and when his father died, there was just enough money from the life insurance policy to pay for his burial and to put them five years ahead on the mortgage. Chris knew that he owed his life to his mother. The fancy home that he lived in, the job he held, the car he drove, his entire life, and now he was letting a woman, a beautiful one that is, come between them. This thought tortured him. He never thought he would betray his mother. She came first in everything, but now he felt that there was something missing in his life, and that something was Keesha.

His voice was calm and calculated. He didn't seem to be hysterical or in denial. Uneasiness came over her. Keesha realized that her friend was upset with her over her only son. Keesha knew that it was nothing personal that Christine had against her. She just wanted the best for her son and for him to make the right choice for the right reasons. Keesha felt like a villain.

"Chris, please give me some time, okay" She stood there with her hand tight around the doorknob with the door slightly ajar.

"Keesha, are you putting me out?"

"No, Chris. I'm just asking you to understand that this is difficult for me. Can you understand that?"

"Yes, I'll give you all the time you need. Just keep in mind I don't want to go on without you being part of my life."

He bent down, kissed her gingerly on the lips and walked out of the door.

"See you tomorrow?" he asked as she started to close the door.

"No, but I'll call you."

"Good enough," he said, leaving.

Keesha closed the door and tears began to fall. She was in love with her friend's son who was too young for her, and now that friendship was in jeopardy. She went upstairs wondering if she had done the right thing dismissing Chris. Why is this happening to me? she thought.

CHAPTER

12

Ebony found herself with a slack day at work and decided that she would give Jamal a call to see if he had been in contact with Keesha lately. At first, she tried him at home. The telephone rang and rang, and she decided that he might have been at the office. She called his office and the nurse answered his line.

"Hello, this is Dr. Warner's office, may I help you?"

"Yes, is Dr. Warner in today?"

"The doctor is in surgery right now, what's this in reference to?"

Ebony was becoming agitated; she hated nurses that didn't know their place, not to mention she had used a preposition at the end of her sentence.

"This is a personal call, ma'am, and you should check your speech, you just used a preposition at the end of a sentence!"

The nurse questioned her . . . "What?"

"You're not supposed to use the word to at the end of a sentence."

"Well then how do you, Dr. Webster, suggest that I ask the question?"

"How can I reference this call? What is this regarding? Better yet, what can he have ready for you when he returns your call? Yes, I think I like that one the best. You won't sound as nosey as you are."

The nurse laughed.

"You always have been a bitch, Ebony!"

"Thank you. I try. When will my friend be back?"

"Call back around two o'clock. There was an emergency today so he was dispatched to do a cesarean early this morning."

"He could have his job!"Ebony said in a disgusted voice.

"You know that's right."

"So what's the news?"

"Girl, ain't nothing going on in this neck of the woods. When are you giving another party?"

"I don't know, I'm still trying to get my place back together from the last one. You girls don't know how to act when you see naked men."

"No. Maybe you don't know how to behave, but I know what to do when I see a naked man!"

"I don't mean wrapping your legs around his neck and feeding him the bush!"

"That's what I'm talking about. By the way, why doesn't Keesha attend any of our parties?"

"You know little miss goody, goody, busy, busy, she'd never come to something like that."

"So how did Jamal and Keesha hit it off when he made his surprise visit?"

"I think things went well."

"Did he hit it?"

"Don't go there, you little biddy. Keesha's my girl and ain't no news being carried about her here!"

"Daaamn, you act like she's sweet on you."

"No, it's just that Keesha's different, and she wouldn't appreciate that kind of conversation. So she deserves the utmost respect!"

"I hear you. Well Jamal's attitude has changed since he's returned to work. I think he's whipped. I don't know what he finds so special about Keesha. There are some beautiful women that come in here with bodies that a man would die for, and he wouldn't give them the time or day. These women actually flirt with him, and he dismisses them. We had this one lady that came in and she actually dropped her dress in his office and stood stark naked in front of him, and he asked her to put her clothes back on."

"Jamal always had this thing for Keesha. Now he has the chance, so I'm going to do all I can to make sure that things work out for them. He deserves her, and she deserves him, they are made for each other."

"I guess they think he's gay."

"Probably, but of course, we know that he isn't."

"Did any of the women score with him?"

"Yeah, matter of fact, there's a doctor on the second floor that he dated for a while. She told everyone that he was the fuck of the century. She said he's huge and got a body on him!"

"He does, and then some!"

"So why are you giving him to Keesha, why not yourself? You've always been out for self."

"He loves Keesha, and Keesha loves him, she's just stubborn and neither of them expressed their feelings for each other when they had the chance. Look, ask Doc to give me a call when he gets a chance. Okay?"

"You got it. Maybe I should push up on him myself!"

"Don't go there. You'll get your feelings hurt. Trust me. His love belongs to Keesha. You should see the rock he put on her finger."

"He gave her a ring?"

"That's right, tramp, so don't even think about it!"

"All right, Linda, I'll talk to you later. As you can see, this is a long-distance call."

Just as Ebony hung up, Jamal walked into the office. He had the look of a tired, overworked gentleman. After greeting his staff, Jamal dragged himself into his office. Not only was he exhausted; Keesha hadn't called him. He couldn't think of one reason why she hadn't. Had she even given him a thought since she returned home? Hesitating for a moment, he decided to give her a call but didn't want to be persistent.

"Dr. Warner, Ebony gave you a call, she wants you to call her when you have time."

"Okay, thanks Linda!"

"Anyone else call?"

"No, are you looking for a call in particular?"

"Linda, I'm in love with Keesha, and I don't know whether she understood the depth of those feelings when I saw her a couple of weeks ago."

"Did you call her?"

"Yes, but I didn't speak to her. I left a message on her phone and she hasn't called me back yet."

"So why didn't you call her again?"

"Because I didn't want her to think I was rushing her! I really do love her, and it's killing me that I haven't heard from her!"

"I've never seen you like this, Dr. Warner! I think you should call her again, right now and let her know how you feel. She's probably thinking you forgot about her and found someone else." With that statement, she turned to leave his office when he began to speak.

"You're right, I'll give her a call right now and see if perhaps I can spend some time with her."

Jamal picked up the telephone and dialed Keesha's number. There was a continuous ring. He decided that he would call her later. He wished that she had picked up the telephone and expressed to him how much she had missed him, and that she wanted to see him. Jamal decided to call Ebony to see if she had heard something from Keesha, or at the very least if she had mentioned him in her conversation. He picked up the telephone and dialed Ebony's number.

"Hello, this is Ebony."

"Hi, Ebony. What's up¿"

"Jamal, how's everything¿"

"Okay, I guess. Have you heard anything from Keesha¿"

"I spoke to her last week. She's doing okay! Jamal you should really call her. Especially now."

"What do you mean¿ Is something wrong¿ What aren't you telling me Ebony¿"

Ebony knew she couldn't tell Jamal about Chris, but with the feud between Keesha and Christine, and her uncertainty about staying with Chris, this is the perfect time for Jamal to step in and pick up the pieces. "I'm not withholding information from you, Jamal, but if you're expecting her to just come running to you, you're sadly mistaken. You're going to have to fight for this one. Don't give up and don't get tired. She's a great woman but Keesha needs a whole lot of pampering. Look, she's been alone for a long time. This is the perfect opportunity to make mistakes. Like dating the wrong guy. You've got to get in her world, Jamal, and stop sitting on the sideline waiting on phone calls. Be spontaneous."

"I didn't want to seem like I was rushing or crowding her!"

"You're not crowding her!"Ebony said through clenched teeth. "Be spontaneous. Call her. "

"I'll do better than that, I'll leave after work and pay her a surprise visit!"

"That's what I'm talking about. Put your all on the line. Call me. Let me know how things work out!"

"Okay, wish me luck."

"Jamal, you don't need luck. Keesha loves you, and all you have to do is nurture what you have already started."

Jamal hung up the telephone with a reassured smile on his face. He thought for a moment and then asked his assistant, Theresa, for his calendar.

"So, anything happening this week?"

"Nothing that Dr. Rich's office can't handle."

He admired his assistant's ability to read his mind. She knew that he needed to get away from the office and that was her way of pushing him to do what was necessary. He had been alone for about a year now with no woman in his life. He had dated this nurse for a little while almost a year ago. She wanted to dominate him not to mention, dip her hands in his pockets. Everything that they did, she had to discuss with her friends and the other staff members. She was probably the cause of lust fads that befell him. The women in the hospital were going crazy over him. They would touch him in places that made him blush. They even went around discussing his genitals with his coworkers. When finally he realized it had been her, he cut her loose.

Now his assistant had a crush on him, and he didn't want to hurt her feelings but nothing would ever come out of it. His heart belonged to Keesha. He wished his assistant would meet a nice, financially stable gentleman who would love and take care of her.

"Dr. Warner?"

"Yes, Theresa, what can I do for you?"

"Can I ask you something?"

"Sure, Theresa, shoot! What's on your mind?"

"I've been working for you for four years now and..."She paused for a moment searching for the words.

"Theresa, are you trying to ask me for a raise? If you are, I have no problem giving one. You are a very hard and reliable worker, I wouldn't trade you for anything in the world! Besides, you understand me and I understand you."

"Good, I'm glad you said that, but that's not what's on my mind."

"Then what is it?"he asked, concerned. He feared for what her next response might be. Had she finally had the courage to approach him about her feelings? How would he let her down without hurting her? Maybe I'm jumping the gun he thought to himself. "Come on, out with it."

"Dr. Warner, Jamal, I've fallen in love with you, and I don't think that I could carry my feelings for you unspoken any longer! I want us to be more than just coworkers. Day in and day out, I think about you, and I think that no one could be more rewarding to you than I am!"

There she thought, I've finally spilled my heart out to him and now he has to answer me and let me know if he feels the same for me. Theresa had no idea what his next response might be but she needed to tell him before he had the chance to speak with Keesha again. Maybe he would realize that there was someone here who loved him and would forget all about Keesha. She had told only one other person about her feelings and that was Linda. Now she had shared them with the one that could make a difference.

Jamal could feel his heart getting heavy. He didn't want to hurt Theresa's feelings. Money he could give her, but his heart belonged to Keesha. Now what was he going to say to this woman to help her understand that there could be nothing between them? She was such a young and beautiful woman, talented in many ways but he could never love her. He didn't want to lose her as his assistant but he just couldn't feel intimate toward her.

"Theresa, I don't know what to say! This catches me by surprise, and I don't know how to respond, I'm stumped for words!"

"Then say you love me too!"

"I can't, I'm in love with another woman."

"What other woman?" she demanded, knowing to whom he was referring. She had met Keesha through Linda at one of her friend's parties. "It's been a year since I've seen you interested in anyone, so is this your way of telling me that I'm not good enough for you?"

"Theresa, please. You know that it's not because I don't think you're good enough. I think you are a very beautiful woman. You are very talented, but there is a woman I knew when I was in high school. I loved her, never had the chance to tell her, but now she is in my life again, and I can't let her get away this time. Can you understand that?"

"Yeah, I guess I can, but I still have these feelings and wish that you could see how I feel about you!"

"I do understand what it means to love someone, that's why I'm asking you to understand how I feel about her and not to think that I'm just giving you the brush off."

"I know, you're right, I'm sorry I mentioned it."

"Don't be sorry. You expressed your feelings and that's good. Just because it didn't work out the way that you hoped it would doesn't make it wrong."

Jamal surprised himself as he reasoned with this woman. It made him more determined than ever to pay Keesha a surprise visit to make the impression even more intense.

CHAPTER
13

Upstairs in her bedroom, Keesha lay on the bed thinking about how this situation could be made right. Should I just settle for Jamal? There's nothing wrong with him. He's very sweet and handsome. He has already reached his goals and status in life. He's my age and wants to make me happy. How can Chris make me happy when he hasn't lived long enough to know what life is all about or not to mention, what it's like being dedicated to a woman?"she wondered. Question after question came to mind as she began to realize that maybe she was making a mistake with Chris.

How did I get myself into this situation, anyway? I've fallen in love with the wrong man and now I have two problems on my hands, well maybe three. She weighed the problems: If she continued her relationship with Chris, his mother would hate her, cause a great deal of grief in her life and embarrass her in front of the neighbors. Chris would never have the opportunity to explore other women or to get a better understanding of him and of what he wanted. Every man needed to explore his options. If she let Chris go and built a relationship with Jamal, then she would have to hurt Chris, proving his mother right, leaving him to be nagged all his youthful life about not listening to his good ol' mother. Not only that, she didn't know if her teenaged feelings for Jamal would surpass her love for Chris. If she didn't try, she might always have this deep longing for Chris in her subconscious. This must be a spell or a punishment for something I did when I was younger,"she rationalized.

The next morning she decided that she would not answer her telephone or the door. Chris would understand that she needed time to get herself together. The telephone had been ringing like crazy all day. Keesha glanced at her machine while browsing her calendar on the computer. The message box read fifteen messages. She decided not to retrieve them. Keesha noted that her schedule was free when a special message flashed on her screen. She wanted to walk away and decided that she would listen to it. Keesha requested that the computer play the message back to her.

"Hello, Keesha, this is Jamal. I've been trying to reach you today but I guess you've been out all day. Please give me a call at 212-686-5722. I love you and hope to see you soon. I miss you so much!" The modem clicked off and told her that she had fourteen other messages then asked her if she wanted to hear them. She typed in no and then closed the screen.

"Two one two, Jamal's here in New York?"she said aloud "What? Okay, pull yourself together, girl,"she said. What to do? What to do? She picked up the telephone to dial the number he left as the doorbell rang!

Keesha paused a moment, deciding to answer it. If it were Chris, ignoring him would not be a healthy thing to do at such a sensitive time.

She went to the door. "Who is it?"

"It's Jamal, sweetheart!"She opened the door for him, and there he stood tall, dark and handsome.

"Hi sweetie, how are you?"

She was too stunned to answer.

"I was worried about you since you didn't answer your telephone all day. I hope I'm not imposing on you or anything, but something in me told me that I should check your house just in case you might be hurt or something."

Keesha finally came to her senses. "Ooh thanks, Jamal, I'm fine. Please come in."

"Are you sure? I can come back at a more convenient time."

"No, no, please, I'm glad you stopped by,"she said puzzled and frightened at the same time.

"Why? What's the matter?"

"Nothing, I'm just glad to see you." Two weeks had passed since she'd seen him, and he was indeed a sight for sore eyes. She ushered him to the living room where they sat and talked.

"So, when did you arrive in New York?"

"Well, I just decided to take a drive, and with you on my mind, my journey ended here. It was only a four and half-hour drive. Nowhere is too distant for me to see you."

He lifted her hand. "This isn't the ring I gave you!"he said with a puzzled look on his face.

"What happened to our ring?" His eyes showed concern. Keesha realized that this was the time to be truthful. Her conscious wouldn't allow her to string him along. She would do the right thing by giving him the opportunity to decide how he wanted to handle the situation. "Jamal, I put your ring in my jewelry box so that I could think about it without being captivated by the diamonds."

"I don't understand. Where did you get the ring that's on your finger now?"

Keesha looked down at her hand realizing that she was still wearing Chris' ring. Jamal's unexpected visit caught her off guard not affording her to make the exchange. She knew there was nothing she could do to keep from hurting his feelings.

"Jamal, it was given to me by a very dear friend, and I wear it most of the time because I like the way it looks on my finger."

He showed a bit of relief but Keesha could still sense his discomfort. One thing about him that she admired was that he knew when to drop the subject. He kissed her ring finger and said, "No matter. I'm just happy that I can spend these few minutes with you, even if this is the last time! Any man who wins you will be eternally happy even if it's for a short while."

Keesha could feel her heart beating with guilt and wished she could find the words to express how sorry she felt about the matter.

"So,"she changed the subject, "how was the trip?"

"It was fine. All I thought about was how I could surprise you and what we could do while I'm up here."

"Why don't we go into the sitting room and watch a movie?"

He accompanied her to the sitting room, and Keesha found one of her favorite movies, Pretty woman. While watching the movie, Jamal watched Keesha from the corner of his eye to see if she felt uncomfortable with him being there. Jamal knew how she must have been feeling, especially since she didn't expect him to show up unannounced. The last thing he wanted was to cause her to be afraid of talking to him about anything, no matter how bad things might seem.

"Keesha, what's wrong? You seem very distant, are you okay? Is there something you need to get off your chest? If you need space, I'll understand!"

"No, Jamal. Please don't go. I appreciate you noticing my feelings. They will subside after a while!"The room fell silent for a while.

Breaking the silence, Jamal began talking about his past. How his parents wanted him to be the success story in the family and raise many children for them to spoil. He talked about his profession, delivering children, what made him tick and how much he wanted things to work out between them.

Keesha found him quite interesting. He had a sense of humor, he was sensitive and she could tell he had a deep respect for women.

"Why is it that a handsome, successful man like you is still running around single and never been tied down?"

"The same as yourself, I haven't found Ms. Right yet! Or maybe I've been waiting for you!"

"Have you?"

"Yes,"he said in that deep sexy voice of his. There was a note of sincerity in his voice. "I have been waiting for you, Keesha, as unbelievable as it may sound. Don't get me wrong. I have dated other women hoping to find someone that I could build a family with and be happy. You know how difficult that is! I want to have children while I'm young enough to enjoy them and young enough to be enjoyed." He looked at her and smiled. "I've dealt with many women, and they were all alike. They are captivated either by my looks, stature, financial status, possessions or just my money! I would love to shower my woman with all the finer things that money can buy, but I need to be loved too. I want a woman to come running home to me after a long day at work. I want her to tell me how much she missed me or maybe cuddle up with me on the chaise and stroke my bald head, neaten my goatee or rub my eyebrows. Men like to be soft sometimes, to be wanted and appreciated. I would love to have my wife look at me with proud eyes and be content with me so that no man can ever come between us. I want to fulfill her every wish so that her fantasies can become reality, not just smoke desires. Is that what you want, Keesha?"

While Jamal expressed his innermost feelings, his charm and sincerity captivated Keesha. He was so soft and gentle. The things he had to offer, any woman would want. How could his search be so difficult? "Yes, Jamal. I haven't found anyone who feels the way I do."

"Yes, you have. You're just afraid to try me! Test me. Give me a chance to be all you want in a man. If you're honest with me about your feelings and not ashamed to share your desires, I will strive to make you happy."

He leaned over and kissed her on the cheek gently and held her face up so that he could look deep into her eyes. He was hoping that she had the same feelings about him that he had about her. Keesha had a funny tingling feeling going on in her chest down to the pit of her stomach. She wanted to hold him but he kept his gaze in her eyes, searching for answers. He saw the beautiful diamond cluster on her ring finger, and wondered how strong his competitor was. Jamal reasoned that the competition must be strong since she still wore his ring. One thing Jamal knew was that asking her now, would be the wrong time.

"Jamal, I don't think that I can start a relationship with you without being honest with you. The ring that I'm wearing is from someone that I think I'm in love with."

Jamal watched her eyes while she spoke. So far, she hadn't surprised him with anything that he hadn't figured out for himself.

"He confessed his love for me and sent me this ring in the plant you saw in the living room."

After she had paused for a while, he realized that she had become speechless.

"Keesha, I don't know what to say or if what I want to say is correct or if this is even the right time. You're telling me that you love this guy but you're here with me. In addition, if you wanted to be with this man he would be where I'm sitting right now and I would be on my way back to Virginia. So, there is something stopping you from committing to him. I don't care about your reasons, I'm just glad I still have a chance."

He understood her well, and she was taken by it.

"When you finally make your decision, I'll be here waiting for you. I have no strings attached, I'm all for you if and when you want me."

They finished watching Pretty Woman." When the movie ended, Jamal informed Keesha that he was going to return to his hotel. He gave her his number telling her that it would be good for a week and that he would like to get together with her again during his stay. Jamal reached for the door but Keesha insisted he stay. He kissed her cheek meaningfully. "Keesha, you're not ready for me to spend the night. We have a whole lifetime to romance each other. Relationships are built over time, and the memories are the cornerstones that help stabilize the foundation. I want to make love to you again with a clear and certain mind. Not one that is confused or in turmoil about two men. I love you, and I'll wait. In fact, I'll take the back burner for now and let you decide where you think your foundation should be built!"

He said good night again, kissed her tenderly on the lips, and then left.

"I'll see you tomorrow?"she asked, concerned that she wouldn't see him again.

"Yes, I'll see you tomorrow if you like." she closed the door, smiling. Keesha was beginning to realize that Jamal really was wonderful.

The night was long. Keesha spent several hours going over presentations for clients. She fell asleep on the lounge chair, waking at eleven-thirty the next morning. She couldn't believe she had slept so late. She took a quick shower then rushed out of the house. She felt so comfortable now that Jamal expressed some understanding about her situation. A sense of relief came over her. She couldn't believe that he even passed up a great body like hers. In a way, she was glad he did, although her body ached for him. Jamal had considered the after effects lovemaking could have on a person, especially a woman.

Hurrying to her car, she was stopped by Chris who caught hold of her arm as she started to open her car door. He stepped in front of her.

"Keesha why didn't you return any of my telephone calls?" His sudden appearance took her by surprise. Where did he come from that quick? Keesha wondered.

"I was busy, Chris. I had a lot of work to get done."

His eyes searched for the truth. He knew that something was going on but he wanted her to tell him before he made any accusations.

"Keesha, I saw a man go into your house last night when I was on my way to visit you. I waited for a while so that I wouldn't impose on you. He never came out. At least not while I was there. I waited for about an hour and decided to go home to get something to eat. I called you several times and no one answered. I decided I'd better stop by again to see if maybe you went out for a bit. I saw that same gentleman leaving your house three hours later. He kissed you good night and proceeded out of your door with the happiest grin on his face. Is there something you want to tell me?"

His impatience was apparent and out of line.

Keesha became infuriated. "No," she said glaring at him. "How dare you stand outside my door and spy on me!"

"Keesha, I wasn't spying on you. I just happened to visit your house as usual, and now all of a sudden I'm spying on you? Another man leaves your house after three long hours, with the same look I have when I leave, and because I noticed, I'm spying on you? Is my mind playing tricks on me or what?"

"I don't owe you any answers. Excuse me." She put her key into the car door and unlocked it. She got in and started to close the door but Chris stopped her by holding it. When he realized what he was doing, he let the door close. Then stepped back continuing to watch her. She started the engine but a twinge of guilt pricked her conscious. She lowered the window staring at the steering wheel. Keesha was afraid to look at Chris fearing what she would see.

Chris remained where he stood and began to admonish her. "How could you do this to me, Keesha? I love you and, you told me that you love me too! If you wanted me out of your life, all you had to do was say it, and I would have left you alone!"

She looked at his face and her heart dropped. The guilt was so thick it showed all over her face like makeup. "Chris, I'm sorry, I shouldn't have answered you that way. I do owe you an explanation. Please forgive me!"

She pleaded with him to excuse her behavior. He took her by the hand and noted that his ring was still on her finger. A spark of reassurance came over him. Certainly, the guy must have seen the ring. Maybe she needed time to explain that she was already in a relationship and let the poor guy down easy and he was trying to hold himself together when he left.

"I guess there is still hope since you haven't removed the ring I gave you."

"Chris, I just have a lot of things going on right now, I'll talk to you about this another time, but right now I have to go somewhere, and I'm running late."

He held her hand for another minute and moved away from her car so that she could drive away. "Speak to you later."

He stooped down and gave her a deep, meaningful kiss on the lips. "I'll miss you!"

He stepped back, allowing her space to drive. He watched her until

she turned the corner and was out of sight. Keesha sat in her car thinking about what had transpired. Why is it that Chris and Jamal seem to
be saying and doing the same things? She thought. Is it all in my head?
She turned on her CD player and listened to her music.

CHAPTER
14

"Ms. Tanner, we received the results back from the blood test, the news is favorable. Your child is all right."

"Thank you, doctor," she said in a relieved voice. "I knew that things would be all right."

"You will need to make monthly visits for prenatal care. Here is a prescription for prenatal vitamins that will help you throughout this pregnancy. Take one every day. Do not take any sort of medication without my consent, and if you experience any unusual bleeding or cramping, please call my office right away."

"Okay, will do."

"I am also giving you a prescription for Iron. You will need it to build up your blood, which will prevent you from becoming anemic. This should be taken once a day also. If you find that you are getting constipated, then take them once every two days."

Ms. Tanner was so happy and excited that their child was going to be okay that she wasn't really listening to what the doctor was telling her. She heard the part about the vitamins and iron but she had not heard the part about bleeding or cramping.

The doctor told her that she should schedule an appointment for four weeks from that day and that he would see if everything was going all right. He called the nurse into the room and told her to take Ms. Tanner's file. He then told Ms. Tanner that she could go home.

Ms. Tanner walked out of the doctor's office a happy woman. She and Chris would be having a child after all. There was nothing that Keesha could do to change that. However, having her out of the way would make things a great deal easier. Chris would be a little more eager to accept his responsibility to her and the child. Right now, he was determined to have this relationship with Keesha.

No matter, she would pay him a visit later in the week. Perhaps he needed a little time to think about it.

She got into her car and proceeded to drive home. She thought about ways that she could cause confusion between Keesha and Chris. Certainly, Christine's unsuspected visit while Chris was over made the situation a little awkward for them.

Chris was sitting at home wondering how he could make things right between himself and his mother. He knew that now wasn't the time to give her a call. He hated himself for letting her down but right now, his heart yearned for the love that only Keesha could give.

His mind wondered to that crazy ex-girlfriend of his. He couldn't imagine why she was so bent on making his life miserable. Now, she had seduced him and may even be carrying his child, a child that should be growing inside Keesha.

He looked out of his window at the nicely cut shrubs. The Lindens provided shade in front of his three-story town house. It was definitely a nice piece of property, and he would be able to make Keesha a happy woman along with the children she would bare for him. He had a twenty-acre grassy yard out back of his house, and an out door pool. There are all kinds of recreation on the property for the residents' use.

He went to his second-floor bedroom and imagined Keesha entering his room in a long flowing royal-blue gown that would show off her perfect body and nicely tanned brown skin. He saw himself laying on champagne satin sheets with nothing on but a royal blue G-string waiting for his wife to come and give him that sweet loving that only she could give. Chris could see Keesha dancing seductively at the door, slowly making her way over to the bed. Every moment that she took to come to him seemed like an eternity. As she teased him, waiting for her to reach the bed, he showed a single red rose that he picked from the bed of roses growing in his yard. He watched her as she made him wait for her. Slowly he picked the petals off the flower trying to decide whether she would make love to him or love him not. Of course, she always would.

Then he went to the window and saw her swimming across the pool, the sun beaming on her body like a spotlight displaying her beauty. "Keesha, I love you so much. No one will come between us. All this is for you, all of it!" Chris loved her so much, but somehow, he knew that there was someone else that loved her just as much and would give him a run for his money.

While still imagining Keesha swimming in the pool, all of a sudden, his ex popped in his head. He now saw her swimming where Keesha once was. Then he saw himself jumping into the pool and swimming over to her. He then wrapped his arms around her, and they kissed passionately. He tore her bikini from her waist and they swam to the edge of the pool where they made waves of passion in the pool. The coolness of the water could not mask the heat of their bodies as they created friction in the water. The water came to a boil as their fire of passion erupted and their juices flowed.

"Damn you for creeping into my fantasies!" Chris cursed aloud. He couldn't understand how she always found her way into his life, even in dreams. Certainly, this couldn't be his destiny. Otherwise he might as well just stab himself right now. He laughed, thinking something as crazy as that. Stab myself, no way. Stab her! he thought.

Meanwhile, Ms. Tanner had nothing on her mind but Chris. No one could "ras her berries" like Chris. Their love was too fervent for words. One thing for sure, Chris could never deny her when it came to sex. He loved it, craved it, and there was no way that Keesha could match it.

She was glad that she told Christine to pay Keesha a visit, and that Keesha said that they didn't spend much time together like they used to. What better time to invite her over than when Chris would be over? "Did she think that she could get away with it forever?" she said aloud as she filled with anger that Keesha would even think that she would get away with stealing her man.

She spent the rest of the drive home talking to the baby and telling her child that Daddy would be coming home to them, very soon.

CHAPTER
15

Keesha spent the day shopping for new outfits and office supplies. At the shopping center, she ran into an old friend from high school.

"David, how are you? Long time no see!"

"I'm doing just fine. What are you doing in this neck of the woods?"

"Just shopping and spending money like it grows on trees!"

They laughed.

"So, have you had lunch yet?"

"No, have you?"

"No."

"So how about it," he asked.

"Sure, I have nothing else to do at this moment."

"So what do you want to eat?"

"How about Japanese?"

"Sounds good. You pick the dish, I'm not very good with Japanese food."

"Okay, I know this place called Sukura of Japan. Have you been there before?"

"No, you lead the way."

They walked to the parking lot together and met at the exit. Keesha waited for David to get his car so that he could follow her to the restaurant, which was only twenty minutes from the mall. She parked the car and waited for David to find a parking spot. They entered the restaurant and the waiter took their jackets and shoes and escorted them to their seats or pillows to be exact. The waiter gave them a nice quiet area where they could talk in privacy.

"So David, what have you been doing with yourself?"

"Oh the same things as always. Working, chores, working and maybe resting every other month."

"Are you in the same line of work?"

"Oh, not at all, I quit that job when I got my degree. Now I spend my days building my business by getting new clients and keeping the old ones happy."

"I don't know, David, sounds to me like you're selling your body."

He laughed.

"No silly, I'm fixing and building computers. As the market changes, so does the equipment needed, that's where I come in."

"Sounds good. Do you like it?"

"Oh yeah, you run into a stick in the mud sometimes, but the overall clientele is the best. How about yourself? Are you still planning other people's finances?"

"Definitely, and it's paying off too!"

"That's great."

The waiter came over to their table to take their order. Keesha decided on the vegetable tempura with the house tea for both of them.

The waiter scribbled on his pad. "Will that be all?"he asked.

"Yes, for now thank you. Oh, waiter, would you bring us some steam fried dumplings with Tempura sauce?"Keesha blurted out.

"Sure." Then he walked away.

They continued talking until the waiter returned with their lunch. Keesha watched David take his first bite of Japanese food. "This is great,"he remarked. She smiled and began eating her own. Time passed as they talked. Minutes seemed like hours. How she missed talking with him. David seemed to be the only man that could listen to a woman and be objective. She never had to worry about him making a pass at her or scheming to get into her panties.

"So David, how do you think I should handle this situation?"

David replied, "Well, Keesha, I think that if you don't know what you want, keep them both and slow down on the bootie outlay. That way you can make an intelligent decision and not depend on that voice on the bottom clouding your thinking!"

Keesha giggled to herself. She could always appreciate how David answered things and knew that he was sincere. David told Keesha that he couldn't believe that after all these years Jamal was still after her. Jamal used to talk to David about Keesha all the time. David told Jamal that Keesha wasn't interested in men, otherwise he would have had her. Keesha found that funny.

"David, are you hitting on me?"

"No, Keesha. You know sex and friendship don't mix. Don't take that last statement seriously."

Keesha looked at him for a moment and then continued to eat and talk.

"So is there a woman in your life yet or are you still being a player?"

"Now that's the wrong terminology! I don't play women, I just hang on to them all until I make a decision like I'm telling you to do. Now what's wrong with that?"

"Well actually there is something wrong with that, if you don't tell them that you're seeing other women."

"You're right, Keesha I should tell them what I'm doing, matter of fact I should just stay by myself since no one will have me if I told them that I was seeing someone besides them anyway! How about that? You and I both know that you can't be honest with women, or men for that matter, these days because they don't understand."

"Now see that's where you're wrong. I told Jamal that I was seeing someone else, and he said he'd wait for me."

"Tell me you didn't!"

"I did!"

"You couldn't have!"

"I did!"

"Do you know what you've done? That is a direct invitation for a man to bang other women. You never tell a man that you want an open relationship because a man will enjoy what he's doing and never think about feelings but women on the hand will torment themselves looking for love."

David shook his head to think that Keesha could do something that was so elementary. He couldn't see how she could break rule number one, never tell your partners that you're cheating on them, in fact, never admit it. No matter how truthful you call yourself being.

"Anyway," he continued, What about this Chris character. Did you tell him about Jamal?"

"No, of course not!"

"Why not?"

"Because Chris is still young, and he wouldn't handle it the same way as Jamal is handling it!"

"So you think that Jamal is understanding, huh? Listen, I hope you don't take me the wrong way and certainly we have been friends for a very long time. Take this in stride, friend to friend, okay? No man wants to know that another man is banging his goods. Whether he loves her or not. It's the fact that she belongs to him. So if you are as smart as you look or at least half as smart as you look, you will keep those thoughts as thoughts and not let them escape again!"

He reminded her that the remark was coming as a friendly gesture. He told her that he never hit on her because he didn't think she'd give it up anyway, but if he knew that he could have, he might have tried.

"This is all just from a man's perspective, you understand?"

"Sure. Thanks, friend!"

"So after you told Jamal that you were seeing someone else, did he sleep with you?"

"No."

"Why not?"

"He said he wanted to."

Before she could finish, David finished her sentence.

"He wanted to give you time to see what you wanted, right? Yeah, yeah. He'll be over tonight ready to help you make up your mind. We all say that when our pride is hurt. That's our way of not telling the woman how she has affected us."

Keesha sat there thinking about it for a while and decided that she'd see for herself if what David said was true. She called the waiter over and asked for the check. David picked up the check and gave the waiter some money. The waiter walked away smiling.

"I take that you gave him a nice tip!"

"Oh yeah, I always give a nice tip. Didn't I give you a nice tip?"

They chuckled at his remark, and he escorted her to her car. They exchanged numbers and promised to keep in touch.

Keesha got into her car and drove off. She could see David in her rearview. He was definitely not the best-looking man in the world but one thing was for sure, the women did go crazy over him. She could see him profiling in his mirror. She turned off when she reached her exit and honked her horn to say good-bye to her friend.

The drive home was relaxing, and Keesha had forgotten about her earlier confrontation with Chris. Running into David rejuvenated her and renewed her spirits. Keesha drove into her driveway since she didn't anticipate leaving the house again that day. The street was full of parked cars and everyone seemed to be at home and resting. Everything was quiet and no one could be seen. She opened the car door, and Christine stepped in front of her.

"So, Keesha, you've been fucking my baby, huh?"

"Christine, look today has been a long day and right about now, I don't need this kind of aggravation."

"You had better leave my son alone and stop playing with his heart. You could never love him. He is too young for you and had never really been out with anyone before."

Keesha laughed to herself. If only Christine knew what kind of lover her son was, she'd know that he had had a lot of experience with women.

"Christine, I know that this must be difficult for you, but Chris has made up his mind. I don't want to talk about it. Quite frankly, I don't feel I owe you an explanation. Your son seduced me, I fell for him, end of story. Please don't come to my house looking to start a fight, I don't need this kind of attention!"

Christine frowned at Keesha stunned and angry, loathing the ground she stood on. Keesha turned her focus from Christine, refusing to acknowledge her interrogation. It wasn't long before Christine realized that she wasn't getting anywhere with Keesha. She left Keesha with her last words of threat and returned to her car, which was double-parked outside Keesha's driveway. Keesha closed her car door then proceeded to her house.

Suddenly, she felt something heavy striking her head. A strange feeling came over her, and she felt herself collapsing to the ground. She heard garbled noises and a voice shouting at her, but she couldn't make out what they were saying. The pain intensified, and she felt pressure on her head. I think that Bitch hit me! She was lying on the floor and a crowd gathered around her. All she could see were silhouettes. People were speaking funny asking her if she was all right. An ambulance came and strapped her to a bed and next thing she knew everything went black.

CHAPTER

16

Jamal sat in his hotel room thinking about Keesha. He remembered how had left her with unfulfilled desires. He hoped that she understood his feelings but he could not bring himself to make love to her wondering if she was focused on him, or someone else. In this kind of situation, he would normally walk away, but his feelings for Keesha went far beyond physical. He wanted her entirely, body, mind and soul. However long it took, he would wait for her and give her as much time as she needed to decide which path she wanted to take.

However, he knew that there must be some reason why she was being hesitant about this other guy. Why else would she risk having another man in her life if this guy was so great? Jamal realized that he should have stayed last night, but he allowed his jealousy get the best of him. Keesha must have some feelings for him, otherwise she would not have wasted her time trying to keep him near.

Jamal couldn't believe that he walked away in defeat. Anything he wanted, he always got, so what made her any different? He picked up the receiver and dialed her number. The telephone rang and rang. Concern struck him when the machine did not pick up as it did the day before. Was she avoiding his call? Had he offended her? Could she be hurt? Jamal couldn't understand why she would be upset with him. Everything he did was in her best interest.

Finally after the telephone had rung countless times, he hung up and wondered whether he should pay her a visit. No, he thought. I would rather she called and invited me herself. I will not invade her privacy again or put myself in the position of seeing something I'm not prepared for. Knowing that there is someone else is bad enough, I don't need to witness it for myself.

After long contemplation, he grabbed his blazer and walked out the door. He stopped at the clerk's desk on his way out and asked directions to the nearest mall. The clerk told him that just five miles from the hotel was the Iverson Mall, which had everything in it. Jamal thanked the man and waited out front while the valet brought his car.

Jamal turned on his music, and the soft melody reminded him of the times he and Keesha had spent together. Sadness befell him as he envisioned her running with another. Had she left him? Did his care and concern for her feelings cause him to lose the woman he loved?

As he pulled into the mall, he saw a gift shop. He decided to buy Keesha a forgive me I'm sorry gift. Then He'd pick her up and take her out to dinner. He would have to find out where the best restaurant in town was. If he couldn't find one here, then he'd take her out of state and introduce her to a little cavern he enjoyed in Maryland.

In the gift shop, nothing he looked at or smelled seemed to be a worthy gift to regain his soul mate's heart.

He then went into a boutique and an attendant helped him find a suitable dress for a night on the town. When Jamal laid his eyes on it, he knew that this dress had been made just for Keesha. He paid for it and had it packaged in a suitable box. He thanked the attendant for her help and gave her a nice tip because he knew he would never have found this dress on his own.

Jamal returned to his car and his beeper summoned him. He looked at the number and realized that his office had been trying to page him for some time now and it had a string of URGENT across the screen. Jamal dialed the office with his mobile telephone, and the nurse answered the telephone.

"Dr. Warner, what happened to you? I've been trying to reach you all morning! We have an emergency here and need you back here at the office."

"What happened to Dr. Rich?"

"Nothing, but Mrs. Taylor won't allow him to do the C-Section! She is insisting that you do it, and she'll wait!"

"Is she stable right now?"

"Yes, but the baby may be in trauma and Dr. Rich suggested that we get you on the telephone before this lady loses her child!"

"Calm down, tell Dr. Rich to get her prepped, I'm on my way. I should be there in about an hour and a half. Dr. Rich can explain that I will be there and if things get out of hand, he can begin the procedure. In the meantime, I will catch the shuttle back. Have a car waiting for me at the airport."

"Okay. Is there anything that I can do to help this thing move more smoothly?"

"Thanks, Linda, I can always count on you to keep things going. I'll make sure you get a bonus for this."

"Thanks, Dr. Warner! I enjoy working for you!"

"Speak to you later. Oh, by the way, do me a favor."

"Sure what is it?"

"Give a call...No I'd better do it myself. Thanks anyway Linda."

Jamal hung up the telephone and called the airline to reserve a seat. There was a flight available which would get him to the hospital as he's planned.

During the flight, he thought about the impression his leaving might give Keesha, but what else could he do?

"Keesha, I'm sorry. I'll make it up to you!" Jamal closed his eyes and tried to get some rest before his busy day at the hospital began.

CHAPTER

17

"You gave us quite a scare,"the doctor said in a concerned voice. "Someone really gave you a whack over the head leaving serious scalp lacerations. Don't worry, we patched them back together."

"Was there any lasting damage done?"

"I'm not sure at this point, but for right now you show signs of con-cussion. We shaved your head. No need to worry, the hair will grow back in no time!"

"What do you mean the hair will grow back?" Keesha asked with trepidation.

"Well, we shaved your head. There was no other way to close the wound if we did not remove the hair, plus you run the risk of infection if it was not removed."

Keesha slumped deeper into her pillow and depression began to take over. She spent the day lying there in the hospital and feeding on painkillers to ease her agonizing headache. The doctor felt that she should stay on a liquid diet for at least a day for observation. She watched out the window and thought about what she'd do to that Bitch Christine when she caught up with her. Just wait till I catch up with that bitch,"she thought. She'll wish she kept her hands to herself. She closed her eyes and prayed for sleep.

When she opened her eyes again, she realized that she must have slept all day.

"Keesha, sweetheart, when I heard you were hurt, I came right over here. How do you feel?"

"Chris, how do you think I feel? Your mother tried to knock my scalp off, which my doctor shaved around, and stitched together. I look like Nemesis." Overwhelmed by everything she was saying, Keesha began to cry.

"Keesha you'll be all right. You look fine."

"Your mother did this to me!"she screamed in a quivering voice.

"You think my mother hit you?"

"Yes, your mother hit me.Who did you think hit me?"

"My mother didn't hit you! Keesha, I know that she's upset, but I assure you that my mother did not stoop to hitting her friend!"

"Chris, I have no doubt that Christine hit me over the head. She threatened me and pretended to walk away. When I turned to go into my house, she struck me from behind, so you put it together!"

Chris looked at her, and he had tears forming in his eyes.

"Keesha, I'm so sorry. I'm going to straighten this all out with my mother tonight as soon as I leave. Are they treating you good in here? Can I get you anything? Do you need anything? I don't know what to say."

"Yes, the nurses have been very attentive to my needs. I don't need anything."Her tone was curt and sharp.

"Keesha, I never wanted you to get hurt. I feel so bad about this. I love you so much, and now because of me, you and my mother are fighting. The two of you have been friends for so long. I would have never seen this coming. I would have suspected that she would have handled this in a mature manner. I'm really at a loss for words. There's really nothing I could say to make this situation better. But no matter what, I will always love you and want you."

He placed a warm, loving kiss on her lips, and Keesha turned her head and let the tears flow. Her heart began to pump rapidly as she longed for his touch. She couldn't understand why she was so in love with him! Why she wanted him so much. He rubbed the tears from her cheeks and again told her how much he loved her. Chris kissed her cheek then proceeded out of the door.

Keesha felt a great loss and emptiness. She knew that she would have to leave Chris. Things had gone too far and there was no turning back. She remained in the hospital for two weeks at which time she had undergone all the necessary tests and observations the doctor found necessary. Dr. Jones came in around noon, looked at her chart and seemed pleased with all the test results.

"Well Keesha, you seem to be alright! I guess this means good-bye!"

"So everything worked out okay?"

"Yes, I've come to sign your discharge papers. If you like, since you may experience some dizziness, I can have a home attendant see about you for a couple of weeks. You know, just until you're back to your old self again."

"No, I think that I will be able to handle things on my own, I'm not used to anyone waiting on me. If I run into trouble, I will call and take you up on that offer."

At that, she was released to go home. An ambulette drove her to her house and the attendant helped her into the house. He suggested that she get someone to stay with her for a few days, at least until she felt strong enough to do her daily routines on her own. She refused assuring him that she would be fine on her own. When the ambulance attendant was leaving, Jamal was standing at the door. He looked at the bandages wrapped around Keesha's head and his heart became sorrow filled.

"Keesha, what happened to you?"

"Someone hit me over the head."

"Why would anyone want to do something like that?"

Keesha considered lying to him but the truth wouldn't let her. She told him it was a friend of hers, who felt that she had overstepped her bounds.

"Do you want to talk about it?"

"No. I'd rather try and handle the situation for myself."

"Okay, but if you need me, I'm here for you."

"Thanks, Jamal."

He picked her up and carried her to her bed. They watched a movie on cable. Jamal fell asleep, and she continued to watch the movie. She watched him sleep and the more she looked at him, the more she realized how handsome he was. His skin had a beautiful tone. His eyebrows and goatee were sexy to the fullest. He had a nice thick chest, with a bulldog neck. His arms were big and muscular. His thighs and legs were strong looking like a thoroughbred. You could tell he was into keeping his body in good health.

She looked at the outline of his penis in his pants and wondered how a man could be so well endowed. She felt a longing growing within her and tried to fight it off. As she continued to watch it, her lust grew stronger and stronger. Keesha turned away from Jamal trying to fight the feeling. His lips looked like someone should kiss them.

She moved close to him and began kissing him. He remained a

sleep. She pressed her tongue between his lips and touched his tongue with her own. It was soft and wet. She climbed atop him and began a motion against his penis. As she rubbed against it, she could feel it growing. It was getting harder and harder. His arms reached up and around her waist. He joined in with ardent kisses.

He pressed her buttocks causing her to grind against him harder. She wanted to tear his clothes off but she waited for him to take control. He continued at her pace, only kissing and touching her. Her heart was on fire, and her body was pulsating. She wanted him so badly it hurt. Her breathing quickened as the desire built.

She stopped and took a position next to him, and he opened his eyes and said,

"Take it!"

She unbuttoned his pants, slid down his zipper and released him from his briefs. It struck out at her touch. She pulled his pants down over his hips continuing to massage his shaft.

"That's right, baby," he said.

She used her other hand to toy with the soft curls on his chest and followed it down the long path to his stomach. His belly was firm. As she continued to stroke him faster, his body began to move up and down. He pulled her up and positioned her over his face and orally pleased her, sending waves of passion through her. It felt so good that she turned around and took his manhood into her mouth, and he moaned with delight. She sucked it so many different ways and at so many different speeds, that he lost control and his gentle sucking became fervent. She cried out for more. When she felt she couldn't take it anymore, she climbed atop him and forced him into her. Keesha rode into rapture as Jamal welcomed her Calvary. When it was over, she let herself drop to his side as they had worn each other out. His gratitude was sealed with a kiss. They went into the bathroom and ran hot, soothing water into the Jacuzzi.

His sympathetic eyes looked at her shaven swollen head, and she could tell he wanted to hurt the person responsible for this hideous crime. Keesha lowered her head to think of how she must look to him right now.

"Keesha, you are still as beautiful as you were before any of this happened. A fire couldn't burn away your beauty."

She was comforted by his words and laid back against his chest and enjoyed the soothing jets that massaged them. After bathing, they got dressed and went downstairs to get something to eat.

"Keesha, why don't you come back with me to Virginia and let me take care of you until you are better? This way, you'll be able to rest and not have any worries."

Keesha thought about it for a moment and realized that he was right. She should be resting and really did need the time away. Keesha knew that if she stayed she would just sit around and feel sorry for herself. She decided that she would take him up on his offer. He helped her pack her bags, escorted her to his car and headed for the highway.

Since traffic was backed up, the trip took longer than normal. He drove for three and a half hours while they talked about his parents and siblings. The more he talked, the more she noticed his humor and adventurous side.

"Jamal, I know that you noticed the other women in our class. Why did you pick me?"

"Because you were a prize to be won! Everyone in the class wanted you, then I saw that you took no interest in anyone in the class. I knew that you had to be special. You were so smart, talented and aggressive. I love a woman that knows where she is going, and as I suspected, you went exactly where you wanted to go!"

"Weren't there any other girls in the class that you took interest in?"

"Like who?"

"Everyone liked Ebony. Why didn't you?"

Jamal chuckled in his sexy way and looked at Keesha to see where she was going with her questions. Then realized that she was just as concerned about his reasons for liking her, as he was about why she resisted him.

"Because Ebony liked attention and had been with quite a number of men! She is a nice-looking woman and has definitely done well for herself. Of course, she isn't quite as beautiful as you!"

He smiled at her, kissed her hand and gave her a wink. Keesha felt so safe in his presence.

"So what made you think that I didn't spend time with men outside of school?"

"Keesha, I knew everything there was to know about you then. Your looks were embedded in my mind, and I took a personal interest in you and your likes. If there was a man in your life, I would have known about him and took care of it!"

Jamal raised his thick, sexy eyebrows and made a mean face and threw a kiss at Keesha. They both laughed but Keesha knew he was serious.

Finally, he pulled up to an elaborate white house with a wide picture window that went all the way across the front of the house with a glass panel running down the middle revealing the stairway. He had a garden of roses and other exotic flowers surrounding the front of the house. They went into the house, and Keesha could tell that he was preparing for a wife. He had every convenience that a woman could ever want and space to add to it if there was something missing. The living room was large but cozy. The dining room was furnished with a cherry-wood dining room ensemble with white cushioned seats. The chandelier must have had about fifty lights on it, and the ceiling was very high. His kitchen floors were made of white marble with silver detailing. Keesha had never seen anything quite like it, at least not in someone's home. They continued through the carpeted corridor, which led them to an indoor pool. The walls and ceiling were glass with an opening roof. It reminded her of a greenhouse without plants.

He asked her how she liked it so far. "I love it!"she said with enthusiasm.

"I designed it myself."Jamal displayed his pride in his architecture. "Well, actually the real credit goes to an old class mate. Do you remember Sean who used to sit next to me in class?"

"Yes."

"Well he built it for me with some of his employees."

"You mean loudmouth Sean owns his own construction business?"

"Yes and interior design. He is doing very well for himself. In fact, he got married about three years ago, and I just delivered his first son."

"That's exciting! What do you think about when you see a baby being born?"

"Will I ever deliver one of my own."Jamal watched her intently hoping that she got his point. Keesha could see that he was sincere, and in a way, he seemed to be hinting his desire to have a child with her.

"You've really given this some thought, haven't you?"

"Come with me,"he said as he led her out of the poolroom and upstairs to a room that would have been heaven for any child.

"This is the playground I've built for my children. I had my nieces and nephews over, and they helped me decide what I needed in here. I watched them and let them pick out the toys and the activities. As you can see, I have indeed given this a great deal of thought but there is more! I want to show you something else."

He led her down the hall and into a room that seemed to have no end. There was no furniture in it and the walls were just plain white. "Well what is this room for?"Keesha asked in awe.

"This room is the master bedroom. This is the room I intend to make my family in. I want my wife to design and furnish it in any way her heart desires."

He pulled her close to him and looked deep into her eyes and said, "I want that person to be you, Keesha!"

He pulled her chin up so that he could kiss her. Then, he held her hand and opened it and placed in it the ring he had given her in Florida.

"Keesha, please wear my ring, even if you only wear it when you come here."

He removed Chris' ring from her finger and placed his cluster of diamonds and rubies on her finger. Keesha felt warm within. He picked her up and carried her down the hall.

"Now this is the room where I sleep now as a bachelor, but I'm sure that my pretty princess will change all of that and save me from this dungeon."

Keesha smiled at that statement but Jamal's face remained serious and intent. Whether or not Keesha realized it, Jamal meant every word he said. There were two other rooms.

"So what are these rooms for?"

"You haven't guessed, huh? These are the bedrooms for my two lovely children that you will bare for me!"

Their eyes met, and he raised his eyebrows in a funny little dance. Keesha couldn't resist the emotions that filled her, so she wrapped her arms around him, and they kissed each other over and over until they stumbled into the bedroom.

He pulled her dress over her head and started to speak softly. "Keesha, you have the most beautiful body I have ever seen. You're so tempting. I love your body and I love you. Your skin is like caramel and your eyes are like almonds. Those eyes of yours are so lovely."

Jamal admired every inch of her. Then they made love repeatedly.

He left her in the room and prepared her bath. After a short while, he returned for her and carried her to the bathroom and bathed her.

"I haven't been washed by anyone fully since I was a little girl."

He washed from her face down to her feet, clipped her toenails and oiled and lotioned her. He put a gown on her and put her to bed.

"You need to get some rest, sweetheart."

He pulled the covers over her, turned the lights out and left the room. Keesha heard the shower running and him singing his little heart out. She closed her eyes and enjoyed the treatment that she received.

The next morning, she felt Jamal easing out of the bed. He went into the bathroom and took another shower. When he returned to the room, he was fully dressed and off to the hospital.

"Sweetheart, I'll be back soon. I have a baby to deliver, which involves minor surgery. After that, I will come back to take care of you. If you like, when I get to the office, I'll have someone come here and take care of you."

"No I think that I'll be okay, but thanks anyway."

"Just make yourself at home because it is your home as long as you are here, and there are no secrets in this house. Whatever I have is yours. My money, cars, land, heart, my body, everything."

They kissed and then he went off to work. Keesha got up and called her house for messages. She put in the code to retrieve her three messages. The first was from one of her clients. "Keesha, this is Jo-Ann, please call me regarding the estate planning we discussed, I'm ready to move ahead."

The machine beeped and then it gave her the next message. "Hi, Keesha this is Chris, when you get a chance, please give me a call. I spoke with my mother, and she said she did not hit you. I love you and I'll speak with you later. In fact, I'll stop by on my way from the office."

Then the machine beeped to give her the last message. "Keesha, you bitch, our friendship is over, and you had better stay away from my son or else I'll be forced to hurt you. Your senseless seduction has come between me and my son, and I won't have that!"

After hearing Christine's message, Keesha realized that she was going to have to take care of her friend once and for all. She showered and put on some clothes. She thought about it for a while and decided to call her friend David who she reacquainted herself with at the mall. David was Billy Bad Ass back in high school. He had a reputation for getting things done. No one wanted to be on his bad list. Well Christine was about to get on David's bad list and Keesha was going to put her there. She told David about everything that took place between she and Christine. He couldn't believe his ears.

"You see, I told you that you needed to leave that woman's baby alone. Now look what has happened. So how do you want to handle it?"

"I need you to do me a solid."Using ghetto terms to emphasize the manner in which she wanted him to handle things.

"Whatever you want Keesha!"

"I want you to get some friends from an outside neighborhood and set that bitch up!"

"Consider it done."

"Thanks, David."

"Hey, anything for you."

"Oh, David."

"Yes, Keesha?"

"I want you to make sure that you don't handle this personally, I don't want this getting back to me, okay."

"Of course, my sweet. Is Chris worth all this?"

"This has nothing to do with Chris, this is personal!"

"Do you want her to die?"

"No, I just want someone to beat her head in and hobble her. Put that bitch in a wheelchair."

"Done. Anything else?"

"No, just make sure that when they beat her, it's done in a way that she'll be forced to think of me."

"You're so wicked when you get mad. No problem, sweets, it's as good as done."

Keesha sat back in the chair thinking about what good news she might find when she returned home in a couple of weeks. She smiled to herself thinking, Christine, you bitch. You're going to wish that you never fucked with this woman. Keesha wanted her to pay tenfold for her act against her, the pain that she now felt would be nothing compared to the legendary suffering she'd feel when she finished sewing.

Keesha went downstairs and reclined in a chair and thought of how wonderful Jamal and Chris were and decided that she would enjoy them both to the fullest. Since Christine didn't want her to have Chris, then she wouldn't. She would make him hate his mother for ruining his life, and at the same time continue to make his yearning for her grow. He would be punished with jealousy, compliments of his dear mother. His mother would be punished with being crippled and having a son that despised her.

Keesha found her way into the kitchen and started to prepare a meal for her lover. She reminisced about how good a lover Jamal was and decided that maybe she'd keep him. Keesha loved everything about him anyway his character, his sexiness and his lack of a bitching mother. She laughed at that thought. Who do you think you're kidding? Your heart belongs to Chris. Well Jamal too. As she turned the two men around in her head, she decided that maybe right now wasn't a good time to think about it. Deep down, she knew that the Jamal was the better choice since there are no strings attached.

Later in the day, Jamal returned and they enjoyed each other's company. He came in looking to cook and found a full dinner prepared.

"Keesha, darling, you shouldn't have done this. How can I spoil you if you're going to be jumping the gun? Sweetheart, I want to take care of you. All I want you to do while you are here is relax, get spoiled and make love to me!"

Keesha laughed and Jamal insisted that she sit and allow him to serve her.

"A woman could get used to this kind of thing,"she told him. She spent the rest of the week enjoying his company. Of course, some of that time was spent alone, especially when he had to go to the hospital or his office. Then there were other times when patients called him late in the night because they were in labor so he had to go to the hospital to deliver another baby. Each time he went into that delivery room he returned with an increased desire to make a child of his own.

As another week passed, Jamal realized that they had not spent enough time together. "Keesha, how about we spend this week totally together? I made plans to stay out of the office all week."

Keesha told him that she should be getting back home.

"Just this last week please?"

He looked so desperate, and sincere, she couldn't deny him.

"Okay, Jamal, I'll stay just one more week."

The first thing he wanted them to do was to go shopping. They went to the mall, and Jamal did not want her to spend any money. He purchased dress clothes and hiking gear for them both. They went food shopping and picked up a freezer box.

"So, where are we going?"

"We're going camping! Have you ever spent a few nights in the woods?"

"No," she said.

"So, this will be your first. I'm glad I'll be the one introducing it. They packed the motor home Jamal had rented with all that they thought they needed. Off they went. Keesha talked about the relationship she had with her mother when she was alive and her younger sister. She also told him all the details that no one knew about her. Jamal took in everything she said and seemed quite amused.

"Keesha, you are definitely an exciting woman, and I'm glad we are taking this opportunity to get to know each other."

The day went by quickly and night was about to take over when they reached the camping site. They drove deep into the woods and found a good spot to build their tent. Keesha tried to help Jamal but he wanted her to just sit and watch. He put the tent up and then they went to gather wood for a fire.

"We'd better start building this fire and heating up something to eat before it gets dark. Keesha gathered as many sticks as she could find. Jamal found her sticks amusing since he was carrying logs.

"Well maybe if I was as strong as you, I would have picked up logs too!"

He chided her with laughter while lighting the logs to start the fire. Keesha sat in front of the fire while Jamal set up his modern roasting rack.

"Now that isn't ranger like now is it?" Keesha teased him.

"No, but it is faster and less energy consuming than holding these ribs over a fire with a stick!" It smelled good.

"Are you sure that we won't attract any vicious forest beasts?"

"Yes, darling, I'm sure, but if so, I'll protect you."

Keesha sat and Jamal. She could tell that he was used to this sort of thing. After a long wait, Jamal passed her a few ribs on a paper plate with bread and then he fixed some for himself. They were good.

After eating, they stretched out on an airbed and stared at the stars. The stars were beautiful. Jamal wrapped his arms around Keesha and talked about the way his father used to bring him camping when he was young and he wanted to share his place of peace with her.

"Isn't this peaceful, Keesha?" he asked.

"Yes, Jamal. I think that this is one of the most extraordinary things I have witnessed about nature."

They listened to the different forest animals making their calls. The wind played its part against the trees creating an orchestra that no one could match.

"Keesha, have you thought about my proposal yet?"

"Oh, Jamal, I think about you constantly, but I really don't want to rush into anything. Marriage is a forever thing, and I'm really afraid that it will be my luck to run into a possessive, arrogant, self-centered and abusive man."

"I'm not any of that Keesha. I am a kind, loving man. I want to be happy just as much as any woman would. I survive on happiness and just like you. I'm scared to get myself hitched to the wrong woman. When I look at you, I can see that you are the woman for me and the one I want to bare my children."

He kissed her and they shared a moment of passion together. Umm, she thought as she enjoyed his soft and gentle kisses. That thin layer of hair that surrounded his mouth and chin gave him a sexy look. His eyes were so brown that when he looked at her she could feel them melting with passion. They made love under the moonlight, and Jamal serenaded her with the songs of his heart. He had a lovely deep voice. He pressed her against his broad, muscular chest. Keesha felt safe from anything while she was with him. She was certain that he would never let his mother beat her up, no matter whom he was seeing. Chris should have known his mother and therefore handled the situation better than he had, she thought. Now he was trying to protect his mother by trying to make her think that she didn't do it.

Keesha snuggled deep into Jamal's arms, buried herself close to his side and enjoyed the warmth of his body. She finally allowed sleep to take over as she found her security in his presence.

CHAPTER
18

Christine stood in her kitchen browsing through her cabinets searching for the components of the feast she wanted to prepare her family and friends. She realized that there were things missing, so she made a list and decided that she'd better go to the all-night supermarket.

Christine realized that it was eight-thirty. She never went shopping that late at night. But with all the cooking that she needed to do the next day, there was no way that she would be able to get it done if she had to go shopping for things in the morning. So she found her purse and keys, and made her way to the car.

Outside the house, just a block away, someone was watching her every move. Patiently the person waited for her to leave. She would not get away, she would be punished for a reason that she would never understand but it was necessary. There was no other way to handle the situation.

Christine got into her car and drove down the road to the shopping center. It seemed that the farther she drove, the darker the sky became. It was as though the sky was closing in on her. Where was Chris when she needed him? As she was suddenly stricken with fear, Christine decided that she had better call Chris at the nearest payphone. She could sure use his company right now. Then she would feel safe even though he was in another car following her.

Never had she felt a sense of fear when going somewhere, but for some reason, tonight was different and she knew that something was destined to happen, the question was what. She drove for what seemed like miles looking for a telephone. All of them seemed to be broken.

Finally, she saw a phone. It was far off from the street in a dark corner. She passed it and decided that she would see if she could find another one in a more populated area, to no avail. The telephone in that desolate area was the only one she could find so she decided to make a quick stop and call her son. Then she would wait for Chris near the mall.

She parked the car in front of the telephone, looked around but there was no one in sight. When she felt that everything was okay, she opened her car door and slowly stepped out of the car. Christine considered leaving the headlights on, but she feared that leaving the lights on would prompt prowlers of her presence, so she left the lights off and relied on the lights in the booth.

She cautiously stepped out of the car. She could feel the hairs standing on her neck. She turned to look behind her. There was no one there. She looked to the left and again saw no one. She looked to the right and still saw no one. She assured herself that her fear was only her imagination. She dialed Chris' number, and the telephone rang before the answering machine finally picked up.

"Hi, this is Chris, at the…"Hello this is Chris,"he said in a sleepy voice.

"Chris, darling, I need you to come and follow me back home, I have a feeling that I'm in danger."

"In danger! What do you mean, Mom? Where are you?"

"I was going to the supermarket to pick up some things I was missing for my dinner tomorrow. The store was closed for some reason so I drove a little farther to the supermarket in the next town."

"Ma, you know you shouldn't be in that area this time at night by yourself. Where are you? I'll be there in about fifteen minutes!"

She gave him the location, and Chris told her to stay in the car and not to let anyone in the car, and wait until he arrived. After thinking about it, he decided that it would be better for his mother to just leave the secluded block, and he'd meet her at home.

"Christopher Walker, I need to get those things tonight, you know the family will be over tomorrow, and it takes me all day to cook!"

"Okay, Mom, have it your way, but I want you to meet me at the mall. You get out of there before something happens to you. Do it right now! Hang up the telephone and go there now."

Just then, Christine heard something that sounded like a footstep.

"Chris, I think there's someone out here but I don't see them!"

"Mom, get into your car."

Christine rushed over to her car and someone struck the light in the telephone booth.

She became afraid. "Who's there?"she asked.

No one answered. She could see three shadowy figures coming toward her. They were slapping something in their hands, taunting her. Christine struggled to get her key into the door-lock, cursing herself for not leaving the lights on. Then right behind her, she felt the presence of someone standing there waiting for her to turn around.

"Go ahead and get it over with!"she said without turning around, fearing for her life and what she might see.

"Do you want my bag? I will give you all of my money if that's what you want!"

The figure still did not offer her any answer. The figure forced her to turn around by pulling her head back by her hair. Christine anticipated her throat being cut or that she would be raped.

She could smell no distinguishing odor or fragrance other than leather. Christine stretched her eyes open hoping to get a glimpse of who was hurting her. She could see nothing.

Finally, before she could scream, a large wad of cloth was stuffed into her mouth and she was mercilessly beat with clubs. The pain was so overwhelming that she tried to close her eyes and wish that she could escape it. Christine was a firm believer that everything happened for a reason, and she couldn't help but think that Keesha had ill-willed her believing that she had something to do with her attack. Christine would never have hurt her. Even after she screwed her son behind her back when she knew that he was off-limits to her, she would never have hurt her. She might go without speaking to her until the hurt went away but never would she stoop to this level.

Then she heard a car coming. It must be Chris, she thought. With one last blow to her thigh, the assailants fled. Shortly after that, Chris was at her side. He had seen nothing and no one.

Chris looked at his mother curled up on the ground, and he cursed himself for not getting to her sooner or calling the police when she told him what was happening. Christine closed her eyes and fell into a state of unconsciousness to escape the pain. Chris feared for his mother's life, and decided that he had better get his mother to a hospital.

At the hospital, Chris sat in the waiting area wondering why this had happened to his mother. This is the second incident like this. First Keesha got hit over the head and blamed his mother, now his mother had been beaten half to death. Could this be Keesha's doing? He prayed not.

Chris tried to reach Keesha again. He had been leaving messages at her house for weeks now. She had left the hospital without telling him and now she was avoiding his calls and not coming out of her house. He erased that thought from his mind. There was no way his loving Keesha would his mother.

Chris spent the next couple of hours waiting to hear something from the doctor. The nurse saw him falling asleep so she covered him with a blanket. She noticed his handsome features while trying to guess his age. He appeared to be about twenty-one.

Around four o'clock in the morning, the doctor told Chris that his mother was going to survive, however, she suffered a great deal of trauma to the spine and head, and her femur was broken.

"Most patients above the age of fifty, rarely have full recovery from this type of injury. I'm afraid she may never walk again. Only time will tell at this point."

Chris tried to listen to the doctor and not get upset. He felt himself going limp as he thought about his mother being attacked in such a violent way. Who could want to do such a thing to her? No money had been taken so whoever did this wanted to make a point.

"May I see her now, doctor?"

"Yes, but only for a few minutes. She won't be able to respond to you now. I sedated her to help with the pain, and to keep her from going into shock again."

Tears were welling in Chris' eyes. He fought to control himself. He slowly walked into his mother's room. Her head looked ten times its normal size, her eyes were swollen shut and her hands were mangled. Chris imagined her hands covering her face attempting to protect it from the blows. From the waist down she was in a cast. Chris couldn't imagine his mother being an invalid, not being able to at the very least, bathe herself.

His mother would never want to have someone washing her. He hurt for her. Chris was thankful for his mother's unconsciousness because she wasn't aware of what she had to look forward to. His heart felt sick, now realizing that because of his relationship with Keesha even after she disagreed caused her to do something so stupid. The only reason he felt that she would have gone out so late without calling him to go with her was to pretend that she didn't need him. And look what had happened. It was his fault. He should have told her about Keesha long before she found out. Then things would not have come to what it did.

The nurse peeped into the room noticing him crying over his mother. She comforted him, and like a scared child, he welcomed her hug. He leaned his head against the top of hers. His body was so weak from crying, that he felt that he was going to fall.

She led him to a seat and gave him time to get himself together. His eyes were so deep that she felt drawn by them. Then, she could see the youth in them. He was just a boy, crying over his mother. The nurse knelt in front of him explaining that things would be all right. "The doctor is good at what he does and your mother will be back to her same old self in no time!"

Chris looked at her and felt that she was just trying to make him feel better, but she assured him that doctors normally give the worse scenario, so that if better came, you would appreciate it.

"If he told you that everything would be all right and she turned out to be a lot worse, then you would doubt his capabilities and think that he lied to you."

Chris listened to her and decided that she was probably telling him the truth. He appreciated the comfort she gave, and then decided that there was nothing more for him to do there. He gave her his numbers at home and at work so she could call him if anything happened or if his mother needed anything.

CHAPTER
19

The next morning, Keesha found Jamal making breakfast. "Thanks, honey,"she said. I don't believe I just said that! she said to herself. Jamal couldn't believe it himself. She could see the surprise and spark of hope in his eyes. He placed the pot on the wood and went to her side.

"You're really beginning to enjoy the idea of us being together, aren't you?"

"Jamal, I enjoy every moment I spend with you, and to tell you the truth, I don't deserve you."

"You deserve every part of my life because I want to give it to you!" He kissed her hands and handed her a plate.

"Enjoy, darling."

After breakfast, they went through the woods and found a lake where they doved in and bathed. They made love again at the edge of the lake and remained there together for a while holding each other. Jamal loved to share his body with her. I think that he would make love to me for a whole week straight if I wanted him to, Keesha thought. The good thing about it was that every time he touched her, she got a brand-new feeling, and it was always different but good.

"Jamal, I think that I am falling in love with you. I find myself thinking about every good thing you do to me and wishing that it could last forever."

"Darling, it can. Our relationship can be whatever you want it to be."

Keesha kissed him, and they got up and went back to their tent. They spent one more night there and packed up early the next morning to head for another destination.

"So, sweetie, where are we going now?"

"Oh, this is a surprise!"he exclaimed. They drove for an hour, and he pulled in front of a beautiful brick house. It was modest but whoever lived in it still had a great deal of grounds to clean.

"So, who lives here?"Keesha asked.

"Come with me."

Jamal grabbed her by the hand and escorted her to the door. He rang the bell and a nicely tanned woman came to the door with an equally tanned man at her side. They were a handsome couple.

"Jamal, how good to see you! I thought you wouldn't be in this neighborhood for a couple of weeks."

"I know but I wanted you to meet someone special!"

"Who is it, darling?

"Mom, Dad, I want you both to meet my fiancee, Keesha!"

Jamal's words took Keesha by surprise but she maintained her composure. Jamal's mother's eyes gleamed with joy, as she looked Keesha over.

"Darling, she is even more beautiful than what you described!"

His father looked her over.

"May, this is a doll baby."

Jamal smiled with pride as they invited them in.

"Come on in, no need to be standing outside,"Jamal's mother said, as she ushered them in. She led them into the living room. Her house wasn't quite as immaculate as Jamal's but it had a unique beauty of its own.

"So, let's see how the ring looks on you!"his mother exclaimed. She picked up Keesha's hand and examined the ring she had given her son a couple of years ago when she thought he was going to marry one of the nurses from the hospital.

"Darling, Jamal must really think something of you because the ring you're wearing is an heirloom that has been in our family for six generations! Jamal's great aunt wanted him to have the ring after she died. Yeah, the diamonds in that ring have been hand-cut and it's priceless."

"Nope, there is no dollar amount that could compare to the quality of that ring!"his father exclaimed. "But it's not quite as pretty as you. We haven't seen many women that Jamal's ever dated, so you must really be special to him for him to even bring you to meet us."

"Yes, darling. We raised our son to never bring the unwanted here. If he wasn't serious about you then there would be no reason for him to waste time bringing her here."

Keesha didn't know whether his mother's statement was a compliment or an insult.

"So, Keesha darling, you must be famished. Jamal will take you upstairs and show you to your room where you can change and get cleaned up and comfortable. I know you must be returning from his special place. So I'm sure you'd want to take a nice hot bath and change your clothes and get into something more comfortable."

She gave her a warm smile to let her know there was no insult intended. Then Jamal took her by the hand and led her upstairs.

"So what do you think of my parents?"

"They're nice Jamal. I love them. But why didn't you warn me that you would be introducing me to your parents? I'm not prepared."

"Prepared for what? They love you the way you are. Just be you. Wait until after dinner, you'll really love them!"

His eyebrows lifted up and down in that funny little dance again, then a kiss followed. She loved when he kissed her. Keesha went into the bedroom and proceeded to get undressed.

Later, after dinner his parents went on and on about Jamal and his childhood. "So Keesha,"Mrs. Warner interrupted. "How did you come about leaving Virginia?"

"Well, after getting my degree, I just wanted a change of pace. New York seemed to be more exciting and offered the best challenges. I worked for an insurance company for a while and decided that I could make more money on my own. I took related courses and became State licensed to do financial planning. I then accumulated high-profile clients, here I am."

"Well Jamal's been in love with you since..."

"High school, Clair,"Jamal's father interrupted.

"That's right, Robert, since High School. Did you know our son had a crush on you?"

Keesha smiled at them bashfully, then cutting her eye at Jamal for help. "I had no idea. He never told me."Keesha spilled her guts. She knew that she was not as well off as well as they were, but she was doing well for herself quite well!

Jamal squeezed her hand to let her know that she was doing just fine and that his parents loved her. His father played music from his time and he taught Keesha a few dance steps. She could tell that this man "cut a little rug"in his time. They laughed and joked for the rest of the night. Jamal's parents were funny, entertaining and very warm toward Keesha. Although Jamal continuously reminded her that his parents adored her, she decided for herself that they really did like her.

They spent another day with them before Jamal said they should be getting back.

He packed the bags in preparation for their departure. Keesha kissed his parents and they invited her to return soon. Jamal gave his parents a big hug and thanked them for their loving hospitality and making Keesha feel comfortable.

"Hey son,"Jamal's dad called, "we really do like her and hope that things do work out for you. Good luck, son, and take care of that flower."

Jamal's mom called Keesha over and spoke with her in private.

"Keesha, you are a very pretty girl and Jamal has been talking about you since high school. He has had girls in the past, none of which he has ever given a ring. Please don't break my son's heart. My husband and I raised him well, and I guarantee you that if you marry him, he will take care of you and make you the happiest woman in the world along with the children you will bare for him. So you think about it. He mentioned to us that you had another engagement ring. So if it is your intention to break his heart, please do it now before you scar him forever."

Keesha was speechless. Why did Jamal bring her here if he told his parents that she had interest in someone else? she thought to herself. Then his mother kissed her on the cheek and bid her good-bye.

"Have a safe trip!"his mother yelled to them as they pulled off. In the car Jamal questioned Keesha about his mother's comment to her in private.

"Keesha, is something wrong? Did my mother say something that caused you to lose that happy look you had? Please tell me now before we get too far so that I can handle it right now!"

"No, sweetheart. I'm okay."

He pulled over to the side of the road.

"Keesha, if my mother said anything to you out of the way, I want to handle it now. I can't have you upset over something one of my parents said or did to you. If my mother hurt you, then she's hurting me, too, because I can't be happy if you're not! So, out with it. What did she say?"

"Jamal, she just mentioned that if I was going to let you go that I should do it now before I scar you forever!"

Keesha's shame in having Jamal's mother point out her infidelity caused her to cry. Jamal held her tight.

"Keesha, you take your time making a decision like this. You're right to be skeptical. Marriage is a lifelong thing, and shouldn't be taken lightly. Would you like me to talk with my mother?"

"No, there's no point in stirring up trouble. She meant well. She did indicate that she was fond of me and that it was nothing personal against me, she's just concerned for you."

Jamal kissed her cheek and thanked her for understanding.

"I'm sorry if you felt that I shouldn't have told my parents about your other relationship. I have never made it a practice to keep things about my life from them, especially when it's as important as this."

"It's understandable, Jamal. You don't have to explain that to me. I would have done the same thing. I tell Ebony about my life and discuss important decisions with her."

"Well now, if you're comfortable, you can share them with me."

He smiled at her and pulled the car back onto the road. They spent the rest of the drive talking about inconsequential things. Keesha wondered if she could really be falling in love with him. He had everything that any woman would want. It was all hers for the taking.

Jamal pulled up to his house.

"So, my sweets, here we are!" He got out of the car and walked around to Keesha's side and opened the door and helped her out of the car. They went into the house holding hands. This man really appreciated every moment we spent together, Keesha told herself.

She told Jamal that she was tired and needed to get some sleep. Then she went upstairs and dove onto the bed and let sleep take over.

The next morning, Jamal woke her up and he had already packed her bags and put them into the car.

"Sweetheart, are you ready yet? You said you wanted to leave early, so I'm ready. Of course, you're welcome to stay forever if you'd like!"

"Oh, Jamal, you're so sweet, but I really have to be getting back."

After taking a shower and getting dressed, Jamal drove Keesha to her humble home. He escorted her to the door and bid her good bye. She asked him to stay at least one day to get some rest. He looked at her and decided that he would spend another day. Especially with the long drive back to Virginia.

Keesha put her clothes upstairs and returned to the living room where Jamal waited for her. She heard the doorbell ringing. Jamal offered to answer, but Keesha had already rushed to the door. "I got it!"

Jamal looked puzzled but returned to his seat. She opened the door and two officers showed her their badges.

"Are you Keesha Smalls?"

"Yes, officers, what can I do for you?"

"You are under arrest for the murder of Christine Walker."

Keesha opened her mouth to explain that she did not kill Christine Walker when Jamal came to the door.

"What's this all about, officers?"he asked in a concerned definitive voice.

"Who are you, sir?"

"I'm Keesha's fiancé."

"Can you validate where Keesha was last Wednesday?"

"Yes, officer, she was with me. We were both up in Virginia camping."

"Do you have any proof of this sir?"

"Yes, inside the car is the registration where we parked the vehicle and received a permit to enter the camp site."

"Is Ms. Smalls' name on this permit?"

"Yes, of course. Everyone must receive a permit in order to enter the camping grounds."

Jamal went to his car and pulled out the permit. He was relieved that the camp site gave such a receipt, otherwise he would have had a hard time proving that she was with him. He returned to the door with the papers and handed it to the officer.

"Okay, sir, you just wait right here, and we will check this out."

The officer went to the car, radioed for assistance to confirm the receipt given to him, while the other officer remained at the door.

When the officer returned, he said that Keesha would have to come into the station anyway to take part in a lineup. Jamal protested. Insisting that a lawyer be present to protect their rights.

"I don't understand why she should have to accompany you to the station when I just gave you proof that she was with me camping."

"Well, sir, my instructions are to bring her to that station. I'm sure that after she accompanies us to the station we can settle this matter quickly. It's probably just a misunderstanding. You know how people think they saw one person and when we put them in a lineup they don't come through.

"But officer,"Keesha protested, "This is clearly a mistake. Why should I need to go with you to the station?"

The officer gestured for Keesha to move toward the squad car. Reluctantly, she obeyed his gesture. Jamal feeling helpless in the matter accompanies Keesha to the car holding onto her hand.

"Stand back sir,"the officer issuing Jamal a command. Jamal steps back avoiding physical contact with the officer who began to wedge himself between them.

"Don't worry Keesha, I'll contact my attorney. He'll take care of this mess."

"Ma'am I need to put these cuffs on you before you enter the car."

Keesha looked from the officer speaking to her back to Jamal indicating for him to say something.

"Officer, that isn't necessary!"

"You're probably right. She seems harmless enough, but we have to follow procedure, otherwise we can get into a great deal of trouble. You understand the predicament, don't you? I'll make sure that the handcuffs are comfortable. In fact, I'll bind her hands in front of her and she can cover them with her coat."

Jamal, dropped his head and assured Keesha that he was right by her side. When they reached the car, the officer stopped Jamal who was following behind them. "I'm sorry sir, but you cannot ride in the car with her. You will have to use your own means of getting to the precinct."

Jamal hurried over to his car and followed the police car to the precinct.

At the precinct, the officers escorted Keesha to a waiting chamber and Jamal was told that he had to wait in the main room. Jamal went to a pay telephone and beeped his attorney and waited for a call back. In about five minutes, the telephone rang. Keesha watched from the waiting chamber, as Jamal explained the situation to his attorney. Relief showed on Jamal's face when he hung up the telephone. Keesha's heart was racing, Jamal had no way of telling her what was going on.

After waiting for what seemed an eternity, a well-dressed man walked in and looked around the precinct. He caught sight of Jamal and walked over to him, and they shook hands. Jamal spent a few moments talking with the man and then they both walked over to the main desk. Keesha wondered what was going on as she saw the man talking with the officer at the desk. The officer shook his head and escorted both Jamal and the man into another room. Keesha assumed that the man must have been Jamal's attorney.

After a while, the nicely dressed man entered the room where Keesha was seated.

"Ms. Smalls, I spoke with the officers that arrested you. I am here to represent you. My name is Jonathan Crammer. Apparently, your name was given in connection with the murder of Christine Walker. Did you have any conflict with Ms. Walker a couple of weeks ago?"

"Yes, Christine and I were friends for a long time, and I had gotten involved with her twenty-one-year-old son. He had proposed to me, and his mother found out and forbid me to see him. Her son told her that this was his life and that he was not going to let me go. His mother didn't like it, so when she saw me getting out of my car about four weeks ago, she told me to stay away from her son. I told her that I didn't want to discuss it, and when I turned to walk toward my house, she hit me over the head with some hard blunt object. As you can see, the top of my head has been shaven, and the wounds have not yet healed."

Keesha tried to explain the entire situation in one breath. Her concern was mainly focused on getting everything out in the open so that it would erase any doubt that she had anything to do with the death of her friend. She explained to the attorney that Chris' mother was a very dear friend, and she would never do anything to hurt her and that there was no animosity in her heart for the woman.

The attorney looked at her with sympathy.

"Ma'am, I need to ask you another question."

"Okay."

"Aren't you engaged to Jamal?"

His question took her by surprise, and caused her to stammer for an answer. "Well, not really, sir. Jamal proposed to me, and we are currently seeing each other, but I didn't actually decide that it was official yet."

"You see the reason I'm asking, Ms. Smalls, is that you told me that Ms. Walker's son proposed to you."

"Well that's true too."

"So you are having a relationship with both men right now?"

"No sir, that's not actually the case either. Chris and I had a rela-

tionship before Jamal had asked me to marry him. So I told Jamal that
I needed some time to weigh my options."

"So what is your current status with Ms. Walker's son?"

"Well, we're kind of on hold at the moment. I told him that I needed time to clear my head,"Keesha said cautiously.

When the attorney felt that he had heard enough, he changed his
mode of questioning. "Ms. Smalls, I want you to know one thing right
now, if things turn out that you need representation, I will represent you
to the best of my ability. I will do this just that because Jamal asked me
to represent you. However, I hope that you for your own sake, are not
playing with his emotions. Jamal is about the most caring man I have
ever known and any woman that can hitch him should count her blessings. He is one of the very few men that is rich who has also maintained
a kind heart."

The attorney poured out his feeling toward Jamal and let Keesha
know that she had better not play with Jamal's heart otherwise, he
would see that things would not go in her favor. Keesha feared for her
future. How could things work out this way? She now feared for her
love for Jamal. Were Jamal's connections so great that she would have
to worry about her own life. She loved him and wanted to be with him
but not in fear.

Johnathan Crammer's questioning was totally unprofessional but
his concern for Jamal's happiness was far more precious than maintain-
ing professionalism. When satisfied with her answers, he returned his
questioning to more pertinent information. "Is there any evidence that
would suggest that you committed this murder?"

"I didn't commit the murder! I know nothing about this murder!"

"That wasn't the question, my question was . . . "

"I know what your question was! No, there is nothing that could
put me at the crime scene!"

"Okay, then we have no problem here."

He scribbled on his pad and walked out of the room. Keesha sat
there stunned and worried about what she had gotten herself into. She
remembered telling David to make sure that they didn't kill Christine!
"Just wait until this is all over with!"she thought.

About a half hour later, the police officer returned to the waiting
room and put handcuffs on her and told her that Chris, had witnessed
her murdering his mother. He told her that she would go to trial and be

convicted of first-degree murder and probably receive a sentence of life in prison. He said it in such a nonchalant manner that Keesha knew that he didn't care about her life and was not interested in helping her.

"That's ridiculous!"she yelled.

The officer wouldn't listen.

"Tell it to the judge, lady. Just tell it to the judge. We've seen your kind before."

He along with another officer escorted her out of the holding chamber and took her to the back room where she was literally thrown in a cell with hostile-looking women. One of the women walked over to her and immediately, she knew that she would have to fight. The other three women in the cell surrounded her.

"Hold her down!"the big one said and two of the women grabbed her by the arms while the others kicked her in the stomach causing her to kneel. The big one pulled her pants down and told Keesha to eat her pussy. Keesha tried to turn her head but her head was held forward.

"No!"she yelled as woke up out of the nightmare.

Jamal was holding her and asking if she was all right.

"Honey, what's wrong? You were having a serious nightmare. Is there something on your mind that you need to get out?"

"No, no, I'm okay. This is the first time that I had such a nightmare!"

Keesha's heart was still racing as though she was still there in the dream.

"Does this have anything to do with that person hitting you over the head?"Jamal asked.

"Jamal, please, sweetheart, I don't want to talk about it. I just want it to go away, to be forgotten."

Jamal looked at her with sympathetic eyes. He had read about people having intense nightmares and felt that she was suffering from repressed thoughts that were trying to surface. But he knew that if she was not ready to talk, then this was not the time to discuss it. He could only offer her as much support as she needed.

"Okay, Darling, if that's what you want. If you change your mind, I'm here for you."

Keesha said Okay and turned her head. Jamal turned her face with his finger on her chin so that she was looking at him again.

"I mean it. I'm here for you, whatever you need to talk about, no matter how bad it may be!"

"Thanks, sweetheart, I know you meant it!"

Keesha needed to get back home especially fast. She felt that there must be something wrong back home. She wondered if she was having a premonition. Could David's friends have killed Christine by accident? She didn't want to think about it anymore, at least not seeing that Jamal already thought she was withholding something from him. As soon as she got home, she would call David to make certain that everything was all right or that nothing had happened. In fact, she would tell him that she would handle the situation herself.

In the car, Keesha told Jamal that she wanted to drive so Jamal moved over to the passenger side of the car, put on his seat belt and told Keesha to knock herself out. She sat in the driver's seat, strapped herself in and put the car in gear. The car shut off. Jamal instructed her on how to work the clutch.

"When you're ready to move into gear, your foot should ease off the brake while the other is depressing the clutch, otherwise it will shut off. Take your time. You'll see it's not hard. Then give it some gas."

It took a couple of tries but she finally got the hang of it. She drove around the neighborhood for a while before going on to the highway. Keesha appreciated Jamal's patience. She had done it before but wanted to never really got the true hang of it. On the highway, he displayed full confidence in her ability. Occasionally he gave instruction or corrected errors.

"Jamal, I truly do love you, and I appreciate everything that you have done for me."

"Does this mean you're ready to marry me?"

"No it means that I'm considering becoming Mrs. Jamal Warner."

"Taking on my name, too, sounds good to me!"

He smiled and put his hand on top of hers and assisted in moving the gear into third. Time seemed to go by fast. Before she knew it, they were pulling up in front of her house. Keesha observed the neighborhood. She peered down the block to see if she would catch sight of Christine. The neighborhood was full of spectators as Jamal stepped out of the car. Michelle who was once talking with one of Keesha's neighbors, hurried over to Jamal's car to get the word.

"Keesha, girl, we have so much to talk about."

"Okay Michelle, I'll be certain to see you tomorrow, but right now,

I have company and I would appreciate you excusing me so that I can get into my house and situate myself."

Jamal was attentive while Michelle introduced herself. Of course, it was only out of politeness, he could see that she was annoying Keesha. He wondered if she was one of Keesha's friends or just someone that was nosey and thrived on gossip.

"So Jamal, what's the scoop between you and Keesha? Are you her new squeeze?"

Jamal smiled at the term. He realized that Michelle definitely had no class.

Keesha had heard just about enough. "Michelle, please,"she said in an annoyed tone. "Excuse me." Keesha hated to show Jamal her bad side but, there was no other way to get rid of Michelle. Michelle didn't understand politeness she was not accustomed to being around people with class. Having money didn't change her. She was just like a street girl from the Bronx. Keesha knew that if she turned her head for even a split second, Michelle would try to seduce Jamal, so she kept her eyes on her long enough for Michelle to understand her point. Michelle shrugged and turned to walk away without the least bit of shame. Michelle turned around again and said, "Keesha, I'm really sorry about what happened to you. I'll catch up with you later. I'm sure that you would be interested in what happened since you were struck from behind!"

Keesha looked at her puzzled. She started to ask her about it but decided that she had better wait.

"I called the ambulance. I saw the whole thing."

Michelle was dying for Keesha to ask her what happened. But Keesha didn't buy into it, not with Jamal there.

"Okay, Michelle. I promise that tomorrow I will stop by your house."

As Keesha got into the house, she checked her messages. Jamal came to her side and put his arms around her waist. The machine gave her the first message.

"Hi Keesha, this is Chris, I stopped by the hospital but they said you were discharged, so I stopped by your house, and you weren't at home. Give me a call if you need anything, I love you."

Jamal considered Chris' behavior, reasoning that if he really loved her, he would have wondered what happened to her after all this time, knowing that she just left the hospital with a head injury. Keesha could have been dead in the house for all Chris knew. Then Jamal remembered that he thought like that because he was a doctor and should not be judgmental. He knew, a lover should go beyond the answering machine. He should push himself to be at his loved one's side when she needed him, even if she didn't realize it at first.

The machine beeped and announced her second message.

"Keesha, are you all right? I stopped by, and no one has seen you around. Please give me a call. I'm worried."

Two other messages played before another of Chris' message came on again.

"Keesha, I know you must be upset about what happened, I promise you that it was not my mother. Please don't shut me out."

Chris had left yet another message. She couldn't bear to hear another message from him so she pushed the stop button.

"I'll listen to the rest of them later," she said to Jamal.

Jamal was glad because he was tired of listening to Chris' whining.

"So Keesha, is that my competition?" Jamal asked jokingly.

She turned and looked at Jamal's handsome face and told him, "There is no competition, just a decision to be made." Hey, she thought, I said that with confidence.

She put her clothes away. Boy, am I glad that Jamal's mother washed them so that I wouldn't have it to do later she thought with relief. Jamal went into the kitchen and found something to drink. He then accompanied Keesha upstairs to watch a movie in the bedroom.

Keesha snuggled close to him, and he squeezed her in his arms. She felt a love she had never known before, and it was only when she was with Jamal. Every moment she spent with him seemed so special. He kissed her forehead and turned his attention back to the movie.

Keesha sat thinking how much her life would change being with Jamal. She enjoyed the warmth his body gave while she was dozing off to sleep.

When she woke up, it was morning. She hadn't realized how tired she was. She realized that she was undressed and in a nightgown. Jamal was gone, leaving only a note in his place. Keesha had no recollection of changing her clothes.

CHAPTER
20

Christine found things that used to be simple more difficult to do as she got around her house in her wheelchair. She looked at her leg casts and wondered why this dreadful thing happened to her. She thought she was spiting Chris by going shopping late at night when she should have waited until morning, and now she may never walk again.

The family dinner that she had planned was ruined. Everyone came down to find her bandaged and cast up in a hospital. The worse part of it was that her son was upset with her because she couldn't understand that he loved her friend. Chris had been trying to reach her for about a month, which made Christine realize how special she must be to him.

Christine listened to her friend Robertha as she tried to convince her old-fashioned friend that times had changed and Chris was not like the average boy at twenty-one. "You've crossed the line of motherhood is what you did. You can only advise him, and it's up to Chris to decide whether or not to take your advise, Robertha counseled.

Christine compared her dear friend Keesha to the other women that her son dated in the past and realized that her maturity was what attracted him to her. Robertha told her that, "If it was an older woman that you didn't know, you would not have thought much of it."

"No, that's not it, Bertha. Keesha is an experienced woman, and she would ruin my son!"

"I know Keesha, of course not as well as you, but from what I know of her, she has pretty high standards, and I can't see her wasting her time with Chris if she didn't love him. I think she would help him reach the horizon that he's looking for. Christine, I think your main concern is that you feel she crossed the line of friendship!"

"Bertha, I love Keesha like a daughter, and I am very proud of her. But, Chris is my son. Look at how he's behaving. He's been calling that girl like crazy person, it's like he won't go on without her."

"That's all the more reason for you to leave them alone! Has it ever occurred to you that, perhaps, Keesha wasn't crossing the line but following her heart? She might very well love your son and make him happy, happier than I can see him being with these silly girls that are flocking around him now. He's too high-class for them!"

"That's true, but he can mold them."

"Honey, Chris doesn't want to mold anybody. He needs companionship. Can't you see he wants to have a family of his own? The man loves children and maybe Keesha's the one he wants to have them with."

Christine thought about it for a moment and wondered why she had reacted the way she did toward Keesha. She would love to have her as a daughter-in-law. Chris has had feelings for her since he was a young teenager. She wondered if Keesha liked him then, too, or if Chris' maturity had something to do with it.

"Listen, Chrissy, give them the chance to see whether this is a fortune or misfortune."

"I think things are already dead as far as Keesha is concerned. She hasn't returned any of his calls in about a month now. By the way, I had a confrontation with her just before her disappearance."

"What happened?"

"Nothing, I just told her how I felt about her seeing my son, and she told me that Chris made up his mind and she wasn't going to discuss it any further."

"So, then what happened?" Robetha questioned expecting the worse.

CHAPTER
21

Keesha shook off the last few cobwebs and went to the bathroom. After taking a shower, she found something comfortable to put on and decided that she would give her good old neighbor a call so that she could give her the news that could not wait. She picked up the telephone and dialed Michelle's number.

"Michelle, hi, This is Keesha. How are you?"

"Oh, hi Keesha. I didn't expect you to be calling me so soon. So who's that hunk you were with yesterday?"

"Oh he's a friend of mine."

"Just a friend?"

"Yeah, just a friend."

"Good then you don't mind me pushing up on him?"

Keesha laughed and decided that she had better tell Michelle the truth about Jamal before the body snatcher attempted to take him.

"Well, actually he's closer than just an ordinary friend, so behave yourself."

"That's what I thought. You know you can't hide anything from me."

"So what are you doing?"

"Nothing."

"So how about stopping by?"

"Okay."

"Good, see you in a little bit."

Keesha waited for Michelle to get there. Finally the doorbell rang and she let her in.

"So Keesha, tell me, who do you think hit you over the head?"

Talk about right to the point, Keesha thought as she looked at Michelle. Of course it didn't surprise her. Michelle rarely had any tact. She told things just as they were.

"I bet you'd never guess!"

"Well Michelle, I don't want to guess. Why don't you just tell me."

"No, no, I want to confirm that you don't know."

"Okay, I think Christine hit me."

Michelle had a mischievous grin on her face as though she proved her point that Keesha didn't know who struck her.

"I knew it, I knew it."

In an exasperated tone, Keesha pleaded with Michelle to stop wearing her patience. "Michelle, please stop the games, how old are you now? You're too old to be acting like a fight-crazed kid. So please get to the point!"

"Keesha, while you were away in Florida, Chris' old girlfriend came around. Word is, he slept with her and she wanted him for keeps."

"You think he actually slept with her or she's just trying to rekindle the old fire?"

"I think he probably didn't intend to but she might have lured him into it. He seemed desperate to see you as though he had done something that he regretted and wanted to get it off his chest. That's when he realized you were gone. Anyway, the girl seemed obsessed with him and decided that she wasn't going to let him go."

Keesha looked surprised, not because someone would be obsessed with Chris but because Michelle had taken so much interest in the matter. Keesha wondered if Chris could have had a fling with someone in his past and brought the woman to her neighborhood to nearly kill her. Keesha thought about it for a moment and wondered why she hadn't noticed someone new in the neighborhood.

She must know someone around here to have sat long enough to take notice that Chris and I were involved with each other. Even Chris' mother didn't notice. The way people act around here, they would have questioned her if she was just sitting around.

"I saw her around the way watching Chris or following him whenever he came on this block. I think the girl's crazy,"Michelle said.

"My question to you is what makes you think that she's the one that hit me? Besides, Chris' mother was there, and she was talking to me."

You're either naive or kick-you-in-the-ass stupid. The girl was close to Christine. Christine always spoke well of that girl. Perhaps she told her about you and Chris, and they both plotted against you but nonetheless, I saw her hit you with an Arizona bottle. "How did you think paramedics got there so fast?"

"So why didn't you help me by calling the police?"

"I called the ambulance since I thought you could use medical attention first before the police started asking you stupid questions."

Michelle told Keesha that she saw her fall to the ground and didn't want to waste time trying to defend her but to get her the help she needed. "Really, I would never have let that happen to you without trying to help you!"Michelle said with sincerity.

"So what happened to Christine?"

"She and the girl got into her car and drove off!"

"That's when I ran over and stayed with you until the ambulance got there."

"So it was Christine's doing?"

"Not directly. She just initiated it. I'm not really sure that she knew that the girl would have done it. The girl wasn't with her when she got there, they just left together."

"Does Chris know anything about it?"

"I don't know about that, I can't hear what goes on behind closed doors. I know you think I have state-of-the-art equipment in my house for spying but I don't. I just get the street news like everyone else on the block! All I know is that the girl has been following Chris around for a while but he wouldn't have anything to do with her."

Keesha wondered what Mr. Walker had to say for himself.

"Keesha, Chris is not worth it. If I were you, I'd take the cute little brownie you had with you last night and leave that young thing alone."

"Thanks, Michelle, but I need to know for myself if Chris knows more than what he's telling me."

"Look, I hear you, girl, I would want to know if he knew something about it myself! Well, do you really want to hear something crazy?"

"What?"

"A week or two ago, someone beat the hell out of Christine. They even shaved her head!"

Keesha was in shock, in fact, she felt kind of sick to think that David's associates would do something as hideous as, that and it was all due to her rage against Christine!

"She was trying to blame you for it, but I'm glad you weren't around for a while, otherwise the cops would have believed her accusations. Chris was around here last week looking for you, and he seemed to be upset. I think he might have thought you had something to do with it too."

"Michelle, how is it that you always seem to get the scoop?"

"I don't know, when you're out here, you get the word. It just seems to fall in my ear."

"Well thanks for looking out for me."

"To tell you the truth, I think she got what she deserves. At least now if you want Chris, she can't get in your way."

"Oh, so you know about our little episode?"

"Of course, the whole block does. She came raging out of your house talking about how you crossed the line. Then there was Chris trying to talk to her and calm her down. Anyway why would Chris return to your house and let his mother leave bitter if there wasn't something he wanted in your house? I think the boy is in love with you and won't settle for anyone else. But I would recommend that you cut your losses while you're ahead and leave him alone!"

"Have you seen that girl around here since when she hit me?"

"Only once. She came around right after Chris showed up."

"How did Chris know about what happened to me so fast?"

"Chris came around seven to see you, like he always do. Everyone was telling him what happened."

"Did they mention to him who did it?"

"I don't know but he seemed pissed off. In fact, if he does know, I think girlfriend will probably get hers."

"So you think Chris will handle the situation?"

"I don't know, but like I said, girlfriend has only showed up once since it happened! For all I know, she could be dead."

Keesha went into the kitchen, fixed herself and Michelle a cup a coffee and listened to Michelle tell her version of the events surrounding Keesha's incident.

"Keesha, I have to go now, but I'll check up on you later in the week, okay."

Keesha thanked Michelle for the input then Michelle turned to leave.

"Keep in touch,"Keesha said. Michelle, left the house and Keesha thought about how to handle the situation. She realized that it was too late to save Christine. She deserved it Keesha thought about bringing danger her way anyway. However, she decided that she would give her old buddy a call. She picked up the telephone and dialed David.

"What's up, friend?"Keesha greeted him.

"Oh, Keesha, how are you? Don't get mad but I didn't get a chance to handle your business!"

"You didn't do it yet?"

"No, I had work that needed tending to. I couldn't very well let money walk away, could I?"

"No, David that's fine, I was calling you to tell you I changed my mind. I'd rather let time handle the situation. She'll get hers in due time."

"I'm glad you said that, because I don't want to live that life anymore. I would have done it for you, however, I didn't want to do it. You understand?"

"Yeah, David, I understand, and I respect you for that. Thanks anyway, and I'm glad you stalled. So how is your business anyway? Did the client buy?"

"I did very well. In fact, my wife's out shopping now."

"You don't have a wife, David."

"I know, I just wanted to know how it would sound to say it."

They laughed.

"So how do you feel, chick?"

"I'm coming along. I guess my head injury is not as bad as I made it out to be! Thanks again, David."

Keesha hung up the telephone wondering if David truly had nothing to do with Christine's injury or if he was severing all ties. "If he didn't do it, who did?"

CHAPTER
22

Pacing in her home, Chris' ex-girlfriend was filled with fury that Keesha could have her cake and eat it too. First, she captivated Chris' soul then she cheated on him. "Who does she think she is, playing with people's hearts?"

She sat back in her easy chair and thought about ways of killing or hurting her. "How dare she think she can just ride off into the sunset with my man! I bashed her head in one time. I guess the next time I'll have to do something a little more drastic--like killing her."She would let nothing or no one come between her and Chris.

Chris' love was embedded deep within her womb, and a child was in the making. She knew that Chris wanted her, otherwise he would have held back and not let things go as far as they did. He was still just as attracted to her as she was to him. For two years straight, she allowed Keesha flaunt her beauty, money and charm in front of her lover's face. She was the cause of him leaving her. Of course, she did not expect things to go as far as they did. But now, she would reclaim what was hers and not allow Keesha to hold on to Chris any longer.

As she continued to think harshly about Keesha, she rubbed her belly where the child continued to grow. She cursed herself for having a body in good shape, which concealed the child growing within her. Chris would never believe that she was pregnant.

She decided that keeping a close eye on her would be the best way to find the right moment and the right action to take against her. One thing she realized was that in order to kill an enemy you had to stay close to them.

That Keesha, she always did think she was too good for anybody and Chris is so blinded by his sexual desires that he can't see what he's doing to himself, she thought.

She knew that her relationship with Christine would win Chris' favor. She thought about how she had caused misery for Keesha so far and knew that the results would be devastating. First she struck Keesha over the head at just the right moment so that Keesha would think that Christine did it. In turn, it caused Keesha to not want to be with Chris. Then to cause Chris to be skeptical of Keesha, she set his mother up and as a mark, shaved her head so that she would think that Keesha had something to do with it since Keesha's hair had been shaven. She was happy knowing that her plot to cause friction between Keesha, Chris and Christine. Now she would take advantage of their turmoil and befriend Christine.

While she continued to think about her devious deeds, the telephone rang and she heard Chris' voice.

"Hello Chris, how are you?"

"This is no social call. I want you to stop visiting my mother before you stir up trouble for me."

"Chris, darling, what would make you think that I would want to hurt you?"

"Why are you making things difficult for me? It is over between us, and you continuously follow me around. I don't want to hurt your feelings but you are pushing me to that point!"

"What about our child? All I want is for you to love us!"

"Why is it so hard for you to understand that things will never go back to the way they were?"

"Because I know you don't mean it. You're just upset now."

"No, I'm not upset, I just know that you are not what I want. We have two different goals and standards."

"Don't say that, sweetheart! I love you. I know that I embarrassed you that time when we went out to dinner, but now I know how you feel, and I won't do it again."

"I'm sorry, I just can't go back there. You are not mature enough for me. I must admit that the sex was great, but it's not enough. I should have stopped things before they went too far but I got caught up in the moment."

"And those moments can last forever. Don't you want things to be like that forever?"

"You see, you don't understand how I feel. I need someone that I can talk to, who will understand how I feel and know when I need a hug for comfort and not a hot night in the sheets! If you are pregnant, I promise that I will take care of the child, but as for us, it will never be. Not now, not ever."

Tears formed in her eyes as she absorbed his words. How could he be so insensitive? She couldn't understand why he continued to love Keesha after she walked away from him and cheated on him with another.

"Chris, let's talk about this. I want to see you."

"No, we don't need to talk about it. I have made up my mind, and you are not the one I want."

Chris hung up the telephone and hoped that she would not call back. He hated to have to treat her unkindly but there was no other way for her to understand how he felt. His life had become complicated since Keesha came into his life. Everything in his life was going wrong and he did not know how to fix anything. He loved Keesha, and she wouldn't even speak to him. It had been two months now since he last spoke to her. No matter how many calls he made or messages he left, she would not call him back.

He was afraid to visit her, not knowing how she would react to him. He knew that there was someone else in her life. The guy he saw leaving her house, he suspected, but there was nothing he could do. How could he win her heart again if he couldn't even speak to her? Did she move away with this guy, leaving everything behind? he wondered.

One time, he thought she might have been home but he soon realized that she had her lights on a timer. Chris admired Keesha for being spontaneous; he never knew what she was doing and neither did she. She just went with the flow. Chris wished that Keesha would pay him a surprise visit and things would go back to normal. He missed her so much. There was nothing that she could have done that he would not forgive her for. Even though his mother thought that Keesha had something to do with her injury, Chris knew that Keesha could never stoop that low. He also knew that his mother didn't hurt keesha. He couldn't think of a soul who would try to hurt the two women in his life and have them fighting each other.

I'll teach her to take me for granted his ex-lover thought as Chris hung up the telephone on her.

I know, I'll work on getting close to Keesha too, gain her trust and then get my opportunity to snatch that worthless life away from her. Chris doesn't love me and here I am pregnant with his child.

A sickness fell over her and she comforted the child within her. "Don't worry baby, Daddy will be coming home to us soon."

CHAPTER

23

Keesha spent the rest of the day wondering who could have hurt Christine and what her condition was. She thought about calling her or paying her a visit. Then she remembered that Michelle said that the girl that hit her left with Christine. Keesha's reasoning led her to understand that Christine had to have something to do with what happened to her. Could Michelle have mistaken? she thought. Maybe she really didn't leave with Christine. Maybe she ran off by herself.

She questioned Christine's reasoning for leaving her there. Keesha considered the fact that they had a disagreement, but nonetheless they were friends, and she never thought Christine could do something so violent to her or at the very least not making sure that she had the proper care.

Keesha sat on her desk staring at a painting of a forest she had on a wall in her study. She remembered the wonderful times she had with Jamal. Maybe I should leave Chris alone and enjoy the love that Jamal has to offer, she reasoned. His sincerity should not be taken for granted and that's exactly what I have been doing all this time. Jamal had everything that she could ever want--or the means of getting it. He could take care of her, and she had been overlooking that for a long time now. For three months, she had allowed this charade to go on between herself and these two men. She wondered what else she could have been looking for? Youth?

After coming to her senses about Jamal, Keesha decided that she would pay Chris one last visit to find out whether she was over him. Of course, she would always love him but she needed to know that if he were to show up at her door if she could she reject his charm and the lovesick spell he had cast on her.

She went upstairs to the bathroom and looked at herself in the mirror. Three months had passed since that dreadful incident. Keesha didn't realize that she allowed so much time to pass without speaking to Chris, her almost husband. Not to mention, her dear friend. The people who once meant so much to her had become a thing of the past as Jamal became more important than anything else in her life. Her wounds had healed, and her hair had grown back. She cut the top down to chin length and let it hang in a nice wrap around her face and the back remained midway down her back. Jamal liked it like that way, which was what was important to her. She remained hesitant about marrying him. Jamal had told her that however long it took, he would wait for her. One thing he did know was that he had her to himself.

Keesha changed clothes and freshened her makeup. She studied herself one last time in the mirror before considering herself presentable. Since it was a little cool out, she decided to wear a light jacket. As she turned to walk away from the mirror, she could feel her reflection staring back at her with disappointment and saying "Girl, you're making a big mistake." She felt a chill and remembered Chris' innocence. Seeing him was something she felt she had to do.

She scrambled through her desk and found his address. In the car she looked down the block and searched for an unfamiliar face. When she saw that everything looked okay, she started the car and drove off to Chris' house. Keesha had never been there in all the time they were seeing each other. Most of their time was spent going out or with him at her house. This would be the first time she would lay eyes on his home, and if those old feelings did not stir, it would be the last.

She read the sign above the gate, "Enclave Town Houses". She could see the homes past the gates far in the back, and they were beautiful. The property was protected by electronic gate. A security booth was stationed right inside the gate and the guard's responsibility was to get verification of visitors and seek authorization to let them onto the premises. She pulled up to the speaker and the security guard asked her for her name and whom she would be visiting. She told him, and he told her to wait just a minute. While she was waiting he dialed Chris' number and received permission for Keesha to enter the grounds. She drove up to the gate and was buzzed in.

Keesha observed her surroundings. The grass was pretty and green. There was a large round island filled with beautiful flowers, the bushes were cut in the shape of different forest animals. There was a deer, a bear, a rabbit, a fox, and farther down was an owl seated in a tree. The place was truly a beauty. Could Chris really live here? she thought. She parked her car in the space as directed by the attendant. Chris was waving to her in front of his stone front home. She walked over to him. He kissed her on the cheek. "what a pleasant surprise,"he said.

Keesha stood a moment longer observing her surroundings. She noticed a stone male statue holding a large vase pouring water into a pool. The place was like a museum. Chris finally ushered her inside and took her jacket.

"So Keesha, what brings you to my humble neighborhood? "

"Chris, we need to talk."

"Okay, about what?"

"Us."

"What about us?"

Chris feared for what was to come. It had been three months since he had last seen her. None of his calls were returned, and the only thing he could imagine her saying was that this was the end.

"Chris, I want you to know that I really do love you and I wanted us to be happy, but with all that has happened, I realized that maybe we should discontinue our relationship and remain friends."

He couldn't believe it. She came all the way out here to disappoint him. He had already figured that things were over or that she didn't want to hear from him again. There was something about face-to-face good-byes that made them more intense.

"Keesha, are you sure that this is what you want?"

"I've thought about it for a long time now, and I can't seem to shake the thought that maybe I did step beyond my bounds. I can't see myself being happy with you when I'm losing the friend. I have been a friend to your mother for quite sometime now and really, I couldn't possibly be happy if we can't continue being friends."

Chris felt a spark of hope as she mentioned his mother. For one, it confirmed that Keesha had nothing to do with his mother's attack and second, his mother had finally realized how he felt about keesha and had given her blessings.

"So, after all we've shared and my going against my mother, you're going to walk away from me?"

"Chris, it's not like that. I really hate to let you go. You will always be special to me, and believe me, the thought of some other woman having you is killing me. But, I'd rather let you go now and keep our friendship as well as your mother's rather than continue the way we're going and having hatred between myself and your mother."

"Keesha, my mother doesn't hate you. We talked about it, and she wishes that you would let her apologize for the way she behaved."

She ignored him, and said, "I'm also returning your ring. I know that you will find someone else who will deserve it more than myself."

Chris felt his heart racing. He had to try to win her over. He knew that nothing was forever until forever came.

"You're returning my ring too? Did my love for you mean nothing?"

"Chris, you're looking at it the wrong way."

"No, Keesha, I'm not looking at it the wrong way. You're treating it the wrong way. When a man gives you something, you never give it back unless he asks for it. You think that I would be so petty as to take the token of my love back from you and give it to someone else. I gave it to you because I wanted you to have it!"

Keesha's action had hurt him deeply. The ring was his only tie to her, and now she was giving it back to him. That ring represented everything that she meant to him and more. He couldn't understand how she could be so insensitive.

"Chris, I'm sorry. I just didn't know how to handle it."

"You know, I thought my being with an older woman would bring happiness and understanding. She'd understand me, and I would understand her. Keesha, I love you, and what do I get, my heart broken. So now that you're dumping me, what are you going to do about the baby?"

"The baby, what are you talking about?"

"You haven't felt different lately?"

"No!"

"Keesha, you're pregnant with my child. I wanted us to have a baby together, that's why I removed the condom while we were having sex."

Keesha felt herself getting sick as she thought about the tenderness of her breasts. Then she realized that after three months, certainly something else would have let her know that she was pregnant. There was no sickness, no change in her figure, no missing a period, nothing. Then when she thought about it she was beginning to get angry.

"Chris, I'm not pregnant, and your new revelation just showed me that you can't be trusted."

"No Keesha, you're the one who can't be trusted. Did you think that I was not aware of your seeing this Jamal character? I saw the ring, Keesha. It was in your jewelry box. So what did you do, switch rings whenever one of us would stop by? And even after that I still loved you. Keesha, I forgive you for that. I know that the reason you want to break up is that you feel guilty for doing what you did, but that's not important to me. What is important is that we can still be a family, and your relationship with Jamal does not have to continue!"

His statement took her by surprise. She didn't know what to do or how to respond. He knew about Jamal all the time and she had been trying to protect Chris from the hurt.

"Chris, you have to listen to me. I really did enjoy the time we spent together but I have to stop seeing you. I'm going to continue seeing Jamal because I have fallen in love with him. I'm sorry Chris. I really didn't want to hurt you!"

Keesha kissed him on the cheek and walked away. As she neared the door, she turned to see him right behind her. He wrapped his arms around her and pleaded for her love.

"Can we make love just one more time? Keesha, you're walking out of my life, and I want something to remember the times we've shared. Could this Jamal character really have replaced that so quickly?"

"Chris, I don't think that our sleeping together again would be healthy for either one of us. It's better to just say good-bye and remember things for what they were."

Something about her actions let him know that there was a spark of desire in her. He hoped that it wasn't buried so deep that he couldn't reach it. He loosened his grip around her arms, and slid his hands up to her chin. Chris raised her lips to meet his, and he gently kissed her. The tenderness of it caused her lips to flinch, and he took advantage of that by placing his tongue in her mouth and pulling her face closer to his. He moved closer to her so that she could feel the warmth of his body.

A yearning from within cried out for him. Keesha returned the kiss as her hands rested on his waist. He pulled her even closer, the blood rushed to his member, and Keesha could feel the need growing in him. As badly as she wanted him at that moment, she pulled away. Chris didn't know where he went wrong. "I love you, Keesha. Please don't take this moment away from me!"he called out to her as she stepped away from him.

"I know you love me, Chris. That's why I can't string you along any longer! Or build a false hope."

Keesha left his house knowing that things would never be the same between them. She sat in her car taking a moment to compose herself with her head resting on the steering wheel, shocked that she just let Chris go. This relationship should never have happened. His mother was right: she had hurt him in the end. The one thing Keesha didn't know was that it would hurt her too.

As she started the engine, Chris knocked on her window. His eyes were moistened with tears as he pleaded for another moment of her time. Rolling the window down, Keesha listened to what he had to say. Chris' voice was unsteady as he whispered in a low solemn tone. "Keesha, don't do this to me. I really love you, and I want things to work out between us. I spoke with my mother about our relationship, and she realizes the mistake she made--she wants us to be together."

Then Keesha remembered that his mother had been attacked shortly after she was attacked. So much had happened surrounding their relationship. Was he so blinded by love that he couldn't see that? She wondered.

"Chris, how is your mother? I heard that she was hurt!"

"She's trying to adjust to the fact that she may never walk again. She was jumped a couple of months ago and some thugs beat her up. When she fell, she fractured her femur. Then they shaved her head."

"Is she home?"

"Yeah, she had surgery on it, and everything is going to be fine. She can't walk right now but I'm still hopeful. My mom is a strong woman and she has come through a great many things, I believe that she would be fine if she wanted to be."

"Look, Chris, Christine needs you more right now. Take care of your mother. Help her get better.

"Keesha wait,"he interrupted but she dismissed him.

"Please don't make this hard for me. I don't take any pleasure in any of this but I think it's in our best interest."

"All I'm asking you, Keesha, is to think about our relationship, and what we had before you make your decision final. Ok? Can you do that for me?"

"Chris! I have made that decision. I have thought about it. This is my final decision."

Chris realizing that his request had fallen on deaths ear, backed away from the car and allowed her to drive away.

I'm sorry Chris, I didn't know any other way to handle this, she thought as she exited the Enclave Town Houses. She knew that there would always be a love for him within her. Take care of yourself, Chris, she said continuing to increase the distance between them.

Keesha reasoned that Chris was a nice guy and would find someone to love him the way he needed. There are just some lines that should not be crossed. Keesha felt sick, her heart was heavy with grief. How could I have let him go so easily? Am I making a mistake?

Just to eliminate any doubt, Keesha decides to drive to the nearest pharmacy and pick up a home pregnancy test. When she arrived at the pharmacy, she proceeded to the register where she knew she would find the pregnancy tests. Someone was standing behind her, "Chris, what are you doing here?"

"I decided to follow you. I want to know just as much as you do. If my child is growing inside you, I would like to be one of the first to know."

"I understand, Chris. In fact, I'm glad to see you. I miss you already. This isn't easy for me."

He avoided looking at her, afraid that she might say something to brush him off again.

"So this guy must really be special, huh? Special enough to take you away from me when all I've ever dreamed of was to make you happy!"

"Chris, I never meant for this to happen. I have always been attracted to you, and now that I have you, realization is hitting me that this would never be able to work out."

"Why not? Why couldn't it work out?"

"Because, you really are too young for me! Look, if I had a son, I would want him to date someone closer to his age. It would make me quite angry if I found out that an older woman was seducing my son, so I can understand where your mother is coming from."

"So this is all because of my mother? Keesha, if I spent my entire life trying to please my mother, doing every thing the way she wanted, I might never find happiness. My happiness is being with you. A younger woman could not replace you. Not because of her age, but because I love you. An older woman could not replace you. I want you and no one else. Did you think my experience with women was limited? I've been with girls my own age, and they can't offer me the things I need emotionally and mentally. They do not meet up to my expectations. I have dated other women, or girls if you want to put it that way, and they have not met my standards."

"Chris, try to understand how this whole situation is making me feel. Even if your mother had never created the scene in front of my house, I still would have eventually come to the same conclusion--we are on two different wavelengths."

Chris could feel his heart dropping. His brain understood the words but, his heart couldn't comprehend how something so trivial, could cause so much hurt.

"This void in my heart has remained vacant waiting for you. Now that I have you and am finally happy, both my mother and the woman I love are breaking my heart. Keesha, promise me that if you are pregnant that you will have my child. It will be the best gift that I could ever give to you or you to me!"

Keesha could see his eyes pleading with her for this one last act of love for him. She still had a longing for him but Jamal had replaced the majority of those feelings with memories of his own. He understood how she felt and considered her feelings in everything he did. She had a mental connection with Jamal that linked them, and she was afraid to let that walk away again. She would do anything for Jamal except destroy Chris' child if it were growing inside her. She loved him just that much!

"Chris, I would never destroy your child, I love you and would never want to scar you. I wanted us to be happy, really I did, but it's causing us both too much grief!"

"If you're willing to hang in there, so am I! I don't care what anyone says about us, not even my mother. My only concern is to make you happy."

The pharmacist was listening to their heart-warming discussion and was moved to comment. "Oh, that is so sweet. Girl I don't know how you could let that man go. It's not often that you get a man to love a woman to that extreme. You'd better keep that man and make him happy. He's gorgeous too!"

Keesha finally chose a pregnancy test she was comfortable with and reached into her purse, but chris handed the cashier a twenty dollar bill before she could pull out any money. "Let me take care of that,"he told her preventing her from retrieving any money from her bag.

Keesha accepted his request. The cashier gave Chris his change and they departed from the pharmacy. Standing outside, Keesha moved toward the McDonalds restaurant only a couple of doors down from the pharmacy. Chris followed, anticipating that she wanted to take the test immediately. She entered the women's restroom, leaving Chris at the door.

Chris ordered a soda to help time pass while waiting for Keesha to emerge from the bathroom with the results. Time seemed to pass slowly while he waited.

At last, she emerged, holding a small, white, plastic box in her hand.

"So,"he asked, almost dropping his soda in anticipation.

"Chris, the results were negative. There is no baby."

"It could be wrong."

"No Chris, it's over. Accept it. Chris, sweetheart, please don't take this so hard"

He put his arms around her; she knew that he was looking to kiss her. As his lips moved closer to hers, she felt that familiar desire building inside. She wanted him close to her. She felt as though she wouldn't be able to live without him. How could she get over him if a simple kiss could win her heart? She stepped away from him."I hope that you will be okay!"

Chris had a look of defeat. He stared hard as he fought back the burning tears that welled in his eyes. Keesha didn't know what to do, as she felt Chris' pain. She wanted to hold him. In reality, she didn't want to be pregnant, not this way. Not with her falling so deeply in love with Jamal. Things couldn't possibly go wrong for her in every situation.

Keesha saw that Chris was taking this very hard. "Chris, honey, do you want to talk about it?"

"Keesha, there is nothing else to talk about. My last hope just went down the drain. The pregnancy test proved that you were not pregnant, which is exactly what you probably wanted to hear, but to me, it just took away my last hope of having you!"

"Chris, I'm sorry that things worked out the way that they did, but you should know that babies don't hold couples together! It takes love and understanding, both of which we had, however, most of that love went to another man, and I'm sorry that this is difficult for you but I've made my decision."

"I hope that he will make you happier than I had planned to!"Then he walked out of the door.

"Goodbye, Chris,"she said softly to herself. "I'll miss you."

CHAPTER
24

Christine had been coming along nicely since the incident. Of course, she wished that she could rekindle her friendship with Keesha. Her good friend Robertha reminded her of the admiration she had for Keesha and that she shouldn't interfere with Chris and Keesha's relationship. Chris had not been himself since that episode at Keesha's house when he finally broke the news that Keesha was the woman he proposed to.

Christine remembered her reaction, realizing that she carried her emotions too far. She knew that the first step was to make amends with Keesha for her own actions and then give Keesha and Chris her blessings.

While Christine continued to think about ways of correcting her error, she heard her doorbell ringing. She rushed over to answer it. "Hello," she called as she opened the door to find Chris' old girlfriend standing there. "Michelle!" she said in surprise. "I would have never guessed that I would ever see you again. What are you doing in this part of town?"

"Oh, I've been around. I just thought that I'd pay my mother-in-law-to-be a visit."

"What do you mean by that?"

"Don't you know? Didn't Chris tell you that we have been seeing each other for some time now, and we're having a baby?"

Christine stared in shock. She knew that Chris was seeing Keesha and that he wanted to marry her. She hadn't heard talk about Michelle in at least . . . she couldn't even think how long it had been, only that it was quite sometime now. "Michelle, are you all right?"

"Yes, I'm happier than a bug in a rug. Why do you ask?"

"Because Chris is seeing someone else. I can't believe that he would jeopardize that by messing with you." Christine's sneer showed her distaste and dislike. Michelle could feel the stab of her piercing eyes.

Cutting right through her plot.

"You must be mistaken. Chris and I are together now. He is no longer seeing that other woman. He said that things didn't work out between them and that she caused too much grief between you and him. Oh, it's going to be great having you as a mom. You know I knew this day was coming, and I'm glad you and I get along so well."

Christine didn't respond. She only watched Michelle wondering if she had lost her mind or this was simply a joke.

"So, how have you been, Christine?"she questioned looking at her cast and bad haircut.

"How do I look like I've been doing?"

"What happened?"

"I was attacked."

"I'm sorry to hear that. Would you like me to do anything for you? I don't have any plans. Since we're going to be seeing a great deal of each other, I hope that we can eventually develop good feelings toward each other."

"Michelle, I have nothing against you. I just don't think you're good for my son. Besides, Chris knows what he wants, and if you were on his agenda, I can assure you that you wouldn't be here telling me this wild and crazy story."

"You know ever since Chris and I parted, all I can think about is him. My life hasn't been the same since he left. You took him from me. Why did you have to move so far away?"

"Well the only thing that I can tell you is to go on with your life and you'll run into someone who will make you happy and stop this fantasy you're on before you hurt yourself."

"Mom, you don't understand, Chris and I are having a child. That part is true, and I am by no means getting rid of it."

"You're really pregnant?"

"Yes, I'm three months now. Didn't Chris mention it to you?"

"No, he didn't tell me that you were carrying his child, but I'm sure that he has the best intentions for the child. I can't see him trying to walk away from his responsibilities. I didn't raise him that way!"

"Chris and I should share every part of our child's life--together. He shouldn't just mail money to take care of it. I have enough money to take care of the child. I need for Chris to be a father to the child as well."

"Well, honey, you can't make him love you if it's not in his heart."

"Maybe you can talk to him and help him to realize how important this is. A child needs its father."

"I know. I just don't know what to say., Chris wouldn't listen to me anyway. His heart is set on another woman."

"You know, I can still remember the time Chris and I used to enjoy each other's company. But now he's in love with someone else, and my child is going to be a bastard."

Christine tried to change the subject. Of course, she realized that this girl wouldn't allow anyone to come between herself and Chris. This was not a healthy attitude that she had about the situation, and Christine knew that she needed to relieve some of the anxiety.

"Don't talk like that. I'll talk to Chris and see if I can get him to realize that he has a responsibility to his child. There's always a silver lining in everything. Right now Chris thinks he's in love with this other woman, he's young, eventually he will grow out of it. It's just a phase. He's had a crush on her since the first time they met. She gave him the opportunity and now he's like a lovesick puppy."

"I know, but it's probably her money that he's after. I know I don't have the status that she has, however, I have feelings and I am willing to take care of him."

Christine thought about what the girl was saying then realized she didn't want Chris to be with her. There was something off about her, and Christine feared for Chris' future if he was in a relationship with Michelle. She had no class about herself, and she was filled with envy and hate. Christine didn't really like her when Chris dealt with her a few years ago, and she certainly wouldn't want to see them patch things up. Christine could only imagine this woman making her son miserable. She would kill his pride, dignity and future. Chris simply didn't need her in his life. Keesha was the best woman for him, and Christine wished that she had not interfered with their relationship. Now that they had broken up, Christine feared Chris might fall right back in Michelle's hands.

"To tell you the truth, I think Chris should concentrate on his success and building himself to where he wants to be before he ties himself down with anyone. Besides, I don't know why you allowed yourself to get into this situation anyway. Are you trying to trap my son? If you are, please just leave him alone."

"Ms. Walker, I don't believe you just said that! You know how much I love your son. I thought you liked me."

"Not enough to see my son miserable. You will bring him down! Besides, if Chris had to choose, he would definitely choose the other woman. He'd give his right arm for her. Hell, he crossed me because I upset her. I have been friends with her for some time, and I can find no fault in her. If it wasn't for her age, I'd say she's the daughter-in-law that any mother would want for her son. I really hope that he can convince her to forgive me for getting in their way and let her know that she has my blessings."

"Mom, what about my feelings? I love Chris!"

"I know you do, sweetheart, but that woman loves my son too. Probably a great deal more. She would make him happy and nurture his dreams. But what's greater than that is that he loves her. He broke my heart when he asked me if I had something to do with her being hurt! I would never have hurt her." Christine remembered that day so clearly. She had been arguing with Keesha, warning her to leave her son alone, but Keesha wouldn't even give her the courtesy of listening and refused to discuss it. She turned her back on her-- something that she had never seen Keesha doing. Feeling hurt, Christine turned and got into her car to visit her friend Robertha to get things off her mind.

"Well, I guess that I'll be going now. You take care and feel better. You will talk to Chris for me, won't you?"

"I'll try but he may not want to hear it."

"Take care."Michelle paused for a moment. "You know what?"she asked observing the patterned dishcloth hanging over the stove handle. "I think I'll tell him myself." She quickly snatched the dishcloth from the stove handle, and pulled the cloth tightly around Christine's neck cutting off her air passage.

Christine struggled, fighting both the pain of her recovering fracture and the wrath of the crazed woman who now was trying to kill her.

"I never did like you anyway. Believe me you won't be missed."

Christine fought for her life.

"Die you old bitch." Michelle cursed her for being so strong. Her hands desperately clawed at Michelle's hands to no avail. She stood too far behind her. Finally Christine collapsed breathlessly. Michelle checked her for a pulse finding none. She wiped the table where she sat and anything else she remembered touching then cautiously left the house.

CHAPTER
25

Keesha left the pharmacy distraught but relieved. She loved Chris and regretted having to end their relationship the way she did. Under other circumstances, she would have chosen him but with the conflict between her and his mother, she didn't think the relationship was worth it. She had spent a great deal of time with Jamal and had grown fond of him.

Jamal understood her feelings and was patient with her. The ride seemed longer than normal but Keesha realized that it was only because her focus was still on Chris. Finally after a long drive she looked up and saw her exit. She had been driving for five hours. There in front of her stood that lovely house, her home. A place where she felt she could be happy, without a care in the world.

Keesha pulled into the driveway, turned off her engine and walked to the door. After ringing the doorbell, a familiar face answered.

"Hello, Jamal, I was on my way home and somehow I just kept driving and ended up here."

"You've been crying! Come in, darling. You never need an explanation to come here!"

"Thanks, Jamal. You are truly the most caring man I have ever known."

"Come here, let me hold you."

"I feel so safe and warm in your arms."

"You are safe in my arms. I will take care of you, Keesha, if you will let me."

He looked deep into her eyes, and she could see that he was pleading with her. Jamal took two steps backward, held both her hands and knelt on one knee.

"Keesha Smalls, darling, sweetheart, love of my life, it would make me the happiest man in the world if you would agree to be my wife! I promise to love, cherish and take care of you for the rest of my life. Even from my grave, I will make sure that you will be taken care of for the rest of your life. Keesha, will you marry me and be my wife forever?"

His eyes searched hers for an answer. A lump formed in Keesha's throat, and her chest became tight as she knew that he meant every word.

"Yes, yes, yes, Jamal, I will marry you. I love you so much, and I don't know how I could have kept you waiting this long."

The words came as a surprise to him as he had expected yet another petition for time. The burden he felt when he first knelt had vanished. Remaining on his knee, he wrapped his arms around her waist. Tears of joy fell from her eyes onto his bald head. He looked up at her and smiled.

"I promise that I will go out of my way to make you happy."

Keesha knelt and faced him, and they kissed. The kiss was so sweet and full of purpose, sealing their agreement. They made love right there on the carpet. For the first time, Keesha made love without protection and didn't worry about getting pregnant. This man would soon be her husband.

"Keesha, I love you ,but I don't want us to have a child out of wedlock, that's important to me. If you want a child now, we can get married tomorrow! Or, I can give you the best wedding you could ever dream of. Personally, I'd rather have the wedding because I've always dreamed of waiting for you to come down the isle in your pretty white dress."

He kissed her tenderly and soon, she ruptured into a sweet climax, but Jamal withdrew before he reached his peak.

"I promise that the night of the wedding I will give you the child we both so urgently want!"

They showered together and that night was filled with talk about wedding plans.

"So Jamal, how many children do you want?"

"As many as you are willing to give me!"

"What if I said ten?"

"Then I would cheerfully give you all ten because I can afford to take care of them."

"What if I said twenty?

"Then I'd say that perhaps you might lose that pretty little shape of yours and that would make you unhappy and then we'd both be unhappy!"

He made his eyebrows do a little dance, and they laughed.

"So what you're saying is that if I got fat and out of shape you wouldn't love me anymore?"

"No, if you're healthy and have no physical problems then whatever weight you carry is fine by me. I love you for you, not how you look! Even though I am fond of that nice little shape of yours! I'll love you no matter what you look like."

"I know, Jamal. I'm just kidding."

"No, you meant it. Every woman has that fear about having a child. I'll take care of you and help you keep that nice figure."

"Good, because I hear that children really stretch you out of place."

He laughed. "What could be more beautiful than a woman with child?"

They talked a little more and went to sleep. "Good night, sweetheart."

"Good night, Keesha. I'm so glad you decided to be my wife."

Jamal cloaked Keesha in his arms, and she fell asleep in serenity. He was warm, strong, clean and smelled of Irish Spring. Clean and fresh. Keesha dreamed of their wedding day: She would wear a long, white fitted dress covered with a sheer material that silhouetted her breasts. The dress would have a long train. Her seven bridesmaids would be standing on her left side in silver satin dresses with a tulle overlay. Jamal would wear a White Dukes' tuxedo with tails. His ushers would wear white tuxedos with silver cummerbunds.

Jamal would stand there with his eyes beckoning her to come to him. At least that's what everyone else would see. Keesha knew the pleasures behind those looks.

Jamal's four nieces would be the flower girls. They would be beautiful with their long curly hair pinned up with the curls falling down around their faces. Their dresses would be an iridescent bone with a floral pattern. They would carry baskets with fresh flowers and toss them into the air to fall fresh on the runner waiting her arrival. After the wedding everyone would strip down to their swimwear and enjoy the rest of the day by the pool. There would be dancing, games and swimming. A day that everyone would remember.

Jamal could see his beautiful bride escorted down the stairs of a Norwegian Cruise ship by her maid and matrons of honor. Her bridesmaids would wait in position for her arrival. Jamal would wait on the deck with the minister flanked by his ushers who would stand to his right. Then Keesha would walk down the stairs slowly with that cute walk of hers. He could see the trepidation in her step. He would smile to show her that everything would be all right. He would make love to her that night, like never before. All that he held back he would give her, and she would never leave his side because he would take care of her every need--physically, emotionally and financially.

Their dreams were so sweet that night. In fact, they almost met in their dreams. Both were the same but different.

CHAPTER
26

She waited outside Chris' house for him to arrive. He had been gone for a long time. As evening started to roll by her will to wait for him diminished. She started to leave just as Chris arrived. "Hello, darling. I've been waiting for you!"

"I told you that I didn't want to see you again! What is it that I have to do to make you understand that I have no feelings for you?"

"Honey, don't talk like that, I have good news!"

"What good news?"

"Well, I have confirmation that I'm pregnant! Isn't that just great? We're having a baby!" Chris' expression changed, and he had a look of disgust. He had just broken up with Keesha and now he runs into the woman that would make his life miserable.

"Chris, honey, don't look at me like that. Where are you going? Chris, talk to me. I'm here for you! I love you and, there's nothing I wouldn't do for you."

Chris turned to return to his car when she called out to him. Chris paused, before speaking. "Then why are you doing this to me? I told you that I didn't love you. Why would you come here, seduce me, get pregnant and expect me to be happy about it? I'm feeling disconsolate, dejected, disheartened and depressed, the worse part about it is that you are the cause of these feelings. I am in love with someone else, and I'm sorry that I didn't send you away before this happened but this can't be, and I don't want you. Now, I'm sorry if this hurts your feelings but I just can't do this!"

"What if this person left you for someone else?"

"She did, and I have to deal with it, but what does that have to do with us? I still wouldn't love you!"

"Don't talk like that, we're having a child"

"No you're having a child!"

"No, it's our child, and don't talk about our child like that!"

"We should not be having a child! My child should be in Keesha's womb, not yours. I don't love you. Why can't you understand that and just leave me alone?"

"Yes, yes, yes, I've heard of the Keesha you were seeing. In fact, I've met her. A very nice woman, but, what you don't seem to understand is that I eat, sleep and breathe you! I don't want anyone else but you."

"Why, is it money? I'll give you money to take care of the child, okay?"

"No, darling. It has nothing to do with money. All I ever wanted was to have a child with you."

"Well this is not the way to do it. Look, as I said before, I'll give you money for the child and be a father to it but we will never be again. I'm sorry, and I hope you can understand that! The child is my responsibility, and it's not here yet so, for now just leave me alone!"

She stormed off loathing Keesha. She came between them. She lived far from Chris for too long and that space gave Keesha all the time she needed to come between her and the only man she could ever love. She couldn't understand how she could have been so stupid. Keesha stole his heart right under her nose.

Everything was going well for them until one summer he changed toward her. She thought that it was just that he needed time or perhaps it was the pressure of working and going to school. Then one day, he came over and ended their three-year relationship. She dated him when he was only thirteen and she was eighteen. Needless to say, she turned him out. He would never leave her side. His mother purchased a car for him during his last year in high school. He would drive to visit her in her small apartment in Brooklyn. At first, his mother thought he was only visiting his cousins who lived around the corner but the truth of the matter was that he would spend the weekend with her. After a while, his mother found out and she didn't seem to mind. Besides, a five-year age difference wasn't much since he was so mature for his age. She taught him everything he knew about making love to a woman and now he was displaying his talents with someone else. Keesha didn't deserve him.

After Chris' father died, right after his graduation, he and his mother moved to Long Island where Chris attended an Ivy League school and majored in Accounting. During his first semester, he would visit her during holidays. She waited patiently for him to stop by. They planned to get married when he turned eighteen but something happened. He didn't visit much and when he did, he seemed to be preoccupied. His visits became ever more scarce until his second semester of college when he stopped coming by altogether.

The car accident that she had gone through when she was younger had finally paid off. She took the opportunity to move closer to Chris and his mother. Chris moved out of his mother's house into another town. That didn't worry her because she was only eight blocks away from his mother and that was good enough. It took some time before she was able to find Chris' new home, and she certainly didn't get the welcome she felt she deserved. Later, she found out that there was a home for sale by sheer coincidence, closer to Christine where she discovered her lover's mistress. She couldn't believe it, he had a crush on a woman that was certainly too old for him, and the woman lived only a few doors away from his mother. At first, she didn't seem to take notice to his advances or notice that he had feelings for her. But then Keesha started inviting him into her house.

He wasn't pleased to see her and treated her as though their long relationship had meant nothing. That's when she knew that she had to get closer to Keesha to find out more about their relationship. Keesha even confessed her love for him and right then they were rivals. Fighting over the love of Chris.

Keesha Smalls, you'll pay for this! she thought. She got into her car and drove back to her home.

CHAPTER
27

"So sweetheart, are you ready to make our announcement to the world?"

"Yes, Jamal, but who will use the telephone first?"

"Hey, there are two separate lines in this house. I'll use the telephone downstairs so that you can call whomever you want to invite up here."

"First, I think we need to discuss what kind of wedding we want and where it will be held."

"So, what is your fantasy, Keesha, since the wedding is for the bride?"

"Well, I've always dreamed of getting married on a huge ship like the Love Boat. I want all my friends to be there and the colors to be silver and white."

Jamal smiled to think that Keesha must have read his mind or really did enter his dream last night.

"I like that, we'll do it on a cruise liner, and that way we won't have to hustle to the airport after the reception, we will sail to wherever you'd like to go! The colors are not important to me, so if silver and white is what you want, then we will have it in silver and white. My seven good friends will be my groomsmen."

"Good, because I have seven bridesmaids."

"You see, we were meant for each other."

"Humm, you're right, we are."

He gave her a hug and went downstairs to begin making his calls.

Keesha called her best friend, Ebony first. She would be her maid of honor. She couldn't think of anyone who could be more deserving of the position than Ebony. In fact, it was Ebony that brought them together. Keesha had known Ebony for a long time and never had she imagined her giving her something that would make her happy for the rest of her life.

She dialed her friend's number. "Hello Ebony, you won't believe this!"

"What is it, darling? Chris' mother decided that she wouldn't mind you dating her young son?"

"Close but not quite! Guess again!"

"I can't."

"Come on, try!"

"Okay, you and Chris are having a child together!"

"Nope."

"I give up. what is it?"

"Jamal and I are getting married."

Ebony screamed on the telephone. "I can't believe it! How did he get you to change your mind?"

"Ebony, he is so wonderful. I don't know how I could have ever let him get away for so long. I will never let that happen again!"

"I'm so happy for you, Keesha. You deserve him. Jamal has been waiting for you for a long time, and all the girls in our school had a crush on him, and look who won his heart. I've always hoped that you two would get together someday."

"I want you to be my maid of honor. Will you?"

"Of course girl! I will represent you well! You're not going to stick me in some old-fashion dress, are you?"

"You, naaa, I've got a dress and color in mind that will knock your socks off!"

"Yeah, what is it?"

"Silver and white! How's that for modern?"

"I like. What kind of dress?"

"Short with a tulle skirt over it!"

"Very good. You're learning. I like your taste and style."

"Thanks, Ebony. You are truly my best friend."

"Not anymore!"

"Why not?"

"Jamal is your best friend!"

"Well then I have two best friends!! Can you do me a favor?"

"Sure, what can I do for you?"

"I'm going to have a great deal of calls to make. Between planning and the invitations, I don't think I can handle it all. Will you help me?

You're really good at that?"

"That's no biggie. Just tell me what you want and need, and I'll get right on it."

"Thanks girl. I'll call you later when Jamal and I talk a little more about our plans, okay."

"Oh, have you guys decided on a date yet?"

"May thirtieth."

"Great, the weather should be excellent. Not too hot and not too cold. Where will it be held?"

"We're having it on a cruise liner."

"Exciting. I definitely won't miss that. Where will it be docked?"

"Probably Virginia."

"Okay, remember, just let me know. I'll talk to you later."

Keesha spent most of the day drafting her list and making telephone calls. She called Michelle and gave her the news.

"Hi, Michelle, I've made up my mind."

"Oh yeah, about what?"

"I decided that I would take you up on your suggestion and marry Jamal."

"Keesha, that's great. Did you tell Chris yet?"

"No, I didn't need to. Chris and I are no longer seeing each other."

"Oh, since when?"

"Since two days ago."

"Ooh, how did he take it?"

"Not very well! But I didn't know any other way to handle the situation."

"So you just dumped him?"

"Hey, I had no other choice. Chris was becoming hazardous to my health! Besides, I've already been hit over the head. I'm still recovering from that."

Michelle told Keesha that Chris really loved her and that with all the girls running behind him that she couldn't believe Keesha would just let him go like that. Michelle considered how Chris must have felt, and she felt sympathy for him. Just the thought of how he must have felt when Keesha told him that it was over made her angry. He was still just a young boy trying to find his manhood, and Keesha had taken his heart and then threw it away for another.

I don't believe Ms. Goodie-Two-Shoes would just drop him.

"Shame on you, Keesha! Hell, I could have had him!"

"Michelle, are you serious? I had no idea you had feelings for Chris."

"Who doesn't? He's drop-dead gorgeous, financially set, and you know he's sexy!"

Keesha felt that Michelle was making too big a deal over their breakup. Keesha almost thought that there was really something personal going on. Michelle never showed any feeling toward Chris. There were many occasions when Michelle would be on her way out when Chris would stop by. Well, actually she would be halfway down the block when he came in but nonetheless, she saw him visiting. She had plenty of time to squeeze in.

"Michelle, I loved Chris from the first time I saw him. I had to let him go, otherwise I wouldn't have!"letting her words trail off. "So don't preach to me. Besides if you wanted him so bad, why didn't you say something before?"

"You were seeing him."

"Well I'm not with him now. Why don't you give it a try--no need in him going to waste! Make him happy."

"You don't mind?"

Keesha couldn't believe what she was hearing. Could Michelle be serious? she wondered. Certainly, she couldn't have had feelings for him. In fact, Michelle was the one to suggest that Keesha go with the flow. Keesha would never have taken him up on his offer if Michelle hadn't tempted her. She was the one to wipe away any guilt that Keesha was feeling.

"No, Michelle, why should I mind, it's not like we were deeply involved,"Keesha said with a note of unnoticed sarcasm. She continued to push the issue, "You are a very nice young lady and closer to his age, I'm sure that he'll love you even more than he could ever have loved me."Keesha laughed to herself.

"You really think so?"Michelle asked feeling flattered and wallowing in her own self-righteousness.

"Yes, I do! So go for it! Get married and have plenty of children."

Michelle considered what Keesha was saying. She wondered if Keesha meant it or was seeing if she would go for it. From the sound in Keesha's voice, Michelle realized that Keesha didn't care one way or the other what she did with Chris. She was with someone else, and they were about to get married, and there was no reason for Keesha to care if Michelle went after Chris.

"Thanks, Keesha. Are you sure? Michelle asked challenging her sincerity.

"Yes, Michelle. I want you to have him!"

"You are truly a special friend."

Keesha remembered how Michelle was looking at Jamal and was glad that she didn't give her enough time to say anything out of the way to him. The word was that Michelle would steal your man right from under your nose. None of the women around here trusted Michelle with their men. Keesha made a mental note not to allow Michelle near Jamal, ever.

"So now that we've squared that away, will you attend my wedding?"

"I'll be there!"

"Thanks, Michelle."

Keesha hung up and wondered if Michelle was pulling her leg or if she was really going to go after Chris. Then she remembered getting hit over the head and decided that it was better that Michelle get crowned over the head than her. More power to you, I hope the two of you will be happy together.

Keesha called her friend, David, and everyone else on her list. She thought about calling her dear friend Christine. She wondered if she would attend her wedding after the grief she had caused her. She decided that she would give her a call since they had been friends for so long.

Keesha picked up the telephone hesitantly then Jamal walked into the room.

"So darling are you finished for the day?"

"Yes, I was going to make one last call."

"Why don't you wait until tomorrow? Let's enjoy each other right now!"

"Okay, what do you have in mind?"

"I want us to go out to dinner, go dancing and when the evening is over, I would like us to come back here and make love over and over. How does that sound to you?"

"Sounds great, when do we start?"

"Right now!"

He handed her a nicely wrapped box and asked her to wear it for him. She opened the box and it was an elegant white oriental dress interwoven with silver threads to add a touch of shimmer.

"Jamal, it's beautiful!"

"Will you wear it for me?"

"Yes, you really know how to make me happy! I love you so much."

Then he handed her a pair of silver high-heeled sandals. "Jamal, how did you know what size to get?"

"How else, I looked at the tag in your clothes and checked your shoes. I told you that I would know everything about you."

"So you've been checking me out?"

"Of course. I don't like surprises. Keesha I hope that when we're married, you will let me in on every aspect of your life and do everything together. I don't mean you can't go away by yourself or spend time with your friends--I would like you to continue doing that--just don't forget about me waiting for you at home, okay?"

"Okay, I can do that."

"So with that thought in mind, how about sharing with me why you were so down when you arrived?"

"Okay Jamal, I know you deserve an explanation. I just broke up with Chris, I told him that I was in love with you and that I had to let him go! It hurt me to tell him that but I had no other choice. If I kept him, I would lose you, and I didn't want to risk losing you."

Jamal wrapped his arms around her, saying he was glad she chose him and not Chris. "Keesha, I'm sorry that you had to break Chris' heart, I'm sure that right now that man must be going through hell. On the other hand, I'm glad that it's not me. Listen, if you need to think a little more, please do, because I don't want to build my hopes up and you let me down in the end."

"Jamal, I want to be your wife! I have never promised anyone my hand in marriage. Yes, it's true that I was given two rings and both of you shocked me, but when I decided that I would let Chris go, I knew right then that I made the right choice for myself and him. I love you Jamal, and I don't want to risk losing you to another woman. There is something so special about you that makes my heart sing whenever I'm with you. That's something that Chris could never give me."

Jamal was satisfied with Keesha's answer so he told her to get dressed so that they could go to dinner. Keesha ran nice warm water into the tub and filled it with jasmine bubble bath. Keesha stepped down

into the tub and enjoyed the aroma. Jamal came in and sat on the side
of the tub and looked at his wife-to-be. "You smell beautiful. I knew
jasmine would be suitable for you. There's a splash to go with it on the
shelf. Jamal washed Keesha's neck, shoulders and back. Then he left her
in the bathroom to finish her bath. He found a suit to match Keesha's
dress. He laid it on the bed and went in the other bathroom. After taking his shower, he stood in front of his mirror and slapped cologne on his
face and neck. Then with the traces on his hand, he rubbed his hands
across his scalp. The room was filled with a pleasant fragrance. Jamal
put on his Calvin Klein briefs on and then in the room, he put on his
suit. He checked his appearance in the mirror, pleased with what he
saw, knowing that his lady would be proud to be with him tonight.
Jamal saw an angel's reflection in the mirror and turned around. Keesha
stood at the door with her hair pinned up in a tight bun with spiraling
curls cascading to one side of her face. Her makeup was light with silver and white shadow accenting her eyes. Her lips were painted with a
sheer frosted mocha lipstick. It looked natural but elegant. Jamal could-
n't believe his eyes. She was simply beautiful. As she walked over to
him, he noticed that her nails were painted to match her lips. Her legs
were shapely and looked totally sexy as she stood with one leg exposed
from a high slit in her dress. She wore shimmering sheer silver stockings
with the silver shoes he had bought her.

"Keesha, you are stunning!"

He took her by the hand and stood her in front of the mirror. He
lifted a velvet case on his dresser, opened it and handed her a pair of two-
carat diamond teardrop earrings to complete the look. He looked at her
to see if anything was missing. She was perfect in every way. The dress
matched every curve of her body. The silver details in the dress twin-
kled like the stars. Her engagement ring sparkled as the light danced
against the stones. "Perfect," he told her.

He held her by the arm and escorted her to the car he had reserved,
a White Bentley with a chauffeur. The chauffeur stood at the passenger
side of the door and waited for them near the car. "Good afternoon. My
name is Charles and I will be your chauffeur for the evening." He opened
the door and helped them into the car. He got into the driver's seat and
lowered the interior window to get instructions.

"Ma'am, I must say that you look stunning!"

"Thank you, Charles."

"So do you, sir. You two make a handsome couple!"

Keesha smiled and knew that this would be a night to remember.

"So, where will we be going first?"

"Charles, first I would like to take my fiancee to the Encarta for dinner."

The driver was familiar with that restaurant. It was very impressive and only the opulent frequented there. "Ma'am, I'm sure you will love the food there and the entertainment!" He smiled at her and raised the window to give them some privacy.

Jamal looked at Keesha and could tell that she was impressed by his display of charisma. He looked stunning in his white oriental suit. His goatee was freshly cut and neat tapering his voluptuous full lips. They were indeed a lovely pair.

When they arrived at the Encarta, the driver opened the door. Jamal stepped out first and all the ladies stopped to look at him. They wanted to see who would get out of the car with him or if he was alone. After what seemed like an eternity, Keesha stepped out of the car and everyone paused. She was simply beautiful.

Jamal was proud to have her on his arm and even more so because she would soon be his wife. They approached the entrance to the Encarta and a waiter told Jamal that his table was ready then escorted them to their table. Jamal helped Keesha into her chair then he went to his seat adjacent to hers. He held her hands and looked into her pretty, light brown eyes. They had so much passion in them that his heart began to race. He wanted to hold her in his arms.

Keesha looked around the room. The decor was better than anything she'd imagined. There were mirrors and chandeliers everywhere. The floor on which their table sat slowly rotated allowing them to see every side of the room. It felt as though they were not moving but whenever she looked up, she was seeing another side of the room.

Keesha had a confused look. "When will we be ordering?" Jamal smiled at her. "Keesha, no orders are taken here, when you reserve your seat, you tell them what you will be having. That way when you get here, they will already have it prepared. Also, there is no one to be harassing you just in case there was something sensitive you were trying to get out."

"What do you mean?"

"Well, say for instance, I wanted to propose to you and was nervous about it, if the waiter kept coming over to us, it would make it more difficult to do because he would always be asking if there was something he could get for us whenever I started to say what I wanted to say."

"What if we wanted more?"

"Then we could summon the waiter, and he would be happy to attend to our needs. Believe me, Keesha, they're trained to see everything. You won't have to call them over!"

Keesha smiled at him and then the lights went dim. Keesha looked up to see what was going on. All the tables seemed to stop rotating and a glass wall opened to reveal a stage. An orchestra descended from above the stage and people dressed in costumes from the Roaring Twenties danced onto it.

Their food arrived and they watched the show while enjoying their steak and seafood entree. The steak was cut in perfect bite-size pieces so that you didn't have to worry about that and the vegetables were in just the right tenderness. Everything was splendid.

CHAPTER
28

After hearing the good news, Michelle looked outside and the day was nice and sunny so she decided to take a drive over to The Enclave Town Houses.

Chris had turned his ringer off and kept his answering machine volume low. He was tired from a long week at work. His workload had increased since the company had let go of one of their senior accountants and Chris was given the position. Even though he knew the position was only temporary, the possibility of earning it was great. His skills, personality and accuracy were better than anyone in the firm. Of course they would try to avoid giving the position to him, but he was the best. Right now the best was tired and drained.

He did realize that part of his workload was figuring out how he could make amends with Keesha. She really did break his heart. He never would have thought that she would actually tell him that she was in love with another man. He would have preferred for her to tell him that she just didn't think that they were right for each other. Her honest nature led her to tell him the truth, and he respected her for that. He wondered if this fascination for this other guy would soon die down and if she would be his again.

He laid there on his champagne satin sheets, in his silk boxers, fantasizing about his doorbell ringing and running down stairs to answer it to find Keesha standing there. He saw himself letting her in and instantly she began to kiss him. Reluctant at first, he finally gave in to her thirsty kisses. The more they kissed the more fervent their desire for each other became.

She ran her hands down his firm chest, past his waist and on to the band of his silky boxers. She placed her fingers inside and lowered the sheet of silk from over his firm buttocks, freeing his throbbing member.

He then pressed her body close to his so that she could experience the fortitude of the staff before her. He pulled her blouse from her pants and lifted it just enough to grasp the firm nuggets hardening beneath her satiny bra. He could feel her pebbly nipple through the soft, thin layer of her brassiere. He stuck his head down beneath her blouse and put his mouth around the satiny mound touching it with his tongue and leaving a moist circle around her nipple. She purred at his gentle touch. He loosened her belt and pulled her pants down over her hips, slowly lowering his face to her navel. She quivered at his touch, and moisture formed between her legs.

Chris could smell the sweetness building in her, and he could tell she wanted him just as much as he wanted her. He pulled her panties to the side and brushed her fuzzy little peach with his hands, then ran his finger down between her seam and into her tunnel. She was so wet. He imagined how it would feel to penetrate her, slipping and sliding in and out of her tender flesh. She pressed her moistness against his hand, and he moved his finger to her rhythm. He knew that she didn't want him to toy with it so he pulled her pants all the way down, and she stepped out of them along with her panties. Then he lifted her, and glided her down his shaft. He felt a slight resistance, but with an easy thrust, he was joined with her.

e laid her on a mount he had intended to get a bust for, and pounded himself into her. She screamed with pleasure while her head hung over the side of the mount. She tightened her muscles around him causing him to rupture into a sweet climax but he continued to thrust his manhood into her until he heard her scream his name on three occasions. Then when her body fell into a slump, he knew that he had fulfilled her lustful binge. He lifted her so that she could sit up straight on the stone mount. She hugged him and told him that she was sorry to have let him go. He wrapped his arms around her. When he woke up, someone was ringing his doorbell. He looked down to find his staff at full attention with a wet circle at the tip. The desire was so intense that he couldn't bear to touch himself. He knew that a cold shower would not heal his sexual craving. He needed to be relieved. The doorbell rang again! He ached with desire as his heart raced. Could fate be on his side? he wondered. He rushed downstairs and answered the door. "Michelle!"

CHAPTER
29

After the show, Jamal escorted Keesha to the dance hall located on the upper level of the restaurant. Everyone was watching them. Keesha decided that it was only her imagination or that they were just admiring their attire. Of course, they were debonair! There was no one in the entire place that could match their radiance.

The music played a nice mixture of rhythm and blues, slow jams and club music. People danced all night long. Occasionally, one of Jamal's friends or associates would come over with their escorts, and he would introduce them to his fiancee. Keesha had never been in a place where everybody was somebody. There wasn't a soul in the place that didn't have a lot of money.

After a while, Jamal asked Keesha if she wanted to check out the jazz hall. When she agreed, Jamal took Keesha to the jazz hall where they were escorted to a table. There was a crowd of women that watched their every move and seemed to be talking about them.

"Jamal, is it me or is everybody watching us?" Jamal laughed and looked at his pretty bride-to-be.

"They're just checking you out, that's all. Whenever someone new comes in here, they watch to see what kind of person they are. They're probably talking about how beautiful you are!" He winked at her, and she was again at ease.

Jamal excused himself and went to the rest room. He kissed Keesha's hands and walked toward the rear of the hall. As he disappeared through the corridors, four nicely dressed women walked over and introduced themselves to her.

"Hi, you must be new around here. My name is Gwen, and this is Barbara,"she said pointing to a tall bright skinned woman. Barbara's hair was cut into a short crop, which suited her nicely. The cut made her look like a doll baby. "She's here with Howard over there."Keesha looked in the direction Gwen had pointed in and saw a white guy who looked too old for this young girl. Then Gwen continued to give her the scoop on them. "He's a multimillionaire and Barbara here is his showpiece." Barbara smiled as though she was just paid a compliment. "Now Candice here, she's with Tom. Tom owns all the jewelry shops you see here in North Virginia. Needless to say, he's filthy rich too!"Gwen said, and Keesha, wondered if all the women in the place were tramps.

Then Gwen introduced her to Denise. "Denise, she used to be close with Jamal some time ago, they say he's a really good lover, but I don't know, I've never had him. So tell us, Denise, what is Mr. Warner like?"

"He's a sexy bald head mother fucker I tasted him many times."

"You must be Jamal's new trick. How long have you been with Jamal?" Keesha was feeling herself losing control when Howard came over.

"So Keesha is it, Jamal tells me that you two are getting married!" Keesha looked at Gwen and the other whore sidekicks and said, "Yes, that's correct!"

"He also mentioned that you were a financial planner and very good at what you do. Jamal is very successful and has thus far invested his money well, and I trust his recommendation along with my other buddies over there--Phil, Tom, Eric, Donald and Peter." Keesha looked at the men standing in a cluster chatting about their success, she imagined.

"Sure, I'd love to take a look at what you have and see if there is anything we can do to make your money grow." Howard gave her some business cards and told her to give them a call when she was ready. Keesha briefly looked at the cards and put them in her silver purse.

Gwen looked at her with scorn and said,"Oh, this is one of those sophisticated bitches. The ones who thinks their men are better than us."Gwen's little crowd looked at her, and Keesha decided that she wouldn't stoop to their level. She got up, and walked to the rear of the hall. As she neared the women's powder room, Gwen stopped her and apologized for her rude behavior at the table. Keesha knew that she wasn't sincere but for the sake of argument, she accepted.

Meanwhile, Jamal turned away from the urinal and walked over to the sink when Denise came in. Jamal saw her through the mirror as she stepped up behind him as he washed his hands in the sink.

"You know you're in the wrong bathroom. The women's room is next door."

Denise smiled at his boyish toying. He knew exactly why she was in there but pretended not to recognize her sluttish gestures. "So Jamal, tell me, where did you find the little poodle?"

"Denise, that woman in there is my fiancee and more woman than you could ever be. Now if you don't mind, I'd like to return to her before she gets worried." Denise walked up to him and grabbed his crotch.

"What's the matter, battery gone dead on you?"

"No, it just doesn't respond to tramps!" He pushed her hand away and gave her a threatening look. She didn't heed his warning and stepped closer to him. Jamal was getting angrier by the second. Just as he reached to push her out of his way, her lips stuck his chest and smeared red lipstick all over the front of his jacket. He started to hit her but decided that he didn't need to make matters worse. He told her to get out and leave him alone before he forbid her from his establishment. She shrugged and walked out.

Keesha saw her leaving the men's room. "What were you doing in the men's room?"

"Rekindling an old flame, and you know what? He's still hot!"Denise walked away with a grin, and Gwen took pleasure in seeing the concern on Keesha's pretty little face. Keesha stood there waiting to see who would come out. No one did. She wondered where Jamal was and if he was in that bathroom. She decided to just wait and see.

Jamal couldn't believe the way Denise acted. He turned to look in the mirror one last time and noticed the lipstick on his jacket. "Shit,"he swore, picking up the telephone in the stall. He asked the attendant to bring him a bottle of club soda and a towel. After a few moments, his friend Kevin walked into the stall and looked at Jamal's stain.

"Lipstick huh, you and your fiancee must be looking forward to a hot night"

"Where is she?"

"She's waiting for you right outside the bathroom! She didn't go far!"

Jamal could feel tension building in his chest. How was he going to explain the lipstick stain to her? Then he thought, maybe she just got there. "How long was she standing there?"

"I don't know, but she's out there with some of your old flings!"

"Kevin, I need to get this stain out of my suit!"

"Hey man, you're not messing around when your girl's right outside, are you?"

"No, I would never do that to her. Denise came in here and deliberately soiled my suit to make it seem like something happened between us."

"Then your best response right now is to tell her the truth!"

Jamal thought about it and decided that he would do just that. Trying to cover the incident up would make matters worse. Most of the lipstick came out but it left a light pink stain that was still noticeable. Keesha would spot it the second he walked out. He took a deep breath and made his exit. Even though he knew that she would be there, the sight of her caused him to pause a split second. Keesha took one look at him and noticed the lipstick on his clothes. She turned from him and started walking away. Jamal took four quick steps and caught up to her. He embraced her tightly in a way that made it seem like he was being affectionate. The last thing he needed was to gain the attention of the crowd or to make Gwen and her league of whores see that they accomplished their vicious deed. He lowered his lips to her ear and told her to walk with him to the car and give him a chance to explain.

Keesha, didn't want her new enemies to notice her hurt so she went along with him. They watched as Jamal held Keesha in his arms and escorted her to their car. A couple of his friends came over to them, but Jamal told them that now was not a good time. He helped Keesha into the car and then got in behind her. He told Charles to drive them home and give them privacy. Charles rolled up the window and started the car.

"Jamal, how could you do this to me? You left me at the table for your ex-girlfriends to torment me with their memories with you, and what kind of lover you were!"

Jamal stopped her as he could see she was on a roll. "Keesha, I didn't know that they would approach you. I'm sorry they did! I'll handle that later. Right now, I need to explain a few things to you."

"Not right now, Jamal. I'm hurting inside, and my anger may cause me to react in a way that may change our future!"

"I'll take that chance because I can't afford to let you walk away from me thinking that I cheated on you! Keesha, it's true that I had a relationship with Denise some time ago. She was not a fling at the time, but I realized that she was not the kind of woman I wanted or needed in my life. I know you don't think that before you and I got together that there was no one else! I ran into many women when I gained my fortune."

"Jamal, please. I don't need you to remind me that you slept with women before me. I already know that."

"Keesha, listen to me. I love you, and I want to make you happy, but if that is going to happen, you have to let your anger go and allow me to explain what just happened." Keesha decided that he deserved a fair hearing and leaned back in the seat. He turned her head to face him, and he told her that she needed to listen and understand how things came to be in his life. Her eyes were swollen with unshed tears, and Jamal could see it. That's why he knew that he needed to wipe away every inch of doubt from her mind right now.

"Keesha, I'm not the same man you knew back in school, and I'm also not exactly what you think I am now. The truth is, I got my degree in medical science and acquired my Ph.D. in gynecological surgery. I am very successful in what I do and make an excellent living off it. That status changed. A good friend of mine named Sean, the same one from school, came to me in my first year as a doctor and asked me to cover him for $100,000 to start a restaurant. His credit was bad, and he couldn't get the money to get his dream off the ground. He was a good friend of mine, and he promised that I would become a fifty percent owner with him if I gave him a chance. Since money was no issue, I loaned it to him, and he and some friends built this restaurant you see.

"You told me he had a construction business!"

"That's true, but it wasn't flying for him until he built the place we dined tonight. At first, everyone could come in and dine, but some really high-class people came in and we made a contract with them to make it a ritzy club. No common people were allowed to come in without an escort. Needless to say that the bunch you met tonight were some of the common people that received an invite. Anyway, the Encarta started off with a net worth of $100,000 but is now pulling in an easy $12 million a year. Keesha when I became worth six million dollars, everyone was after me. I wanted someone to love but I couldn't find anyone. Of course there were a few women that I ran into that fulfilled my manly needs but there was never one that made me feel the way I do when I'm with you. Ebony can tell you how long I've waited for you. I don't flaunt my possessions in front of anybody because I want to know if they can love me for me. You are the only one that gave me what I needed--love! Can you understand that?"

Keesha fought to hold back her emotions, but there was one thing she needed to know. "What happened in the men's room tonight?"

"Denise came in and I told her that you were my fiancee after she tried to seduce me."

"What did she do?"

Jamal didn't know how to answer her. He didn't want her to think he enjoyed it or if she would understand that nothing happened. "When I turned around she grabbed my crotch, and I pushed her hand away."

"Did she stimulate you?"

"No, she did not get me aroused, It angered me! I don't see why you're asking me these questions, I told you nothing happened!"

"Something happened, you had lipstick all over the front of your jacket not to mention the smear that's still on the front of your pants where it appears her lips must have been!" Keesha's voice held a hint of sarcasm. Jamal looked down and saw the stain that laid directly on top the imprint of his penis. He hadn't noticed that. He wondered how it got there. She didn't kneel in front of him. He wondered how he would explain that since he didn't know how it got there.

"She must have had it on her hand when she grabbed me!"

"Are you sure she didn't go down on you and you rejected her after she got there or maybe she did it for you and you ended it there!" Jamal could feel himself getting angry.

"Okay, if you don't believe me, then take it out and see if it's been touched!" Keesha looked at him shocked but took him up on his offer. He slouched in his seat so that she could unzip his pants and released his member. It didn't even harden to her touch. She inspected it and saw no traces of anything. Nothing. She massaged it and received no response. She looked up at him, and he had a look of hurt and frustration on his face. He realized that she didn't hear a word he said or didn't believe him. There was no way he would allow himself to get erect now so that she would think someone else could have encouraged his feelings.

She kissed his neck and moved to his lips. No response. She could see he was hurt by what she said. She released his member and sat back in her seat and looked out of the window. Jamal returned his penis to his pants and zipped up his pants and sat back in the seat.

"Now do you see that it takes more than a touch to turn me on? Keesha, I'm not that twenty-one-year-old boy that I once was. I've slept with many women, and I know all about sex, and there's nothing new. I'm turned on by you because I want to be, not because I get an urge in my pants, the wind blows or a woman touches it or twists her buttocks in front of me. I'm past all that. You hurt my feelings and thought that I would perform for you. Keesha, I'm sorry that this happened, and I don't know how to make it right. All I can say is sorry and hope that you will forgive me and forget about that part of the night and remember how it was without any of the disruptions."

Keesha continued to stare outside. She couldn't bring herself to face him after carrying things too far. He touched her hand, and the tears that she fought back streamed down her face. She turned around and told him that she was sorry for overreacting. He removed his handkerchief from his jacket and dried her eyes. Then he kissed her. She trembled at his touch and tried to pull back. Jamal realized that she was suffering from the woman's pride syndrome so he cupped her face with both his hands and forced her to continue kissing him. He took her hand and placed it on his erection so that she knew that he was responding to her and wanted her. He looked out of the window and saw that they were near his home. He used his handkerchief to correct the smudges of lipstick on her face so that when Charles helped her out of the car she would look just as fresh and innocent as she did when he first met her. Charles drove the Bentley to the front of the house, opening the door for Jamal. Then he stepped back so that Jamal could help Keesha from the car. He reminded her how lovely she looked and escorted them to the door. After they were safely in the house, Charles returned to the car. There was an envelope on the backseat with his name on it. He opened it and found a personalized thank-you card from Jamal with a five-thousand-dollar check in it.

Lovemaking was sweet between them that night as Jamal gave of himself until Keesha had climaxed seven times and finally fell asleep in his arms.

CHAPTER
30

There she stood with those long swan legs and tight belly at his door. She was beautiful. Tasteful. He felt a twinge of guilt but his body needed her, cried out for her, to give him release. He stepped back and as she entered she could feel the heat radiating from his body. A fume she recognized. She stepped closer to him pressing against his throbbing organ. If he wanted it, he would have to take it. She would not make it easy for him this time.

He opened the belt to his silk robe and let it swing open revealing his obvious lust. He pressed his body closer to hers, letting her know that there was no doubt, the fever is on! He picked her up and carried her to his bed. Not like the last time, he would be gentle and passionate. It would last. He pulled a blade from his draw and cut off the buttons of her short crop blouse, revealing her firm but tender breasts. Her nipples hardened at his touch and stood at attention. They were good. He tickled them with his tongue moving from the left to the right, then back again.

He removed her pants and panties at once exposing her neatly shaved nanny. Raising her leg, he buried his head deep into her flesh. It was so good. Her body wasted no time releasing its love juices. She moved up and down, making love to his lips as his tongue teased her opening, in and out. That gentle motion made her crave for him to enter her until she could wait no more. She called him to come to her. "Give it to me," she pleaded. He lay on his back beckoning her to come and get it.

She turned on her side pulling his silkies over his hips. Then using his blade she cut them away from his body. As the material loosened, his staff plunged forward. It had been released from its bondage. She let her mouth move slowly over its head moistening it with her saliva. He trembled with pleasure. She was indeed good at it, and no one else could bring those feelings out of him like her. He remembered his first time, when she turned him out. He vowed to never leave her bedside. She was just as good now as she was then. "Oh God, Michelle, you're so good!"

He ran his hands over her soft curly hair. He felt himself wanting to cum, but he didn't want to, he wanted it to last. He stopped himself and made her lie down on the bed so that he could enter her. He massaged her vagina with soft, easy strokes. She moved with him. On and on they made love like the first time again until all was spent. Then unlike before, he cuddled close to her and wondered why it couldn't be Keesha next to him. As Michelle continued to lie there, she decided that there was no need to break the news to him about Keesha after all. His obsession for Keesha was over. Things were back to the way they used to be.

The next morning, Chris woke up early. He remembered bits and pieces of his dream. Michelle had again crept into his dreams. He had made love to the two women that left lasting impressions on his life. The funny thing about it was it seemed so real. He even made passionate love to Michelle. Even the time he really slept with her, it wasn't passionate. She must have a spell on him, he thought. Chris sat up on his bed and decided that he'd better get going. He walked sluggishly to his bathroom. He opened the door, and in his tub was a nightmare-- Michelle soaking in his Jacuzzi. He backed out of the bathroom, looked at his bed and around it in disbelief. His sheets were rumpled. Buttons were all over the floor along with panties and underwear. Could he really have slept with her? he wondered. Now, how would he get rid of her, he couldn't just treat her callus. He walked back into the bathroom, and she took note of him this time.

"Chris, how do you feel this morning?"

"Michelle," he said, looking for words but sounding surprised to see her there.

"Last night was great. I knew that you would be back. Chris, we're meant for each other."

"Michelle, I don't know how to say this, especially after what apparently happened last night but this thing between us just can't be."

"What, Chris? We just made love last night, that had to mean something, nobody displays passion like that without meaning!"

"Michelle, I needed someone last night, and you were there."

"Are you trying to make me think last night meant nothing to you?"

"Michelle, it didn't, I mean it did but not for the right reasons. I made love to you but my heart wanted Keesha."

"Keesha!, Keesha!"she repeated in disgust as if the name left a vile taste in her mouth. "Why are you so hung up on her? You don't even have her. She doesn't love you. Matter of fact, Keesha is getting married!"

"Keesha and I are engaged. We split up for a while so that she could get her head together."

"Well she's seeing someone else!"

"I know about that too!"

"Her wedding is set for May thirtieth."

"You don't give up, do you Michelle? Why do you have such a fixation on me? There must be plenty of guys knocking at your door and wanting to be with you. You deserve better. You need someone to love you, and I can't do that. What we have is purely sexual. I mean that is the way we met, isn't it? You taught me how to make love to a woman, now I know! What is it now? You want me to be your sex slave?"

Michelle couldn't believe it. She poured her feelings out to this man and he continued to want something he couldn't have. She couldn't understand what was so special about Keesha. There was no doubt that she was pretty, so was Michelle. Her body was shapely, so was Michelle's. Keesha had money and so did Michelle, just not as much. In Chris' case, he wouldn't be interested in money anyway. He had his own and did quite well on his own. There was something that Keesha had that made men go crazy over her. Michelle decided that she wouldn't bother with Chris anymore. His mind was made up--he wanted Keesha. There wasn't anyone else who could take Keesha's place so there was no point in Michelle trying to pursue Chris anymore.

She quietly got out of the tub, dried herself off and searched Chris' wardrobe for something suitable to wear. She found a shirt that matched her pants and put it on. She tied it at the waist and looked at herself in the mirror. She looked good. She found her shoes and bag and made her way downstairs.

Chris was staggered by her display of nonchalance and recognition of defeat. He wondered if she was feeling suicidal. "Michelle, are you okay?"

"Sure Chris, I understand now. Things will never be between us so there is no need in me chasing behind you. I hope that you will be happy with your illusion of Keesha! I could have loved you but you don't deserve me or Keesha. You are selfish, insensitive and deserve to be by yourself. Good-bye Chris!"

He watched her leave his house and go to her car. Chris stood at his window, and something inside him was crying. He realized that he hurt her. When he first met her, he couldn't get enough of her and now his heart belonged to someone that was with someone else. He knew things were over between him and Keesha but he just couldn't get her off his mind. He didn't want to be tied down with anyone else if she decided to come back to him. Nothing would be in their way if and when she decided to come back. He watched the woman of his past drive off and knew that he wouldn't make love to that beautiful body again.

Chris wondered what would happen to the child Michelle carried. Now that he thought about it, he wanted to be close to it. To watch it grow and take care of it. Somehow he knew that would never come to fruition. She would torture him by keeping the fruit of his loins away from him. He could see his mother holding her, playing with her, and he never having the chance because she would not be around when he was near. How did his life start so perfect, and end so wrong? Was he selfish? he wondered. Should he have loved Michelle? Did she deserve him or was it his conscience talking to him? Whatever the case he knew how he felt and what he wanted--Keesha.

CHAPTER
31

Keesha had a lot of planning to do. Her wedding was in three months and she wanted everything to be perfect. She sat in her office and opened the mail that had accumulated since Thursday when she visited Jamal. She found a check and other correspondence letters being answered. He took care of them and reclined in her leather swivel chair with her feet propped up on the desk.

Keesha went into her telephone book in the computer and wrote a note inviting her closest friends over for a celebration of her upcoming wedding. She tagged the names she wanted to invite and sent the messages out by e-mail. The others she printed and mailed.

The day seemed to go smoothly. She saw clients and in between called more friends to inform them of her wedding plans. She looked around and decided that she had better start working on getting things ready for the get-together she planned to have in three weeks. Keesha found her dust mop, sprayed it with Pledge and ran it over her floors. She removed her draperies and put them aside so that she could drop them off to the cleaner.

She dusted her lamps and cleaned her chandelier. She shampooed her living room carpet along with the carpet in the gallery. She checked her portraits for any dust that might have settled and everything looked perfect. She wished she had help. It seemed like the more she did, the more she had to do. Of course, she could hire someone to do it but she didn't want to bother with having someone come in because she would have to keep an eye on her merchandise. The last time she had someone come in and clean, she was missing some valuable things so she didn't want to chance it.

She did, however, make arrangements for someone to come in and clean her furniture. There was no way she would be able to get that done. There was nothing wrong with it but she wanted everything to look new.

The week seemed to go by fast. She hadn't spoken with Jamal since she returned on Monday. She looked at the clock and decided to give him a call.

"Hello, this is Dr. Warner's office may I help you?"the assistant answered.

"Hello this is Keesha, is Dr. Warner in?"

"Oh yes, hold on a moment, I'm sure he'll be glad to hear from you!" She put Keesha on hold and summoned her boss to pick up the telephone. The day had been very long and tiresome. He delivered four babies, one of which was a stillborn. He had never in his eight years of delivering babies experienced the anguish and sorrow that followed the birth of a dead child. His heart went out to the parents. It was their first child, and nowhere during the pregnancy did he detect any problems. Now sitting in his office, with papers to fill out, he went over the patient's file to see if there was something he had overlooked that would have changed the outcome of this delivery. He looked at her medical history along with the blood tests, nothing. He looked at the sonogram, nothing. He reviewed the chart of urine and vital signs, nothing. He couldn't understand it. Everything seemed to be perfect, so how could this child's birth turn out to be such a disaster?

He heard the mother's scream in his head over and over. The sound was recorded in his heart, and her expression etched in his brain. He wished that there were something that he could do to reverse what had just happened. Nothing would brighten up his day.

When Linda realized that Jamal wasn't picking up, she decided that she had better pay him a visit. "Dr. Warner, are you alright? I hope you're not beating yourself up about the tragedy that happened earlier! It wasn't your fault, you are a very good doctor, and I'm sure that Mrs. Felix feels the same way."

"I can't Linda. If I had just noticed that one little thing, I might have saved that child!"

"Dr. Warner, you are only a man and you can't fix everything. Now I know that you are a doctor and very good at what you do but there are times when not even the best can foresee these tragedies, so please, pick up the telephone and talk to your fiancee and stop hurting yourself!"

She left his office and hoped that he heard her that time. Jamal thought about what she said and decided that he had better at least pick up the telephone, and talk with his bride-to-be before she thought that he doesn't want to speak to her.

"Hello, darling, how are you?"

"Jamal, what's wrong? You don't sound like yourself. Is everything alright?" Jamal took a deep breath and started to speak.

"Keesha, I lost a child today!"

"Oh, sweetheart, I'm sorry, that must be hard on you." Keesha stumbled to find comforting words. As much as he loves children, this must be eating him up, and she knew that he was taking it personal. "Darling, I'm sure that it was not your fault."

"Keesha, I don't know what happened, everything I've looked at so far indicates that things were perfect but when the child was born, it had no life. Keesha, I don't understand what happened."

"Jamal, darling, sweetheart, sometimes these things happen, and they can't be detected. It just happens. I wish I was there to hold you!"

"I do, too, I need it."

"Sweetheart, why don't you go home and take a few days off if you need to?"

"I can't, I have at least ten mothers that are expecting to deliver any day now, and they are counting on me to be there!"

"Then you have to pull yourself together before you start doubting your skills or they begin to doubt your abilities!" Jamal knew that she was right and appreciated her knack to get through to him. He thanked her and told her that he loved her. Then they bided each other good-bye and hung up. Jamal took one last glance at the file and wrote cause of death unknown then closed the file. He felt a little relieved when he shut the door on that episode and prayed that he would never have to see a situation like that again. It would have been different if he had known that something was wrong with the mother or the child but for the baby to die with no apparent reason made him feel as though it was his fault by negligence.

He buzzed Linda to come into his office. When she walked in, she saw him standing by the closet. He had already removed his smock. "Doctor, are you leaving for the day?"

"Yes, Linda, I would like you to clear my calendar for the rest of the week. The only appointments I will see this week are deliveries or extreme emergencies. In the case of an emergency, you can conference the call to me at home, and I will decide then if I will come in to see them."

"Okay, are you going to be all right?"

"Yes, both you and Keesha have helped me get over today's tragedy. Of course, I'm still sad about it but I think that I can handle it better now. I really appreciate your display of aggression earlier." She laughed and told him anytime.

Keesha wondered if Jamal was doing all right. As much as she wanted to be there for him, she had so much to do. Besides, she knew that he needed this time to himself so that he could get over it on his own. She would only divert his attention and keep him from facing the real problem.

CHAPTER
32

"Hi. We spoke on the telephone the other day. Do you have the stuff ready for me?"

"Yes, do you have the money?"

She reached in her purse, pulling out a check then sliding it through the window. She tried to peer in but nothing could be seen through the tinted glass. He looked at it then pushed it back through the glass returning it to her..."We only accept cash. What are you stupid or something? This thing's traceable!" Feeling embarrassed for not realizing, she returned the check to her purse and turned and walked out the door. She returned to her car and drove around until she found a bank which she could cash her check. Finally at 2:30 she pulled into the parking lot of the bank. The attendant told her that they were closing. She pleaded with him to allow her to come in. He apologized and told her that she would have to return on Monday. "Monday is too late!"She stammered, "I need the money today."

He could see the urgency in her face and felt sympathy. He stepped back and allowed her to enter the bank. When she came in, she saw that only two people on the line and one at the new accounts counter. She hurried to the line and waited her turn. In ten minutes, she walked up to the teller and handed him a check made out to cash. He looked at the amount and called his manager over.

"Is there something wrong with the check?"

The teller told her that he had to get an approval for the amount of money she was requesting. She waited for the manager to finish talking with another client then he came over to where they stood. He looked at the check and then the account. She had plenty of money in the account and there was no reason to decline the transaction. He signed the approval slip and started to give her a certified check.

"No, I need that in cash please!"They looked at her for a moment

and told her that it would dangerous for her to walk out of there with
that kind of money. She told him that she needed it right away and to
put it in large bills. They looked at her and wondered if she was doing
something illegal.

"Listen, you're holding me up, and I need the money tonight for a
car. I tried to use a check but the dealer wanted cash for it. If I don't get
back by five o'clock, he's going to sell it to someone else. I will never get
a deal like this one again. They went into the vault and returned with
an envelope containing five-thousand-dollars all in fifty-dollar bills. She
watched him count it then put it into an envelope. He had her sign a
release form documenting that she received the cash and verified the
amount given.

She raced out of the bank and jumped into her car and returned to
the pawnshop on Gunhill Road. She knocked on the glass and the voice
returned to the window. As before, she could not see his face. Forcing
the bulky envelope through the slot in the glass, she waited for the guy
to finish counting the money. When he was satisfied that the agreed
amount was in the envelope, he handed her a bottle, emphasizing they
never met. "Make sure you forget this place when you leave. This is a
one-time service operation." His voice was cold and stern. He reminded
her that the stuff was illegal and he had to go through his foreign connections to get it. Then he explained to her how it worked and how long
it took. He reminded her that too much could be fatal. She nodded and
took the bottle. She returned to her car and drove home. When she
arrived, she turned on her computer and wrote a letter. This was the
first step to her plot to get even with the two people who tried to ruin
her life.

Dear Chris,
I know that things didn't turn out the way that we
planned, and I'm sorry about that. I've decided that
maybe we should get together and try to work this
thing out. I need you, Chris, and I hope that it's not
too late for us to rekindle what we had.
P.S. I will be away until Friday. I hope that you will
come by around eight o'clock on Friday. I will have my
telephone off so no need calling. Just come by. I miss you.
Love Keesha.

She sprayed the letter with the same fragrance Keesha wore and
sealed it in one of Keesha's personalized envelopes. She calculated the

days, making certain there was enough delivery time to make her plan work. Then placing a stamp on the envelope, she hurried to the post office. She returned to her house, feeling good, knowing that she would get Keesha after all.

CHAPTER
33

Chris received Keesha's letter. Things were working out just as he had expected. He knew that if given the space and time she needed that she would realize that they were meant for each other. Michelle had come over and tried to break his spirits by telling him that Keesha was marrying this Jamal character.

Chris knew that she couldn't possibly be capable of making a permanent decision about another man when her feelings for him still resided in her heart. He loved her more than anything in the world. His mother had been calling him all week and leaving messages. He felt that she would only discourage him from his quest to regain Keesha's heart.

He sat at the foot of his stairs and wondered how he could have fallen into Michelle's hands again. They had made love, and it was passionate, sweet. Chris couldn't believe how gentle he was with her and conscious of her sexual needs. It was good and of course, it was memorable.

He shook that thought from his head as he recalled that he was to meet with Keesha later that evening. He looked at the letter again and noted that it said to stop by at eight.

Meanwhile, Michelle decided that she had better give Keesha a call to see if there was something she could do to help her get this shower along. She grabbed her bag hurrying to Keesha's house. She smiled to herself knowing that she would kill two birds with one stone. Going over the arrangements made with her friend to meet her around midnight to deliver an urgent package, airmail, she knew that her plan would work.

She approached Keesha's home and rung the bell. Keesha answered the door shortly after. She was glad to see Michelle since she was working on cleaning her china and champagne glasses. That was the job she hated the most. It seemed tedious.

"Michelle, girl you don't know how glad I am to see you."

"Thought you might need a hand for the get-together Saturday!" Keesha invited her in, and she led her into the kitchen where she had a sink full of champagne glasses. She expressed to Michelle how important it was to get all the water spots off them.

"Hey, I know how to clean crystal. My mother used to have me clean hers when she was entertaining. You just relax and let me handle things."

Keesha returned to the living room and started folding napkins in the shape of swans. She was relieved that she didn't have to clean those champagne glasses.

Michelle had finally finished cleaning the glasses and checked them one last time. She had also taken the liberty of cleaning the china. Looking at her watch, she realized that she had better get her plan into action as Chris would be over in another hour.

"Hey, Keesh, I'm fixing myself something cool to drink. Can I get you anything?"

"Thanks, I really could use something to drink right about now!"

Michelle looked in Keesha's refrigerator and found a pitcher of tea.

"How about tea?"

"That will be fine, thank you. Anything will do!"

Michelle poured Keesha a glass of tea when she realized that her bag was in the other room. She went into the living room where Keesha was sitting and found her purse.

"Michelle, I thought you were fixing us some tea!"

"Oh, I'm sorry, I left it on the counter."

"All right, I'll get it."

"No, no, please let me get it, I just forgot it."

She hurried back into the kitchen and quickly poured the liquid from the vile into Keesha's glass. She shook the glass around and hoped that it wouldn't taste funny. The man she purchased it from told her it would only sweeten the taste but not change the taste. She knew that Keesha would be in to check on her drink any moment so she didn't have time to measure it properly. Besides, she didn't care whether she lived or died anyway.

"Here you are, nice and cold."

"Thanks, Michelle. I could never have gotten this work done without your help."

They sat back and enjoyed their drinks and talked like two school-girls. Michelle asked Keesha about Jamal, how they met and where he lived. Keesha gave Michelle a general idea of where he lived. Michelle took everything in she said. Keesha's description was just as good as giving an address as Jamal lived in a ritzy neighborhood. That wouldn't be hard to find, not with his name on the invitation.

Michelle stayed for another half hour. Then Keesha started feeling funny. Looking at her watch, Michelle realized that it was almost eight o'clock.

"Well, Keesh, I guess I'd better be going. I have a lot to do to get ready for this party tomorrow."

"Okay, Michelle, I'm gonna lay down now anyway. I'm feeling a little strange myself. Thanks again for your help."

Michelle went to the door and let herself out. Keesha had a strange sexual urge. She wished Jamal were around. I wonder where this feeling came from, she questioned herself.

Chris would not be late for his appointment tonight. Keesha wanted him, and he would be there for her. After parking his car, Chris mounted the few steps and rung the doorbell. He waited before ringing it again. Then Keesha came to the door. She looked so seductive. Chris walked in and Keesha stood there shocked that he was there.

He could see her taunt nipples through her blouse. She wanted him.

"I missed you," he said in a low, even tone. He couldn't wait another second. He wanted to hug her so bad it hurt. His arms lifted in anticipation of hugging her when she attacked him. Her kiss was wild and fervent. He welcomed it with the same intensity of passion.

His manhood stood at attention and was ready for anything she wanted. Her blood was rushing, and she couldn't control herself. She needed him, his body, and his manhood. Keesha reached down between his legs and felt his erection, squeezing it with hunger. Chris' muscle throbbed hard against his vessel's wall, excited by Keesha's strange lascivious behavior.

"Fuck me, Chris!"

Chris was more than willing to oblige her. Even if this passion was for this night only. Keesha impatiently forced him into her office pulling his pants open exposing his silk boxers.

"Take them off,"she demanded, and he obeyed. He kicked his shoes from his feet while stepping out of his pants. She snatched his boxers down. She wrapped her arms around his neck, pulling herself up. Her legs clasped around his waist moving and writhing with uncountable movements causing Chris to stumble backwards a couple of paces before catching himself. Keesha propelled herself against him, kissing and biting at his lips hungrily. She pleaded for his strong masculinity. Chris obliging, laid her on the desk placing her legs over his shoulders and aggressively pressing forward. "Harder,"she demanded, trying to satisfy the unrelenting craving. Tightening his hands around her thighs, Keesha's inner muscles contracted around him. He did as she requested. His force he thought brutal but she beckoned more. Her lust for him was insatiably insane. Nothing he did pleased or satisfied her climatic crave. He turned her over remembering her preferred position and deepened his plunge.

Her climax was great, even shocking him. She pushed him to the floor mounting him with skill and authority. Her inner wall that previously marked her end now crumbled at her force. He feared the damage gripping her sides trying to slow her pace but she resisted. It was like she wanted him to hurt her. She bit his tongue and then his neck. He had never seen her in such a lustful fury. Her juices came down like lava. Her ending was as abrupt as was her beginning. Her eyes, though unfocused were on his and a single teardrop fell from her eye into his. He waited for a response but received none. She collapsed to the side sleeping instantaneously. He tried to whisper in her ear but received no response.

Chris carried her upstairs to her bed then ran water in a pan. He bathed her then placed her on the bed covering her. Her hair was in a wild frenzy. He brushed it away from her face with his hand. She responded to none of his touches. He felt used. Chris decided to go home and wait for her to call him.

He found his clothes after cleaning himself and made his way out of her house. In his car, he couldn't believe what just happened. Keesha was like another person. Never in a million years would he have expected her to respond to him like that and just turn off. He looked up at her window one last time to see if she might have gotten up...nothing...he drove off.

Michelle had taken all the pictures she needed and she even took the liberty of videotaping the act. She placed the tape and film in an envelope and headed to her friend's house so that he could develop the film and deliver it. She waited patiently for him to tell her that they were ready. Finally, he handed them to her and she looked at them. At first, she felt a twinge of jealousy then remembered the purpose of the pictures.

She put them in the envelope and addressed it to Jamal Warner then handed it to her friend along with an envelope with money. She left his house and returned to her own. He grabbed his bags and drove to the airport. He would first deliver the package to Jamal. Then he would continue on to his mother's house as he had originally planned. The only difference was that since he was doing this favor for Michelle, his trip was free plus he had spending money.

It was a two hour flight and as planned, he had a cab take him to Jamal Warner's residence, and he placed the package on his door step, then rung the bell so that Jamal would pick it up. He returned to the cab and told the driver to hurry up.

The driver sped up and they were off of Jamal's property before he could get to the door. Jamal looked down the road and could see nothing but taillights from a car speeding up the road. He looked both ways and saw nothing. As he was about to go back into the house, he saw a package on his step. He reached down and picked it up then thought, this is a strange time for someone to be delivering a package! He brought the envelope into the house and put his ear to it. The label read urgent--view immediately. He opened it,and found a videotape dated with tonight's date. He also found an envelope full of pictures.

His first thought was Keesha must have been surprising him with something but when he put the tape into the VCR, and saw the intense sex being carried out by his fiancee and her ex-lover, he became confused and hurt at the same time. He knew that the tape was devised to hurt him but he had to find out why she would cheat on him after accepting his proposal.

Jamal didn't bother packing any clothes, knowing that his stay would be short. He picked up his car keys and made his way to his car. It was three o'clock in the morning and there was no traffic to slow down his journey. He didn't know exactly what he would say or do when he got to Keesha's but she would give him a decent explanation for deliberately breaking his heart. How could she do something so deceitful? She received nothing less than love and kindness from him, and she betrayed his trust.

Then he wondered whether or not this was a trick to make him think it happened tonight when it was a long time ago. He picked up the pictures, noticing his ring on her finger wrapped around the hips of another man while his body was joined with hers. He could feel his heart racing as he neared her house.

At seven o'clock in the morning, there was nothing stirring in her house. He looked at the keys she had given him wondering if he should use them. He thought about it for a moment and decided that he'd better ring her bell and let her answer it. He took a deep breath and rung the bell. He waited receiving no answer. He pressed it again, still no answer. He gave it one more try before using his keys. He knew that she should have been home as her car was parked right outside.

The house was quiet, nothing stirring. He saw her clothes scattered in her office. They were the same clothes she had on in the pictures. Everything looked as it did in the pictures. His heart sank when he realized that it had to be true. He continued upstairs wondering if he would find them cloaked in each other's arms. He opened her room door and found her asleep in her bed. There was no one next to her but by the looks of her hair, he could tell that she went to bed without doing her usual ritual. Keesha would never go to bed without wrapping her hair or braiding it. She couldn't stand for it to be out of order like that.

He moved to her bedside fighting emotion.

"Keesha," he called. "Keesha." His first thought was that she was ignoring him. No matter what, he loved her and would give her the opportunity to explain. He knelt at her side placing his hands on her face. It was hot. His cheek descended to her nose and her breath was hot against his skin. He lifted her eyelid and she stared blankly. There was no response to anything he did.

Jamal began to worry. He found a towel and ran cold water on it then placed it on her head. He sat her up to see if she would at least respond to him. Her skin was so hot it scared him. "Keesha," he called, "please answer me!"

"Jamal," she said in a weak tone. "I'm so sorry, Jamal. I let you down." Then she blacked out again. Jamal carried her to his car and quickly headed to the hospital. When he arrived, he identified himself as a doctor and told them that Keesha had a high fever and wasn't coherent. The staff brought out a bed and wheeled her into an examining room. Blood was drawn and she was put on watch until the results came back.

Sitting at her bedside, Jamal wondered what had happened to her and why Chris would leave her if he knew she was sick. Had he taken advantage of her in her weak state? he wondered. His nerves caused him to pace back and fourth, to and from her window. The nurse told him that maybe he should wait outside in the waiting room until the results returned. Sitting here would do no good.

"No, I think my place is here by her side just in case something goes wrong or she opens her eyes and is frightened because of her whereabouts." The nurse understood his concern and assured him that her vital signs were being monitored and any movements would be detected. Jamal told her that he would remain in the room until he at least knew what was wrong with her.

He sat in the chair at the side of her bed. Leaning back sleep called him. Jamal pulled his chair closer to Keesha, clasping her hand in his. He kissed it then said a silent prayer. Becoming fatigued from the long drive and course of events, Jamal fell asleep.

The doctor returned to Keesha's room along with three police officers. He had contacted the local police upon getting the results of her blood test. Jamal looked confused, he wondered why the doctor would need police to give him the results of her tests. The doctor told Jamal that Keesha had been given a substance called Cantharidin. He said it has an undeserved reputation for being an aphrodisiac. It's a drug used for sexual manipulation. The street name for it is Spanish Fly. He turned to face Keesha's unconscious body and injected something into her intravenous tube. This medication should stabilize her until the drug leaves her system although there is no real cure for this drug. The effects can be devastating. It's really up to her to pull through this. Jamal couldn't believe that Chris would sink so low to give her such a drug. He guessed he just wouldn't accept the fact that she had left him. Without warning, the police grabbed Jamal by the arms telling him that they had to take him into custody until they could speak with Keesha to find out who gave her the drug.

Jamal was enraged. "You think I did it? I would never do a thing like that, I had no need to, we are getting married in May." The officers only listened to him then interrupted him to say rape may be a charge as well. Jamal felt sick. Since medicine was his field he imagined the worst. The tears which needed repairing, the child they may never have due to her damaged uterus. If   only they would listen, he could fix her. He didn't think about the pictures dropped on his doorstep last night. He went along quietly and asked the doctor to please get an answer from Keesha when she woke up and to keep him informed of her condition.

The officers escorted Jamal to their vehicle and took him to the station to make up a report. When Jamal got there, he was seated in an office and was questioned by the arresting officers.

"So, Mr. Warner, where did you get the drugs you used to impair that woman into having sex with you?"

"I have no idea what you're talking about. When I came into New York this morning just before I brought her in, she was lying on her bed sleeping. I tried to wake her, and she didn't respond. When I touched her face, I realized that she had a fever so I picked her up and brought her to the hospital."

"Are you denying that you gave her the drug or that you fucked her?" Jamal was appalled at the officer's use of that word when he spoke of what they shared.

"No, I did not make love to her last night. As I said before, she was unconscious when I got there and I thought she was asleep at first." The officer looked at him and could tell that something was missing from the story.

"You said you found her asleep in the bed when you arrived, is that right?"

"Yes."

"Then who let you into her house?"

"I have keys to her house, as I said before, we are engaged to be married in May. She gave me her keys so that when I'm in New York, I could let myself in until she arrived if she wasn't at home."

"Well, sir, what I can't seem to understand is why you would be visiting her so late at night. Didn't you say earlier that you live in Virginia?"

"Yes, I do live in Virginia. I received a package last night that disturbed me so I decided to pay her a visit."

"What was in the package?"

"Pictures and a videotape."

"What kind of pictures." Jamal took a deep breath because he didn't want to mention what he saw on the tape but it would be the only thing that would clear his name, at least as far as possible rape was concerned.

"Someone had dropped off this package to my home last night, rung my doorbell and drove away. When I got to the door, they were gone. The only thing I saw was a package on my step. So I brought it into the house and took a look at it. They were pictures of Keesha and a man in compromising positions."

"What do you mean when you say compromising positions?" Jamal looked at him with scorn because he knew exactly what he meant.

"The package contains pictures of Keesha and another man having sex. The video confirmed that they were having sex."

"What makes you think they were taken the same night. Someone would have had to really go out of their way to get that to you the same night it happened!"

"Whoever sent it must want us to break up!"

"Do you know the man in the picture?"

"No, I can only guess that his name may be Chris, someone I've heard a great deal about. He and Keesha had a thing before we met, and Keesha left him for me."

"Do you think he would have to drug her to coerce her into bed?"

"I would guess so since we are getting married. I couldn't see Keesha jeopardizing our relationship for something like sex."

"This guy seems to be young, maybe he does it better!" The officer was trying to make Jamal lose his temper so he would incriminate himself.

Jamal only looked at him. He wouldn't even dignify that statement with an answer. Besides, he knew that he didn't have to prove himself to this officer; he knew how Keesha felt about their lovemaking.

When the officer was satisfied with Jamal's answers, he told the officer to fingerprint him and take him to his cell.

"Don't I get to make a call?"

"Oh yeah, but no long-distance calls are allowed."

The officer led Jamal to the telephone and Jamal put in his calling card number and punched in his attorney's number. His attorney's secretary picked up the telephone. "Hi, Diane, let me speak to Jonathan." He waited a couple of seconds and Jonathan picked up the line. "Hi, Jonathan, I can't speak long, but I ran into a situation and I need your help." I've been arrested here in New York for something I didn't do, and I need you to help me straighten out this situation and protect my rights."

Jonathan knew that right now was not the time to ask questions. He got the information to Jamal's whereabouts and told him that he would be there as fast as he could. Jamal hung up the telephone as his time was up and followed the officer to the cell. He was glad he didn't have to share the cell with anyone at the moment, giving him time to rest a little. He hoped that his attorney would get there soon.

CHAPTER
34

The day seemed to go by slowly as Chris wondered whether Keesha would give him a call. Her behavior last night had taken him by surprise. They had made love on several occasions but never as rough and uncontrolled as the way she performed the previous night. He didn't know whether he liked it that way or not. The thing he couldn't understand was how she could go from a roaring tiger to a deep sleep. Chris had planned to discuss Keesha's change of heart but before he could talk to her she had attacked him. He wanted to know where their relationship was going or if she was just putting him on another roller coaster ride.

How could she have just fallen asleep like that? he wondered. A relaxed state he could understand, but not out cold. Had he been used? He couldn't put the pieces together. Chris retraced his steps that night to see if maybe he had gotten the wrong idea from her, and she was just submitting to his own lascivious desires. Then he remembered that she had attacked him first.

The telephone did not ring the entire day, and he wondered whether he would see Keesha again.

Ebony had arrived at the airport early Saturday morning. She wanted to get to Keesha's first thing, so that if Keesha needed to get some last-minute things done, she would be there to help her. She waited and waited but Keesha never showed up. Ebony found a pay telephone to call Keesha to see if she had forgotten to pick her up or over slept. Her telephone rang three times and then her machine picked up. There was no special message on it, which was strange for Keesha. If she stepped out, she would leave a detailed message to let her guest know that she was around and that she would call them back soon or when she would be returning. Ebony waited another fifteen minutes and decided that she had better try her line again. When the machine picked up, Ebony left a message telling Keesha that she was going to catch a cab. If Keesha got to the airport after she left, she would know that she was on her way to the house.

Ebony picked up a cab and gave the driver Keesha's address. Ebony was worried about Keesha and wondered what could have kept her for two hours. One thing she knew about Keesha was that she was punctual. If she told you eight o'clock, then she meant eight o'clock. The cab finally pulled up in front of Keesha's suburban home. Ebony noticed Keesha's car parked in front of her house so she knew that she should be home. Ebony rung the bell, but no one answered. She rang the bell again, still no answer. She waited a moment and wondered what was going on. Ebony sat on the step and wondered what to do next.

While sitting there, Michelle walked up to her. "Hi, I'm Michelle, looking for Keesha, huh?" Ebony looked up at her. She hadn't noticed her coming down the block. She just seemed to appear in front of her.

"Yes, I'm looking for Keesha. Have you seen her today?"

"No, I haven't seen her since yesterday. I stopped by to help her with any last-minute things she needed to do. After we had gotten the china and crystal out of the way, Keesha said she was going to lie down because she wasn't feeling very well."

"What do you mean she wasn't feeling well? What did she say was bothering her?"

"She didn't say, she just said that she felt funny and would see me tomorrow." The two women looked at each other and wondered what to do.

"You can wait at my house if you want to, and I'll try to call Keesha." Ebony said she'd appreciate her calling Keesha for her but she'd rather wait in front of the house.

"suit yourself, but you're welcome to come in,"Michelle said.

Ebony sat there and waited for Michelle to reach her house. She got up close to the door and listened for the telephone to ring. When she heard it, she waited to see if she would hear Keesha stirring or if she could tell if the machine picked up. When she didn't hear any response, she sat back down in front of the house.

Time elapsed while Ebony waited for Keesha. She waited for her for more than an hour and still no Keesha. Ebony left her bags in front of Keesha's house and decided that she had better start asking the neighbors if they had seen Keesha today. When she neared the first neighbor's house, a car pulled up. An attractive young fellow walked up to Keesha's house. He saw the bags and wondered if Keesha was taking one of her spontaneous trips again.

Ebony called out to him, and he looked in her direction. She figured that it must have been the guy that Keesha had talked about. She hurried over in his direction.

Chris wondered who she was. He had never seen her before but she was indeed pretty. Keesha had a nice group of friends.

"Hi, I'm Ebony, one of Keesha's friends. I've been looking for her all morning, and no one has seen her today."

"I'm Chris. I haven't seen or heard from her since last night. I decided to stop by to pay her a visit."

"Did she appear to be sick when you saw her?"

"No, she didn't seem to be sick at all. I saw nothing wrong with her." Ebony thought to herself. She recalled the woman, Michelle down the street mentioning that she was sick and now this Chris character was saying that he saw her last night, and she was fine.

"I see her car is here, how long have you been waiting for her?"

"She was supposed to pick me up at the airport at seven this morning, but she never came."Ebony explained that she had taken a cab to Keesha's house. Keesha wasn't answering the telephone or anything. Chris wondered about that himself. Keesha didn't call or answer his many calls today.

"Maybe she stepped out with someone else and didn't realize that time was passing as quickly as it did." Chris heard his car telephone ringing so he returned to answer it. Ebony watched him talk to someone. Then he returned to where she stood. Chris hated to leave her standing there waiting for her friend outside by herself, but he had business to attend. "Keesha isn't the type of person to stand anyone up, so I guess that she will be back soon." Then he walked away and told Ebony to tell Keesha that he stopped by, and he would catch up with her later.

Considering that he hadn't seen his mother in a week, Chris went down the block. He didn't bother ringing the bell since she was in a wheelchair and didn't want to put her out of the way answering the door. There was a foul odor reeking around the house. Chris checked the garbage cans to see if it was full. But there was nothing in it. He returned to the door and unlocked it. Instantly upon opening the door, the vestige liked to take his breath. "Damn,"he swore. "Mom, are you alright? What is that repugnant odor?"His mother didn't answer. Chris had never smelled anything like it. He made his way to the kitchen and his mother sat at the table in her wheelchair unmoving. Chris called out to her again while approaching her. "Ma."His mother was dead. She was sitting in excrements, which must have been there some time now. Maggots swarmed in her lap with flies swarming like buzzards over her body. "Get away from he!"he screamed fanning at the flies, fighting them away from his mother. She was gone. He walked around to face her. There was nothing he could do. He neglected her and she died right in her chair. "Damnit, I should have been her for her."Chris picked up the phone and called the police. Feeling weak, he hurried outside and sat on the steps. Ebony could see him and he seemed distraught.

"Hey Chris, are you alright?"she yelled bout he didn't respond. Ebony took quick steps in his direction and a disturbing odor hit her. She felt like turning around but continued over to him. She recognized that scent. Someone was dead. "Chris who was it?"

"My mother,"he said standing up and collapsing in her arms. The cry he tried so hard to hold in, burst out like a wild beast. Uncontrollable tears streamed down onto Ebony's shoulder.

"I'm so sorry. What happened? Was she sick?"

"She had been attacked a few weeks ago and was recovering. I don't know what happened. I should have been here to take care of her. I let this happen because I resented her for interfering with my relationship with Keesha. I couldn't bring myself to speak to her. I didn't know she was sick."

"Where is your father?"

"He died a few years ago. I have no one now."

Ebony tried to comfort him. After a while, the police arrived along with someone from the coroners' office. Chris told Ebony that he would be all right and that she should go back to Keesha's house and wait for her to return.

"Will you tell her that Christine is dead? And that I stopped by to see her."

"I will. You take care of yourself."Ebony returned to Keesha's porch. She watched at a distance as the police questioned Chris. At long last, the body was removed from the house and Chris got into his car and drove off.

As much as Chris hurt, he knew that he had to get to the office. Hopefully he could keep his emotions in check long enough to get through the meeting. Saturday meetings were rare but when they came up, he knew that he couldn't miss it. The job was becoming ever more demanding as he climbed the success ladder. Chris was by himself now. No mother, no father, and no Keesha.

Keesha had regained consciousness sometime that afternoon. The doctor came in to see how she was coming along. He checked her vital signs and temperature. Everything seemed to be in order. Keesha had a slight headache but that was all. She had calmed down since she first woke up as she was not sure of her whereabouts. Now that she knew where she was, she wondered why and how she got there.

"Hello, Ms. Smalls, how do you feel today?"

"I have a slight headache, but I'm all right I guess. Why am I here?"

"You don't know?"

"No, all I know is that I woke up here in the hospital. Am I all right?"

"Yes, according to your tests, you should be just fine in a couple of days."

"How did I get here?"

"A man by the name of Jamal Warner brought you in. You were unconscious at the time. He waited to see if you were all right but when the results from your blood test came back, I had to contact the police." Keesha became confused. The last person she remembered being with was Chris. How did Jamal get there?

"Why would the police be interested in my blood test?"

"There was a large dose of a drug known as Spanish Fly in your system. The drug causes the victim to become aroused. If this drug is misused, the results can be deadly or cause a permanent psychological imbalance."

"So where is Jamal? I'm glad he got me here in time before any damage could be done."

"Well, Jamal was arrested."

"Arrested, why?"The doctor could see the alarm in Keesha's face as she fought to sit up. He tried to make her relax. "Understand that when someone does something like this to you, he doesn't love you. He's only looking for fulfillment of his own sexual desires.

"Excuse me. Jamal would never do anything like that to hurt me.

He would never use such a thing. He doesn't need to use drugs to arouse me."

"Then if he didn't give you the drug, who did?" Keesha thought about it, and she couldn't figure out when it might have gotten into her system. She realized that she was taken by an unusual sexual craving and Chris had stopped by but he didn't have time to give her anything.

"I don't know,"she said, confused.

"Did you take it yourself?"

"No, where would I have gotten a thing like that?"

"Well, if you didn't take it yourself, and you don't want to give up the person who gave it to you, then there is nothing that will prove that your friend didn't give it to you. He said that he was your fiancé so I presume that he was the one that did the damage to your vaginal canal.

"What damage?"

"You have several tears in your vagina that were caused by an act of violent sexual intercourse. We had a hard time patching it up. You don't feel it right now because we have been giving you pain killers intravenously. Now are you going to tell me that your friend didn't do that?" Keesha didn't know how to answer that as her lover was not Jamal last night, it was Chris.

"No, he didn't. I slept with someone else last night." Keesha tried to say it with a straight face and not allow the doctor to notice her shame in seeming promiscuous.

"Do you have multiple partners?"

"No!"

"Is Jamal Warner your fiance'?"

"Yes, he is but I did not sleep with him last night."

"Are you sure you're not just trying to cover for his mistreatment of you?"

"Yes I'm sure." The doctor shook his head and told Keesha that the officers should be returning sometime that day to get her statement. She would also be required to reveal the name and location of the person responsible for her present condition. Then he turned and left the room.

Keesha was worried about Jamal. Whatever was happening in he life was pulling him into it. Now he was sitting in jail because she wa attacked. She realized that it must have been Saturday. She buzzed the nurse to confirm the day. When the nurse came into the room, she tol her that she was sorry about what happened to her and that Jamal ha told her that when she woke up to tell Keesha he love her. Keesha felt something swelling within her heart.

"Would you do me a favor?"

"Sure, what can I do for you?"

"Would you call the precinct and ask the arresting officer to please stop by the hospital?"

"No problem. Girl, you get that man out of there, I can tell he doesn't belong. I'm sure that whatever happened to you, he couldn't have done it. I mean I couldn't even pry him from your side."

"Thanks, nurse. I really appreciate that." The nurse winked and squeezed Keesha's hand to let her know that she understood what she's going through. When the nurse returned to her station, she dialed the precinct number the officer left for her in case Keesha woke up. She asked for Officer Thompson. When the call was switched over to him, the nurse informed him that Keesha had awakened.

"Did she say anything?"he asked.

"Yes, she wants you to release Mr. Warner. She said that he had nothing to do with her condition."

"Well, I can't do that until I speak with her in person."

"I understand."

"I will be there shortly." He hung up the telephone and went to Jamal's holding cell. He was sitting on a hard bench with his hands clasped around the back of his head. He had his head between his knees.

"Hey, Mr. Warner"the officer called to him. "It's a possibility that you will be out of here soon. Apparently your fiancee has awakened, and she told the nurse to have you released, however, I can't let you go until I get back from the hospital with her statement."

Jamal nodded in understanding and thanked the officer for going out of his way to help him. The officer told him that he was sorry Jamal was arrested, but it was procedure.

The officer left the holding area and made his way to the hospital. He realized that time was of the essence and the sooner he could get there the sooner he could free an innocent man.

CHAPTER
35

Every minute seemed like an eternity as Jamal sat in his cell wondering how long it would take them to clear his name. He wondered whether Keesha knew her assailant, and if she did, he wondered how he was able to drug her.

He envisioned his lovely wife-to-be in the compromising positions displayed in the photos he had received. Seeing Keesha with someone else sexually sickened him to his stomach. Of course, he knew that it was not her fault. In fact, he was glad that it wasn't at her own moral will because that would have meant that she wanted it to happen, which would have tainted his high opinion of her.

She seemed so helpless as her limp, unconscious body lay on the hospital bed. What would her mental state be like now that she was awake? he wondered. Would she be able to function as she used to? He wondered how he could have let her out of his sight. He should have made her stay with him. This wouldn't have happened if she stayed at his home in Virginia, and he wouldn't be spending the night in Long Island County Jail. There was no way that he could have slept another wink after receiving those pictures without confronting her, and it was not something that he could speak with her about over the telephone. Eye contact was very important although he still didn't get the eye contact that he wanted. He knew that it wasn't her fault. The person who did this to her would pay for this hideous crime.

Why were these things happening to her? Who was doing them and why? Could Chris want to hurt her? Why would he need to give her such a powerful stimulate to excite her? Just the thought of Chris taking her with her senses impaired made Jamal angry. Keesha meant everything to him, and he was not going to let him get away with it. Then the nerve of him to send photos to his house was totally out of line. As Jamal continued to ponder the hurtful things of his heart, a officer came to his cell.

"Mr. Warner?"

"Yes."

"There is an attorney outside. He says he's here to represent you. His name is Jonathan Kranzler. Do you recognize that name?"

"Yes, I do." The officer waved to someone down the hall, and Jamal could hear footsteps nearing his cell. After a few seconds, a handsome, tall, well-built Jewish man appeared at Jamal's cell door.

"Hello, Jamal. It's been a long time since I've heard from you!" He smiled to see Jamal helpless behind steel doors, like a bird in a cage. "So..."Just as he was about to finish his sentence, the officer opened Jamal's cell and let the well-dressed man in. The officer waited until he saw that Jonathan appeared to be alright then told him that he'd be right down the corridor if he needed him. Jamal looked at Jonathan with scorn then stood up to shake his friend's hand.

"Thanks for coming to see me on such short notice!"

"These situations are always short notice, unless of course, it's premeditated and you had already let me know that you were going to be arrested!" He smiled to let Jamal know that everything was okay. He took a seat next to Jamal on the bench, removed his pad from his briefcase and prepared to take notes. "So, tell me, what did they accuse you of? I want to know what happened, when, where and why if you know!" He looked at Jamal, anxious to hear the charges since the officers at the front desk wouldn't give him any information.

"First of all, they are accusing me of administering an illegal and banned drug."

"Ooh, serious business. Did they find it on you?"

"No. When I brought my Fiancee to the hospital yesterday, the blood tests showed this drug and the doctor called the cops and I was arrested since I was the one to bring her in." The attorney looked at him as though to say, "something is missing out of this picture." He raised his eyebrows and decided that he should ask a question before he went further in his explanation.

"So if you brought her to the hospital, why didn't she clear your name?"

"Because she was unconscious when we got there, I had no idea that she was overdosed. All I knew is that when I got there, she was asleep, and her face was hot and feverish. When I received no response from her after trying to talk to her, I rushed her to the hospital."

"So in other words, the doctor assumed that you were the one to have given her the drug! Why?"

"Because I indicated that she was my fiancee and the doctor automatically inferred that I must have given her this drug to stimulate her."

"Did the officers give you a chance to explain your side of the story?"

"No, the officers just read me my rights and brought me here where I've been since yesterday."

The attorney squirmed in his seat and tried to think of a way to ask his next question. He knew that it would be a touchy situation but it had to come out. He looked at his friend, and Jamal could see that he was uncomfortable about asking him something.

"Look Jonathan, if there is something you need to say, please just say it. We've been friends for a very long time, and I know that whatever you have to say to me is all in the name of helping me out of this situation."

Jonathan was relieved to hear Jamal say that so he proceeded. "Jamal, if your fiancee was found to have a drug in her system, that would mean that she had to have taken it within a twenty-four-hour period, otherwise, her blood would have cleaned it out. So I need to know where you were within that period of time before you found her in that condition. I need to know what made you drive to New York at that time and how you got into her house and finally, it would also mean that she must have been sleeping with someone else unless she expected you and was preparing for you."

Jamal took a deep breath before answering the questions. He hated to explain what transpired but it was the only way. "I received pictures on my doorstep the night before last, and they were pictures of Keesha with another man. I was hurt and angry about it so I decided that I would pay her a visit and find out why she would do such a thing to me. When I arrived, I rang her bell several times. When no one answered, I decided that I would use the keys she gave me. I opened the door and walked through her house calling her name. She never responded. I saw the same clothes in her study that she was wearing in the picture. When I saw that, I assumed that the guy was still there, and I wanted to catch them in the act so that she wouldn't lie to me. When I finally made it up to her bedroom, I saw her sleeping in her bed. Her hair was in a tangled mass, and Keesha would never go to bed without grooming herself. She can't stand for her hair to be out of place while she's sleeping." Jamal paused to recalculate the events of the night he found his beloved in her bed near death.

"I called her name and lightly shook her waiting for a response. When she didn't answer, I became worried. At first I thought she was ignoring me and hoping that I would see that she was sleeping and leave her alone, but when I touched her cheeks the heat that radiated from her skin was like fire. Right then I knew that she was sick. I rushed into the bathroom and wet a cloth with cold water when something told me to take her to the hospital. She didn't say or do anything the entire time...no wait, she mumbled I'm sorry Jamal, in a low, faint voice, which didn't seem coherent anyway. I called the hospital from my cellular telephone and told the hospital to have a staff ready as I was bringing a comatose patient over, and she needed immediate assistance. When I arrived, they rushed her into a room and started looking to stabilize her. The doctor took blood and I waited a couple of hours for the results to come back. When the results came back, the doctor returned with two police officers who instead of giving me a handshake for saving her life, slapped handcuffs around my wrists and welcomed me with this uncomfortable cell!"

It was only when Jamal saw the attorney sitting at the far edge of the bunk that he became aware of his composure. Jamal had clasped his hand around his fists and started banging on the bed making it tremble. The recollection of the past events brought nothing less than pure anger and frustration out of him. He wanted to lash out but couldn't. His demeanor wouldn't let him. His sophisticated mannerism wouldn't let him. His desire to maintain his sanity and composure compelled him to regain control of himself and not alarm his fear-stricken attorney. Even though the attorney knew the depth of their friendship, he also recognized the power of anger, especially in a black man.

"Jamal,"his attorney called. "calm down. You're getting a little excited here! I'm only asking questions to help me defend you. Not for a moment, did I think that you could have done such a thing."

"Jonathan, I know you're not taking a coward seat toward me? I didn't mean to raise my voice, it's just that this situation makes me angry when I think about it." He clasped his hands around the back of his head and fought to hold back his tears.

"Do you have any idea who the other guy might be?"

"No, not really. I do know that she was seeing a young man by the name of Chris who she had been engaged to."

"Did she every give you any indication that he was the jealous type or perhaps had became enraged when she broke off the engagement?"

"No, she just told me that she was hurt by it, and was sorry that she had to do that to him. She didn't say anything else that would make me feel that her life was in danger." The attorney shook his head and asked Jamal where he could find the pictures that were sent to his house. Jamal told him that they were left in his car, which was probably in the police impound. He patted Jamal on the knee and told him that he would get him out of this situation. As he turned to the cell door, Jamal told him that he might be cleared in a matter of hours now, because the arresting officer was on his way to the hospital to get a statement from Keesha.

"You didn't tell me that she regained consciousness."

"I just found out a few minutes before you came in!"

"Would you like me to hold off until the officer returns with information?"

"No, you gather up as much information as you can, that way, if something goes wrong, at least I will have you working on my behalf to clear my name." The attorney nodded in agreement, then summoned the officer to let him out. "Thanks, man, I really appreciate this," Jamal said.

"By the way, give me Keesha's home address so that I can tag along with the officers, have a look at her home and see if there is any evidence of foul play." Jamal gave him the address then the attorney exited the cell along with the officer.

Jamal remained seated. The last thing he needed was for the officer to think that he was trying to attack him by standing near the cell door while he was closing it. As he continued to wait for the word from the arresting officer, Jamal decided that he would take the quiet time to relax. He wondered how things were going back at the office. He had a couple of patients who were due to deliver any day now, and he wasn't there to attend to them.

The attorney received authorization to have Jamal's car released. He paid the three-hundred-dollar fee to have it removed from impound. Of course, their price was steep as his car was only there for one day. He would take up that issue at a later date. The important thing right now was to find out what was in the envelope Jamal talked about. He got into the car. The officer waited to see if he would look for something in particular. The attorney sat in the driver's seat and started the car. He looked at the officer and waited instructions to leave the lot. The officer stood there a moment just to keep him waiting, he then directed him to bear to the left until he reached the guard at the gate where he would have to show his pass.

At the gate, the officer checked his pass then allowed him to proceed through the exit. He looked at the directions Jamal gave him to Keesha's residence. He found the highway and drove until he reached exit 18b. He looked at his watch and noticed it was noon. He pulled in front of Keesha's house and noticed a woman sitting on the porch with her bags at the door.

"Hello ma'am, my name is Jonathan Kranzler, I'm an attorney." Ebony looked at him wondering why Keesha would need an attorney the day of her party. Then she wondered if it might have been a client.

"Hi, I'm Ebony, a friend of Keesha's. Are you one of her clients?"

"No, I'm here to get a look around the house."

"Well Keesha isn't home right now. I've been waiting for her since seven o'clock this morning. No one has seen nor heard from her since last night."

"How come you've been waiting for her so long?"

"Because she is supposed to be having a get-together, and I wanted to help her get some last-minute things done. Keesha is normally prepared and would never stand anyone up, I hope that everything is alright!" He noticed a note of concern in her voice and decided that he would let her know what was going on.

"Your friend Keesha is in the hospital."

"In the hospital! What happened?"

"She's recovering from an overdose of a hormonal stimulant!"

"Why would Keesha be taking something like that?"

"Someone must have slipped it to her and took advantage of her sexually."

"Did they catch the guy that did it?"

"They have the guy that brought her to the hospital, her Fiancee."

"Jamal? He would never give her a thing like that. He loves her and would do anything for her. Not to mention, that she loves him. There is no way he would need to take advantage of her. In fact, they are scheduled to get married the thirtieth of next month!" Ebony became confused. None of the answers given to her made sense. She knew Jamal for a very long time and knew that he was certainly not capable of committing such a nefarious crime.

"I know, that's why I'm here, I'm trying to get him out of there."

"Why didn't Keesha clear his name?"

"Because she was unconscious when they arrested him, and the police assumed that Jamal gave Keesha the stimulant during one of their sexual escapades!"

"Is Keesha all right? I've got to get there to see her. Do you know where she is? Can you take me there? Besides, there is nothing I could imagine in the house to clear Jamal's name. We've got to talk to her. She's the only one who can say who did this to her." The attorney opened the manila envelope in his hands and showed her a picture of a man engaging in a sexual act with Keesha.

"Do you know this man?" Ebony looked at the picture, then another where the man's features were more defined.

"He was here earlier looking for Keesha. His name is Chris. Keesha used to be involved with him before she decided to marry Jamal. Keesha never mentioned that he had an obsession with her! He loved her too. I don't think he would have done something like that either. Not based on what I've heard about him."

"Are you saying that Keesha consented to having sex with him last night?"

"Hey, only she could answer that. Besides, if his intentions were to hurt her, he certainly wouldn't show up at her house the next day looking for her with a handful of beautiful flowers."

"Maybe they were, 'I'm sorry' flowers."

"No, if brother love overdosed her with drugs, he would have taken her to the hospital and brought her flowers to say `I'm sorry,' not pretend he had no clue why she didn't call him. That just wouldn't make sense."

"Well look, Jamal gave me the keys to her house. Let me take a quick look around. You can put your bags in and then we'll go to the hospital to see if Keesha can straighten this whole mess out! There is one problem though, the drug is illegal in this country and someone will have to answer for it. They will not let the issue go. Anyone who came in contact with her and a drink that night will be arrested as a suspect." Ebony shrugged her shoulders as they walked into the house. Ebony looked into Keesha's study where she saw Keesha's clothes and underwear.

"Umm seems like it was a wild, freaky night to me. That must be some good stuff because I didn't think Keesha had it in her! She definitely wouldn't leave her clothes thrown wildly about the house. Keesha is very neat. Knowing her, she would neatly fold each piece before she would engage in sex," Ebony said.

The attorney looked at her and wondered how she was in bed. There was something about her that gave him the sense that she would give his body a new definition of the term turned out.

Ebony walked off with her tight belly exposed, knowing that her movements teased the attorney. He would never get to taste her brown sugar. His clear blue eyes were like a microscope as he slowly dissected her inch by inch.

Every step she took seemed sensuous. She tantalized him with her movements, although Ebony hadn't given him any thought, in fact, she hadn't paid his wondering eyes any attention.

They headed for the kitchen. They noticed china and crystal champagne glasses stacked on the table. Then there were two dirty glasses in the sink. The attorney wrote that down and told Ebony not to touch anything. The glasses in the sink would probably be the just the evidence needed to clear his client and friend's name as well as expose the real adversary.

"Keesha had to be drugged no more than an hour before the attack. Well not attack because I'm sure she was more than willing with that drug in her system, so the traces of the drug should be in these glasses. The assailant probably didn't have time to clean up his act if these are indeed the glasses used. We need to find out who was drinking with her that night. Jamal said he took her to the hospital from her bed. That means we should take a look upstairs to see if there might be another glass or set of glasses up there."

"I would think that since her clothes are all down here that she must have been drugged down here. Who would leave the bedroom upstairs to return downstairs to engage in sex?"Ebony asked.

"Hey, maybe the stuff didn't kick in while they were upstairs and she was escorting him out when she attacked him or he touched her to see if she was ready!"

"Well, Keesha is engaged to Jamal so she wouldn't have had Chris upstairs in her right mind anyway, so no, I don't think they would have been upstairs. He did the whole thing right down here. Not to mention, if Keesha had to wait an hour to be stimulated, she would have cleaned these glasses. She would never allow dirty dishes to just sit around in her sink--not even one minute after use. As soon as he finished, she would have taken the glass from him and into the kitchen to clean it. That's just the way she is!"

The attorney could see that Ebony was taking offense to his suggestions, so he decided that he would just make his way to the hospital and try to get some answers from Keesha.

"Why don't we go over to the hospital and see how your friend is doing and see if maybe she feels like answering some questions? Besides, Jamal said that the officer was on his way to the hospital to ask her some questions since she had regained consciousness."

CHAPTER
36

Officer Thompson waited at the nurses' station for permission to enter Keesha's room. The doctor returned to acknowledge that Keesha was awake and coherent enough to answer any questions that he might have. He followed the doctor into Keesha's room.

When he entered the room. He realized how beautiful she was. Her hair had been brushed into a neat, radiant ponytail pulled around to her left shoulder so that she wouldn't be resting on it.

"Hello, Ms. Smalls.How do you feel today?"

"I guess I'm all right, a little worn, that's all."

"Are you up for some questions right now, or should I come back later?"

"No, no, please, the sooner, the better." Keesha pressed the button on her bed to raise her back into a reclining position so that she didn't have to look up at the officer. He noted her discomfort and decided that he would have a seat so that she could be more comfortable. It wasn't normal procedure to sit on the job but he didn't want her to strain her neck trying to look at him.

"So, tell me from the beginning, what you remember happening the night of the incident,"he said in a low, even tone so that he wouldn't startle her.

"I was planning a get-together with some of my girlfriends to let them know that I would be getting married next month. So I spent the day trying to get my china and crystal cleaned and set up for them by the time they would be arriving today."

"Then what happened?"

"Chris, an ex-boyfriend of mine came over, and for some reason, I had this strange, insatiable desire to make love to him. I tried to shake it off, but the feeling was so intense that I couldn't resist him. I guess he sensed those urges, and everything just started to happen."

"What do you mean by `everything started to happen¿' "

"Well, we started kissing, and the next thing I knew, we were engaging in a rough but passionate sexual intercourse."

"Do you think he might have drugged you¿"

"Chris would never do a thing like that. Besides, he didn't have a chance to do it!"

"Ma'am, these things happen while the victim is occupied and not paying attention. He could have slipped it into a drink. It could have been in any medication you might have taken at that time or whatever."

"No, you don't understand, when he arrived, I was already feeling that way. He just came in the nick of time to satisfy those feelings."

"Then when did it occur¿"

"I don't know, no one was over before that." The officer sympathized with her then wondered if maybe she might have taken it herself and administered more than she needed to."

"Did you take anything that day for headache or any other reason¿"

"No, not that I remember."

"Do you normally use stimulants before or during intercourse¿"

"No, what for¿ I have no problem being stimulated!"

"These answers are not helping me. The only conclusion I can draw is you're either not remembering the events properly and don't remember sharing a drink with this Chris character or perhaps Jamal gave it to you, or you took it yourself and bit off more than you could chew!"

"Listen, officer. I'm not really sure when Jamal arrived, but right now the only thing I know is that he was not around when it happened, and I'm sure that he is already hurting because it did. We were engaged to be married in a month, but I've just broken our engagement by sleeping with my ex-lover. I don't know why he showed up when he did or when this drug could have been given to me. The only thing I know is that neither Chris nor Jamal could have or would have done such a thing to me! I'm requesting that you let my Jamal out of there so that he can go on with his life."

"Well, you have given me no evidence to let him go, and we will have to find this Chris character to question him and get to the bottom of this situation. Someone gave you the drug, and someone will be convicted for this crime, even if it's you!"

The officer got up from his chair informing Keesha that he would be getting back to her after having had the opportunity to speak with

Chris. "Give me a call if you remember anything else that might aid in the arrest of the right person."

He walked out of her room suggesting she get some rest because she would be seeing quite a bit of him. He returned to the nurses' station where he ran into Jamal's attorney and Ebony.

"Are you Officer Thompson?"

"Yes, I am, what can I do for you?"

"My name is Jonathan Kranzler, I am the attorney representing Jamal Warner who was arrested yesterday for the administering of an illegal drug and committing a crime against Keesha Smalls."

"Okay, what can I do for you?"he repeated in a nonchalant tone.

"I just left Keesha Smalls' house, and I found something that might be of interest to you, and I wanted you to get forensics over so that we can find out who shared a drink with Keesha Smalls the night before last. That may be the key to who gave her the drug, especially if there are traces of the residue still in the glasses." A spark came to the officer's eyes. Keesha had just told him that she didn't share a drink with either man and now there were two glasses in her sink.

"Okay, please take me there." He called over to the police lab and requested that the forensics people meet him at Keesha's house. Ebony asked the attorney if he needed her to return with him to the house.

"No, you can go in to see your friend. I'm sure you want to see her." Ebony received directions from the nurse, and she walked into Keesha's room.

"Keesha, how are you? I was so worried about you."

"Ebony, how did you know that I was here?"

"I ran into Jamal's attorney while sitting on your porch, and he explained everything. The attorney found something that he wants the officer and forensics to take a look at. This may clear up who did this to you!"

"I'm glad, because I would hate for either Chris, Jamal or me to go to jail for something we didn't do."

"You mean their suggesting that you took it yourself and attacked Chris on your own?"

"You got it. How's Jamal holding up?"

"I don't know. I haven't spoken with him yet. The attorney just showed up at your house, and that's all I know. By the way, Chris has been trying to reach you. He's a handsome man. I can see why you had trouble deciding which man you wanted. He is fine!" Keesha laughed at her friend's statement. It was the first laugh she had shared with anyone since the incident. She needed it.

Ebony had evaded the subject long enough. "Keesha, Chris wanted me to tell you that his mother died."

"Christine is dead? How? What happened?"he asked, not half believing what her friend was telling her.

"I don't know. When he went to the house, he found her dead. She must have been dead for a while because the odor was all outside."

"That's too bad. How did he take the news? Was he distraught?"

"Yeah, he cried on my shoulder. That guy really loves you. He said he hadn't seen his mother since you left him."

Keesha began to cry.

"What's wrong?"

"This is my fault,"Keesha managed to say weakly.

"No it isn't'. Don't you even think that her death was your fault, Chris might have killed his own mother,"Ebony said, not half believing her own words, though she did believe that he must have known something about Keesha's condition after hearing the events that led up to Keesha's injury.

"Ebony, how could you say that? Chris loves his mother. He might have been angry with her but he certainly wouldn't kill her."

"So you don't even have the slightest doubt that Chris might have done this to you since you broke up with him?"Look at how he just showed up at your house, not to mention, leaving you in the condition you were in. He could have laced your glasses with that drug some other time."

"Ebony, I don't want to think that he could have done something as vile as that. I don't believe it. I won't believe it!"

"I know honey, but you're going to have to be reasonable. This kind of thing doesn't just happen. Think about it and stop being naive."

"Can we just talk about something else while we wait for the answers to come back? I really don't want to think about this."

"Okay, I'm sorry. I should have been more sensitive about the situation. Look, I had better be getting back to the house just in case the others start coming by."

"No, don't leave me. I could really use the company right now!"

"Whatever you want, friend."

"I think I've just lost the best man I've ever known. I can't see Jamal forgiving me for this!"

"Keesha, it wasn't your fault and I'm sure that Jamal knows that. He loves you more than life itself. You were drugged, Keesha. There was no way of you resisting what happened."

"I just wonder what made Jamal stop by when he did. I mean, he does make surprise visits, but not early in the morning like that. Normally when he comes by like that he would let me know that he was in New York, and then he would come by. He showed up as though he knew something was wrong."

"You know, that is strange. Not to mention the pictures of you and Chris making love. His attorney showed them to me. They were delivered to Jamal the same night this happened," Ebony told her friend.

"What, you mean someone set this up?"

"That's what I'm telling you. Who else would benefit from Jamal's knowledge of your rekindled flame with Chris but Chris?"

"As much as I would love to deny that, it makes sense. You think he hired someone to take pictures of us having sex and had them sent to Jamal? I can imagine the torment Jamal must be feeling right now. No wonder he showed up when he did!" Keesha was concerned for her love's feelings. She had to let Chris be punished for what he'd done to her, and her Jamal."

CHAPTER
37

Michelle sat on a neighbor's porch watching the officers enter Keesha's house and wondered what was going on. She noticed that Ebony was no longer waiting for her and her bags weren't on the porch. Could Keesha have died? she wondered. Had she given her too much? She had to get rid of the rest of it before people started asking questions. Then she told herself that they would be looking for a man and not a woman.

Michelle stood so that she could get a better look at what was going on. Then she saw Chris' car pull up. He got out of the car when he saw all the police cars. He rushed over to the house and started calling for Keesha. The officer asked his identity and relationship to the resident.

"She's a friend of mine," Chris said, giving the officers his name. Jamal's attorney heard Chris' name and recognized Chris from the picture. He told the officer that Chris was wanted for questioning.

The attorney summoned Officer Thompson, telling him that Chris shown up and had been taken into custody. He recommended that he be held until the results from the fingerprints came back along with whatever substance was found in the glasses.

Michelle saw them putting handcuffs on Chris and reading him his rights. Then they seated him in the backseat of the police car. After a while two officers got into the car with him and they took him away. Michelle smiled, pleased with the outcome. Chris deserved all of it for what he did to her and their unborn child.

Keesha never showed up, and Michelle wondered how serious her damages were. She became so happy that she decided to go out and celebrate her victory over Keesha. That goes to show you that you should never come between lovers, She said to herself. Chris should have known that their love was meant to last forever. Life as he knew it, would never be the same. He would spend the rest of his life in jail for this crime, she imagined. Michelle was extremely pleased with the outcome. She couldn't control her excitement. It even caused her unborn child to leap in her belly. "That's right baby. Daddy is paying for his crime against us. He thought he would leave us for Keesha and now he will be saddling with some man named Bull in a cell."

The officers made themselves comfortable in Keesha's living room as they waited for the results.

"How long will it take for the results to come back?"Jonathan asked.

"Not long at all. I would say about two to three hours. Sometimes a match comes up quick and then again, you may not come up with one right away. We have both men into custody. Certainly one of them will prove to be the one. The question is whether or not the drug will show up in the glass."

Jonathan decided that he would pay Jamal another visit to see how he was getting along and to let him know that Chris was in custody. He told the officers that he would be at the precinct with his client, and he wanted to be contacted as soon as the results were in. Jonathan gave the officer's his pager number, and told them a code to put in so that he would know that it was them calling.

He made his way to his car and drove back to the Westchester Precinct. When he arrived, he went to the normal process to receive admittance to the holding area. When they escorted him to Jamal's cell, he saw that Jamal looked depressed. At first, Jamal didn't notice him outside his cell but then he looked up and there his friend stood. He knew that he must be bringing news to him and hoped that it would be good.

The officer opened the cell door and let the attorney in. Jonathan walked over to his friend and their hands locked in a handshake and their shoulders met in a manly hug.

"So, what's the word?"Jamal asked as he couldn't wait a second longer.

"Right now, we're waiting for results to come back from forensics regarding two glasses found in Keesha's sink. If they find traces of the drug on the glasses, they will do a fingerprint check to see who shared that drink with her. Whichever fingerprint match up, that will be the one who will take the rap. Did you by any chance have a drink before you found Keesha upstairs in her bed or maybe fix a glass of something for her to drink?"

"No, I wasn't thinking about having a relaxing moment with her, I wanted to know about the pictures I received on my door step."

"You have no idea who could have sent them to you?"

"None whatsoever. The only thing I saw was the tail-lights of a fleeing car!"

"Well, they have that Chris character in custody. It's just a matter of time before they realize that he had something to do with it and along with the pictures, it will build an even bigger case against him."

In the meantime, the officers were questioning Chris about his relationship with Keesha and confirming that he was at her house the night before. Chris considered the questions and decided that he would tell them everything as he remembered it to be.

"I received a letter from Keesha on Monday telling me that she would be away all week and that she was sorry about the way things worked out between us and wanted us to get together and talk about it. It also said that I shouldn't call first, just be there at eight o'clock sharp on Friday, which is exactly what I did. When I got there, she didn't seem to want to talk. She started kissing me and fumbling with my zipper."

"Are you sure that you didn't drug her while you had the chance so that the night would be memorable?"

"No, I would never give Keesha a drug for any reason other than to help her if she was sick and not even then unless she asked for it. I would just as soon take her to the hospital before playing doctor. You should be asking her doctor friend. He would probably have a faster access to that kind of thing than I would. I would never even think of such a thing. For all I know, he could have been giving it to her all the time and that's why she thinks she's so in love with him." The officer took in what Chris was saying and decided that he wasn't buying it. Something was missing from this story, and he would get it out of Chris if it was the last thing he did'. He was known for getting a suspect to open up.

"So, you said that she just wanted you to stop by, and she started removing your clothes but she had told you previously that things were over between you and she was seeing another man. Did she also mention to you that she was about to marry that man?"

"No, she just said that she was in love with him and that it was over between us."

"Then what I can't understand is why she would send you a letter telling you to come over when she made plans to marry someone else!"

"I don't know. The letter is right here in my pocket. I was coming over today to ask her about it, thinking she would at least give me a call to talk about what transpired between us last night, but when I didn't hear from her, I became concerned. I figured that maybe she was having second thoughts about us or maybe she just wanted to make love for one last time. I don't know. I'm just as baffled about it as you are." The officer considered what he was saying, but it just didn't seem right.

"So, how old are you fellow? You look to be no more than twenty-five if that!"

"I'm twenty-one. What does that have to do with anything?"

"Why would a thirty-five-year-old woman be interested in a young boy like you other than for sexual gratification?"

"Look, I don't know why any of this came to be. All I know is that we were lovers, and now it's over. We made love last night, and I haven't heard from her since then. I have been trying to reach her all day."

"Well, that pretty little lady is in the hospital recovering from an overdose of a deadly drug called Spanish fly and claims she doesn't know how it got into her system. Her friend Jamal received pictures of the two of you having hot sex along with a video showing the act. You were the only one benefiting from it. My speculation is that you had someone deliver the package as an attempt to break them up, hoping that things would go back to the way they were!"

Chris couldn't believe what he was hearing. He didn't know anything about someone taking pictures of them. He would never do such a thing. Chris wondered who could have done such a thing and why. Then for some strange reason, he thought of Michelle. Could she be capable of doing something like that? He decided that he wouldn't mention her until the results came back. If neither his nor the other man's prints showed up, he would ask he officer to check her out.

CHAPTER
38

In the lab the glasses were tested to see if any traces of any illegal substances could be found. Only one of the two glasses showed traces of Spanish Fly. Keesha's fingerprints were found on only the contaminated glass. The next test was to see whose prints would show on the other glass. After comparing Jamal's prints with the ones on the glasses, Jamal was found innocent of the crime.

Chris' prints were scanned into the computer. His prints took a little longer to process, they seemed to have been altered. An officer was instructed to get another sample of Chris' fingerprints.

Chris was brought up for new prints and when his fingers were examined he was asked when he had burned them.

"I scorched them on a pot about two days ago."

"Why didn't you mention that when we were taking your prints?"

"I didn't think about it, besides, I didn't expect to be spending my afternoon here anyway."

"Did you burn both hands?"

"No, just the right one." The prints of his left hand were taken and he was returned to his cell.

The technician took the copy of the prints and said they would have to wait a couple of minutes for the prints to dry, otherwise, they might be damaged and we will have to get another set of prints.

"It's better to be careful the first time. After about fifteen minutes, he looked at the prints again and decided that they were dry enough to run through the scanner. They waited to see what the computer would read. After a few minutes, they realized that it was definitely a complete print. It took twenty minutes before the computer told that it was definite, without a shadow of doubt that these prints did not match the prints on the glass.

Officer Thompson, felt a thickness building in his throat. He just knew that it had to be one of them. He would have to go back and speak to the man who was with her when it occurred. In fact, he would pay Keesha another visit. This thing would be solved no later than tomorrow even if he had to take the prints of everyone on her block. Then he thought, that's what he would do, he would subpoena the prints of everyone who lived on her block. Certainly one of them must have visited her that week. Maybe it wasn't the intention of arousing her but to kill her and make it seem like it was a sexual thing.

He decided that he couldn't do it that way anyway. He needed reasonable cause to get that kind of permission. It was a direct evasion of privacy so he went back to square one: to ask Keesha if there was anyone else who was with her the day or night of the incident.

Officer Thompson accompanied by another officer named Richardson went back to the car.

"So, where to now?" asked Officer Richardson.

"Back to the hospital to talk to Ms. Smalls and see if she can remember a little more about that day. There is certainly something missing in her story. Someone else was certainly there because we have prints on both glasses and one of them is the assailant so she is just going to have to think a little harder."

At the hospital, Keesha waited with Ebony for word of the findings. Ebony spent most of the time calling the people who were invited to Keesha's get-together letting them know that it was canceled. She had finally made the last call on the list when Officer Thompson and Officer Richardson walked in.

"So, did you find out anything?" Keesha asked of the officer.

"Yes, but not enough to convict, which is what I'm looking to do, so I need to go over your story in a little more detail."

"I've told you everything that I remember about that night. I don't have anything else to say about it."

"Sure you do. What I need to know from you right now will solve this mystery."

"So what is it?"

"Who gave you something to drink yesterday or last night?"

"Oh, I had my friend Michelle over earlier in the day, and she helped me clean my china and glasses. Why?"

"Because we found two glasses in your sink. Only one glass had your prints, the other had both prints and you both were drinking the same thing but only you overdosed so did you and this friend Michelle share a drink together?"

"Yes, she fixed me a glass of tea."

"Did you wash those glasses?"

"No, I started feeling funny after that, and she told me that she had to be on her way and that she would see me today at the party."

"Approximately what time was it when she had to leave?"

"I would say about six-thirty or seven. I don't have any quarrels with her. What reason could she have in wanting to hurt me?"

"I don't know, but one thing is for sure, we have two men locked up and neither of their prints is on the glasses. Maybe she is the missing link to all of this. I need to know one more thing. Did you send a letter to Chris asking him to come over on Friday to talk about what happened between the two of you?"

"No, he just happened to have shown up. In fact, he came over about an hour after Michelle left."

"Well guess what, Chris received a letter that told him to come over at eight which is one hour after your friend, Michelle left your house. Don't you think that a little strange?"

"Well, not really. I'm sure she must have been tired after cleaning all those dishes for me." Officer Thompson wasn't interested in hearing anymore. He asked Keesha where he could find Michelle. Then Ebony told him that Michelle had come by that morning. She said that Keesha said she was feeling sick when she left and told her she was going to lie down. When she spoke with Chris, he wasn't aware of Keesha being sick. He said she was fine when he last saw her.

Officer Thompson and his assisting officers left the room and headed to the precinct to get authorization to request Michelle's prints. After receiving the required subpoena, they hurried over to Michelle's house. When they rang her bell, she answered the door with a surprised look on her face.

"What can I do for you officer?"

"I have a subpoena here that authorizes me to escort you to the precinct for fingerprints. It also gives our officers the right to check your premises for anything that might link you to what happened to Ms. Smalls. This is just to see if your prints match with the prints we found in her house."

"Well, can I get my purse, then I will be right out."

"Sure, but we will have to accompany you just in case you try to destroy any evidence." Michelle looked surprised and cursed herself for not getting rid of the vial when she had the chance. She grabbed her purse, continuing through the door with the officers. The balance of them remained to check her house for any incriminating evidence.

At the precinct, they took her prints. Afterwards, she asked for permission to go home. They told her that she wouldn't be able to leave until the officers returned from her house just in case what they're looking for was found.

"What is it that they're looking for?"

"Anything, signs of foul play."

Michelle wondered what he meant by that. She knew that he was looking for the drug but she had it right in her purse, so they certainly wouldn't find it there. She sat in the room they escorted her to and waited to be released. Officer Thompson wouldn't chance sending those prints in the hands of anyone but himself. He personally drove over to the lab and gave them to the technician. When the prints were put into the computer, there was a definite match. Thompson then hurried back to the precinct with the results. Michelle denied everything. She said that of course her prints would show on the glasses since she was washing the glasses and gave Keesha something to drink.

When his chief told him that he couldn't hold her without proof of administering the drug, Thompson stormed out of her office and called Officer Robertson to his side. They then went back to Michelle's house to see if anything had been found.

When they arrived, the officers told him that they checked everything and nothing was found. Not even on her clothes. Officer Thompson knew in his gut Michelle had something to do with poisoning Keesha and was determined to find evidence.

He and his partner returned to the precinct so Officer Thompson could talk to Jamal to find out what kind of relationship Keesha had with Michelle. Jamal told him that as far as he knew they got along fine, Michelle was just a pest to her, nothing serious. Then he went to Chris cell.

"What kind of relationship would you say that Michelle and Keesha had?"

"Michelle, what does she have to do with this?"

"Her prints were found on the glasses in Keesha's sink the night of the incident. We're trying to prove that she had reasonable cause."

"Well she and I used to be lovers, and she was jealous of Keesha and me, but as far and I know, they got along fine." Officer Thompson started thinking, this woman didn't just let bygones be bygones. She was trying to get back at Keesha. Who else would want to make Jamal think that she was having an affair with Chris? He was willing to bet that if he checked the airport, something would show up. He called the airport and asked them to check to see if they had a Michelle Tanner on the roster. Nothing.

He cursed. "The proof is right under my nose, and I'm not getting it. I can see that she's guilty. There is something about that girl I just don't trust. Richardson, did our men check absolutely everything?"

"Yeah, maybe she got rid of it already!"

"Nah, she's not smart enough to have gotten rid of it. I bet she's laughing at us right now. Besides, she wanted to go back in the house and when I told her that she would have to be accompanied, she almost froze. If she had been given the chance, she would have gotten rid of it then. I bet we can make her tell on herself. There must be something we didn't check." Suddenly he realized the one place the officers didn't check.

The officers tripped over each other as they hurried to the releasing station.

"Ms. Tanner, we need to check one more thing!"

She looked at them with disgust. "What is it now officers? You've wasted enough of my time. How do you think this is going to look to the neighbors?"

"I know, and we're sorry for any inconvenience. We will in fact, return you to your home after this search if it proves to be false."

Michelle grinned and gave consent.

"May we see your bag, Ms. Tanner?"

Her face almost changed color as they waited for her to hand over her purse.

When the purse was searched, nothing out of the ordinary was found. Officer Thompson handed her back the bag. "Sorry for the inconvenience, ma'am. We'll take you home as promised. Then Officer Thompson noticed one last compartment on the bottom of her bag where she would keep an umbrella.

"Can I see your bag one last time?"

Her patience was just about to run out and she looked up at the clerk as to say that this had gone far enough.

"I hope that your men did not ransack my house!"

"Ma'am, if there is anything out of order, we will personally straighten it up." He knew that she was displaying annoyance to cover her fear. The vial was in her bag somewhere. When he turned the bag over, her head dropped as the little vial was exposed as they opened the compartment. Officer Thompson handed it to Officer Richardson. He didn't have to say anything. He knew to take it right over to the lab. He told Michelle that it would only take about twenty minutes to verify what it was. Thompson knew by the look on her face that he had hit the jackpot.

Officer Richardson quickly returned with the results. "Lock her up, it was a perfect match. We got her, buddy!" Officer Thompson looked at Michelle and smiled.

"I just want you to know that I always get my man--that goes for women too!" He put the handcuffs on her to escort her to a cell. He read her rights. Officer Thompson handed Michelle over to Officer Richardson then personally went to Jamal's cell to release him. His attorney had spent all that time with him waiting for the results to come back. Officer Thompson shook Jonathan's hand and thanked him for all his help and apologized to Jamal for any inconvenience this incident caused.

The officer made his way to Chris' cell to release him. He gave him the same apology suggesting that in the future he consider informing his girlfriends of other women that they might come in contact with.

At the front desk, Chris and Jamal stood side by side as they waited for the appropriate release papers to be signed.

"Hi, I'm Jamal. Are you Chris?"

"Yes, I guess you must be the man that won my Keesha's heart!"

"That's correct. Look, man, I'm sorry that things came down the way they did but I love Keesha with everything in me, and I've wanted no one else but her from the moment I laid eyes on her. We are getting married next month, and I hope that this ends your pursuit of her. I've got her now, and I'm not going to let her go!" Chris looked at him and told him that he understood. If Keesha had given him half the chance, he wouldn't have let her go either.

"This course of events just lets me know that we don't stand a chance. Keesha really must love you, and if she were in her right state of mind, what happened last night would never have occurred. I'm sorry that I didn't know that then. I thought that she really wanted to make things like they were again. Take care of her!"

Jamal shook Chris' hand and thanked him for understanding and told him that he would find someone else that would make him feel just as good as Keesha did.

When they finished signing the papers, Chris and Jamal went their separate ways. Chris found his car waiting for him outside of the precinct and Jamal also found his car out front. The attorney received his three-hundred-dollars back for the impound fee. Jamal wrote him a check for ten-thousand-dollars and shook his hand. They went their separate ways and Jamal drove to the hospital.

When he got there, he saw Keesha on the bed with her eyes closed. Ebony caught sight of him at the door and almost screamed his name but he covered his lips with his finger to tell her to keep quiet. Ebony got up and walked out of the door and told Keesha she would return shortly.

Jamal slowly walked over to her with a perfectly formed long-stem red rose. He knelt at her bedside gently rubbing it across her cheek. She opened her eyes and couldn't believe what she was seeing. Her prince had returned to her side.

"Jamal, I didn't think that you would want me!"

"Keesha, I love you and recognize that none of this was your fault. I hope that you can get past it so that we can go on with our lives." He pulled her up and cradled her in his arms. The warmth welcomed her. She was cloaked by his affection. "Nothing will come between us but you if that's what you want!"

"I don't!" He kissed her again and took a seat next to her on the bed. Ebony returned to the room and gave Jamal a hug.

"Jamal, I knew that you were innocent. I'm glad I ran into your attorney and we put our heads together and everyone worked together to free you. Was Michelle guilty?"

"Yes, she even had the vial in her purse. She almost walked away because there wasn't enough evidence to convict her!"

"Yeah, well the guilty never win in the end!" All three of them hugged like a family.

CHAPTER
39

On May thirtieth, Keesha and Jamal were married. The ceremony was a success. Just as discussed, they had it on a ship. Jamal had his four brothers and three best friends represent him as ushers. They looked elegant in their white jackets and silver cummerbunds just like Keesha imagined. The girls in their silver dresses with silver overlays looked beautiful. Everything was just as they wanted it.

After the wedding, Jamal and Keesha went to their cabin suite and made love. Jamal projected the seed of his loins into her. She would carry his child and he would love it just as much as he loved her. Of course, nothing would be as precious as she.

In mid March, Keesha gave birth to fraternal twins. Jamal was there to help her bring them into the world. That day marked the second happiest day of his life. Ebony became the godparent.

Things went on between Keesha and Jamal, and he loved her ever more as the days went by.

Preview of forthcoming book
Missing Births

Tracey cringed, as she watched the menacing light dance along a scalpel's razor-sharp edge. She had never felt the bite of a knife before. Tracey desperately clinched her restraints, while she prayed for a quick ending. A light too bright for her eyes, and too hot for her skin, lingered above her, not even three feet from where she lay. She felt a tremble in her stomach that let her know it was time.

Her blood felt hot, escaping her body in rhythmical spurts when the blade tore into her flesh. She desperately fought the urge to scream, though the pain was more than she could bare. A masked face stood over her with only narrowed eyes revealing an identity. The person intently penetratrated layer after layer. Perspiration stung her eyes and Tracey turned her head trying to clear it. The burning wasn't as intense as the probing hands that pealed her flesh back pulling at her muscles and tissue, robbing her of the child she patiently awaited for nine long months.

She cursed Daniel for leaving her. If he were there, he could save her, but he wasn't. Tracey realized for the first time how alone she was. Her boyfriend had abandoned her, the projects didn't offer the best of friends and her parents put her out when she told them she was pregnant. Many times she tried to reconcile their differences but they didn't understand, at least they didn't seem to understand.

Tracey felt a tug and out popped her baby. She could see the child's penis saluting proudly between his bowed legs. "It's a boy." The voice behind the mask said narcissistically. She wiped the child with the towel she pulled from her bag, then wrapped it in a receiving blanket followed by another blanket.

Things were getting dark by the second. Tracey knew she couldn't hold on much longer. The agonizing pain subsided and her legs ceased to writhe then the sensations ended. She began to feel faint, and instantly, her heart stopped beating.

One out of every thousand children being born are kidnapped within the ages of one and five. Half that number are taken from local parks while unattended, while the other half wander away from their parent or guardian while shopping in a supermarket.

Five children are missing,there are no records of their births and the only evidence of their existence are the gutted cadavers which once harbored them.

No clues, no evidence and no refuge. Missing Births is a mother's worst nightmare, and her last.

Coming Soon.

Now In Stores
Shadow Lover
He heard her cries and out from the shadows he came.

Shadow Lover is an erotic horror about a battered woman's plight to escape the hands of her abusive husband and his determination not to let her go. After a miraculous surgery, an unyielding love drives a surgeon to desperately fight to save this woman's life but it may cost him his own and everyone he knows.

Shadow Lover delivers horror with a new note...with its breath taking suspense, perfectly illustrated, orgasm producing romance and trendsetting language.